Professor Astor

CATHARINA MAURA

This one is for myself and my Desi girls.

Playlist

You can find Leia and Adrian's playlist on my Spotify profile. Just search for 'Catharina Maura Spotify'

Songs

Tere Liye
Save The Hero
Agar Tum Mil Jao
My Boy
When You Love Someone
Read All About It
Samjhawan
Soulmate
Tere Bina
Rise Up

Contents

One

LEIA

"You ready to go, sweetheart?" Mom asks, her head popping into my room. There's concern in her voice that she tries to hide behind a smile, but I know my mother well enough to see through it.

"Yes, Mom," I tell her, pasting a reassuring smile onto my face, even though my heart is racing, a familiar ache spreading with each heartbeat. I grab my favorite handbag with fingers that tremble just slightly, tightening my grip around the luxurious leather straps as I lift it onto my shoulder.

"Can you believe Asha was in labor for fourteen hours? That's not something you ever want to experience," Mom says, her voice high-pitched, the way it always is when she's rambling. "It'll take her months to recover from that, you know? Pregnancy is so hard on women."

I nod and smile, swallowing down my misery. The truth is that I do want to be in labor for fourteen hours. Hell, I'll happily breathe through three full days of labor if it means I get to have a child of my own.

Mom often does this. She tries to downplay the significance of having children, as though that'll make me want them less. She'll take my sister as an example of how tired I'd be, how hard it is, and how many things I'd have to sacrifice. Her intentions are good, they always are, but she fails to realize that I want all the bad right along with the good.

"Sounds awful," I tell her absentmindedly, and she smiles shakily, a hint of relief in her eyes. Sometimes I wonder if her attempts to console me are more for her own benefit. I bite down on my lip and shake my head slightly, berating myself for my thoughts.

It's not my mother's fault I had ovarian cancer in my teens, and it definitely isn't her fault I developed primary ovarian insufficiency from the chemo, rendering me as good as infertile. I know she's as heartbroken as I am, but it doesn't make her attempts to console me feel any better. It's pity at its finest, and I hate being pitied.

"There you two are," Dad says, his expression as blank as it always is. "Let's go. Always late, we are," he grumbles in his best Yoda impression, his attempt to lighten the mood. I force a smile for his benefit as I follow him to the car.

I'm quiet as we drive to my sister's house, wishing I could've made an excuse not to go. I desperately wanted to stay home, but I know that if I'd done that, Mom would've worried about me.

I'm overcome with dread as we park in front of Asha's house. Somehow I don't mind children when they aren't family. I have no problem working as a nanny for my sister's business, but when someone close to me has a baby, it hits me hard. It doesn't help that my mother watches me closely at the mere mention of anyone in the family having a child, which these days seems to be every few months. I'm so scared of her hurting on my behalf, yet I'm also tired of hurting in silence.

Mom clutches the gifts she brought Asha to her chest as we walk up to the front door, her eyes beaming with excitement. I wonder what she'd be like if I ever had a child of my own. I wish I could be at the receiving end of her joy someday.

"Mom, Dad," Rohan, my sister's husband, says as he opens the door. His smile widens when his eyes land on me. "Leia! Asha is going to be so happy to see you."

He offers each of us a hug as he ushers us in, and I grin when I notice the milk stains on his t-shirt. Looks like they haven't had an easy time since the baby's birth.

Rohan leads us into their living room, where Asha is seated with the baby in her arms, their two-year-old son, Rohit, next to her, iPad in hand. Asha looks up, her eyes lighting up when she sees me. "Leia!"

I grin and grab some hand sanitizer from the coffee table before sitting down beside her. She's trying to console her baby daughter who won't stop crying, and the sounds of the baby's soft sobs tug at my heartstrings. "How have you been?" I ask, pressing a kiss to my sister's cheek.

She sighs and shakes her head, her eyes briefly lifting to our mother who is making her way to Asha's kitchen, while my dad stands in the corner, chatting to Rohan. "I'm tired," she murmurs. "The feedings are driving me crazy, and she just cries so much, Ley. Please tell me you're okay to take over from me at work," she says, referring to the highly exclusive nanny business she's been running for years now. Her waiting lists are years long, and her clients are some of the richest people in the country. I get why she's worried, but I know her company as well as she does, and I'm certain I can handle it just fine.

"Of course. You know I've got this. Don't you worry. The company won't fall apart while you're on maternity leave, I promise you." I hold my arms out, and Asha smiles as she hands me the baby. My heart skips a beat as I place the baby on my chest. "Hi, Nalini," I whisper, patting her back.

"Oh my, she stopped crying," Asha whispers, the relief in her voice palpable. I grin, my heart overflowing with equal parts need and happiness. "You're so great with children, Ley. Once you have some of your own, you'll put us all to shame. I have a feeling you're going to be one of those annoying perfect supermoms with perfectly behaved annoying little children."

I chuckle, even as my heart skips a beat. I glance at my sister and smile. She knows how low my chances of ever having children are, yet she has so much faith. I wish I could borrow some of it every once in a while. "I'd have to find a husband first," I say, knowing that that's not something I'll ever do. Even if I wanted to, most of the men in our community would never accept me. We might be living in modern times, but in our culture, too much is still far too backward.

"I've been meaning to talk to you about that," Asha says, her tone careful. "Rohan has a really nice colleague that I think you should meet. He's incredibly kind, and he's an accountant."

I tense, unsure what to say. The older I get, the more often family members try to introduce me to someone, and I hate it.

"You're twenty-nine, Leia. You can't stay single all your life. You have so much love to give, so much left to experience. Just grab a coffee with him, okay? I'll text him your number."

I swallow hard, unable to form a reply. "I'm just focusing on finishing my PhD," I tell her eventually.

Asha sighs. "You've been doing that PhD of yours for years now. You're hiding behind it, and don't even try to deny it. You've been using it as an excuse not to live your life, and I'm not going to let you keep that up. I love you, Ley. You deserve the world, but you can't have it if you hide yourself away."

The baby squirms in my arms, and my heart shatters as I blink away my tears. I want to scream at Asha, tell her that I wish I could have everything she wants for me, that I'd want nothing more than to be happily married with children of my own, but it isn't that simple. Something like this isn't reserved for everyone. She knows about the medical issues I've been dealing with, the hormone replacement therapy, the endless supplements. Despite that, she never lost faith. There's no use trying to talk any sense into her. My big sister is adamant that I'll be a mother someday, but it just isn't that simple.

Nalini starts to cry, and I hand her back to her mother instead of consoling her. Asha takes Nalini from me, but her eyes never leave mine.

"Leia," she murmurs, but I don't turn to look at her.

"I've got some data I need to analyze tonight, Asha. I'd better get going," I murmur as I rise to my feet.

"Leia!" she repeats. "Don't go, okay? I won't *rishta* you again," she says, using the word we've come to replace the word matchmaking with.

"Where are you going, Leia?" Dad asks, a hint of concern in her eyes.

I smile at him as brightly as I can. "Sorry, Dad. I've got to get back to school. I'm so sorry, but I completely forgot about something I had to finalize tonight. I've just been so busy that it slipped my mind."

He falls silent, as though he's seeing straight through me. "Do you want me to drop you off at the college?" he asks, his voice soft.

I shake my head and head to the door. "Amara is picking me up," I say, lying and using my best friend as an excuse. "I'll see you tonight, okay?"

Dad nods, and for a moment I'm scared he'll insist on walking me to the door and seeing me off. He adores Amara, and he usually loves seeing her, so I wouldn't put it past him. Thankfully, Rohan distracts him, and I slip past him before he can change his mind.

The door closes behind me, and I take a deep breath, oxygen filling my lungs as though I've been suffocating. I glance back at the door and walk away before anyone sees me standing here, my thoughts reeling as I walk through the unfamiliar neighborhood.

My emotions are all over the place tonight. I thought I was stronger than I am, and I can't help but feel disappointed in myself. I thought I'd accepted the future I'm heading toward, but Asha reopened old wounds.

I take a deep breath and pause by the bar in the corner. I should know better than drinking away my sorrows, but I'm weak tonight.

Two

ADRIAN

I stand in the doorway of my grandfather's office, taking in the room that looks identical to my memories of it. I always found Grandpa's office intimidating, and I still do. I watch him as he works behind his desk, jabbing at his keys instead of typing the way he should. I wonder who pissed him off. I'd hate to be on the receiving end of whatever email I'm sure he's typing.

I smile when he looks up, surprise lighting up his eyes. He rises from his seat, speechless for a moment.

"Never thought I'd see you at a loss for words, Gramps."

He chuckles and shakes his head. "Adrian, you're home."

Home. Yeah, I guess that's what this place has always been to me. Home. I've been away for far too long.

Grandpa gestures toward the seat opposite him, and I push away from the wall, taking a seat in front of his desk.

"It's good to have you back, son," Grandpa says, and I smile. He looks older, and my mood drops at the thought of everything I've missed here. I didn't get to see my little cousin, Amara, grow up. She's the closest thing to a sister I have, and the distance has made us grow further apart than I'd like. I wasn't here to support my grandfather with the company, either.

"It's good to be home," I tell him, and it is. I've been away for years, and it feels good to be back. If things go to plan, I'll be back here permanently.

I glance around my grandfather's office, appreciating the years he spent building this business. "I've never told you this, Grandpa, but you are the most inspiring man I've ever met."

Grandpa looks away, like I expected him to. He's never been good with compliments. Neither am I, to be fair, but my daughter is a sensitive one, so I've learned to voice compliments whenever I can.

"What brings you home, Adrian?" Grandpa asks, making me chuckle. He never beats around the bush. His directness is in stark contrast with what I've grown accustomed to in London.

"Alice and I are getting a divorce," I say simply. The words no longer hurt, not even in the slightest. It came as a shock to me. I thought we were happy, that our family was thriving. I never even realized that my wife was miserable, and she reminds me of it every time I ask her to stay.

Grandpa sits back, his eyes widening. He falls silent for a moment, and it doesn't surprise me. Everyone always thought Alice and I were perfect together — and so did I. We met when I was at university in London, and we've been together ever since. I always thought we were on the same page about what we wanted out of life, that she was as happy as I was.

"I'm sorry to hear that, Son."

I nod. "The kids don't know yet. We haven't told them yet, but we've formally separated. I've been sleeping in the guest room for months now, and the paperwork has been signed. It's all being handled right now."

"I take it you're finally ready to come home?"

"Yes," I tell him. "I'd like to come home, and I'll take the kids with me. Alice and I are discussing custody, but it looks like I'll get the kids, and she gets visitation. She says she wants to focus on her own career after sacrificing years being a stay-at-home parent, and that's fine by me."

I try my hardest to suppress the ache I feel at those words. I have no idea how the kids are going to take the news, and while I don't want to take them away from all they know, I think a fresh start surrounded by my family is exactly what they'll need.

"Will you at last be joining the company, or are you going to continue to teach?"

"If I can, I'll do both. I'm not ready to step away from teaching, Grandpa. I know you'd rather have me join the company full-time, but I can't at this time."

He nods. "You have your mother's and your grandmother's heart, that's why. Your grandmother was always a teacher at heart, too. If I'd allowed her to follow her dreams, she'd be a tenured professor now, but I never wanted her to work." The regret in his voice grabs my attention, and I frown. My grandfather is a proud man, and he isn't known to admit his faults.

"Tenure," I murmur. It doesn't exist in England, but it's something I've always wanted. If nothing else, it'll give me something to aim for, something to focus on.

"Adrian," Grandpa says, his voice weary. "Amara isn't ready to take over the company. I know you've always said that you weren't interested, and I've always allowed you to chase your own dreams because you weren't here, and I was certain Amara would be the perfect heir for my role. It looks like she's changed her mind about what she wants out of her future. You understand what that means, right?"

I nod. "I'll be there, Grandpa. I'll need to be trained, but I can support Amara. She and I can do this together, if that's what she wishes."

Grandpa looks relieved, and I smile. He's always been strict and no-nonsense, his mannerisms rough. When I was a child, I was certain he didn't even like me, and I know Amara felt the same way. With age comes understanding, though. I see the worry in his eyes, his need for us to land on our feet. I see in him the parent I've now become.

"Don't worry," I tell him. "I'll be home soon, and I'll do all I can to support the company."

Grandpa nods. "If you agree to come work for me, I'll ensure you and the kids have everything you need."

"Very well," I tell him, knowing full well that he'd do so even if I declined. My grandfather loves making us feel like we earned the things he'd give us regardless. "Then I'll have to ask you to contact your property manager to select a suitable home for the kids and me. I expect us to move back before the year is over, but it depends on how they respond to the news. I want to make sure that I put their needs first."

"As you should," Grandpa, says, rising to his feet.

He walks me to the door and claps me on the back. "Don't forget to go see your cousin and aunt, if you haven't yet," he reminds me, and I nod.

"As if I'd ever forget. Amara would never forgive me."

Grandpa smiles, but it doesn't reach his eyes. I suspect something might be going on with Amara, but I'll have to ask her myself.

I'm absentminded as I walk to the truck I borrowed from Silas, my best friend — perhaps my only friend. Instead of unlocking it, I lean against it, taking a moment to ground myself. I can't believe how much my life has changed in a matter of months, how much it'll change further still. I can't believe I'm getting a divorce at thirty-nine.

I push away from the truck and pull a hand through my hair, my eyes dropping to the bar opposite me. I walk in, intending to call Silas to meet me here, but my every thought fades away when my gaze falls to the woman sitting on the barstool by the entrance.

She's alone, her eyes filled with sorrow as she sips her cosmopolitan. She's wearing a yellow sundress that looks stunning against her caramel skin, with a pair of yellow heels that have a large sunflower on the back. My mind instantly drifts to me grabbing her ankles and pushing those sexy legs of hers up over her shoulder, those shoes of hers still on. Long dark hair cascades down her back, and when she lifts her dark eyes to mine, my heart skips a beat.

Before I realize what I'm doing, I'm taking the seat next to hers. The last thing I need right now is further complications in my life, but something about that look in her eyes keeps me enthralled. She looks the way I feel, sadness coated in sheer stubbornness.

"Tough day, huh?" I murmur.

She looks up from her glass, and I'm instantly nervous. When is the last time a woman made me nervous? Something about her simultaneously puts me on edge and eases my soul.

"You have no idea."

"What's your name?"

She smiles. "You can call me Ley."

Not sharing her name, huh? "I guess you can call me Thor." No one other than Silas calls me that. It's a stupid play on my last name, but if we aren't sharing names, then I guess this'll do.

Ley smiles at me, and I suck in a breath. Fucking hell. I didn't think she could get more beautiful, but she did.

"Now tell me, Layla, what's got you frowning like that?"

She chuckles. "It's not Layla, but it's a good guess."

"Lorelei?"

She shakes her head again.

"I'll figure this out eventually, Ley. But first, I'm going to buy you a drink."

Three

LEIA

I take in the handsome stranger seated beside me and let my gaze wander over his sharp cheekbones and those bright blue eyes. There are a few grays peeking through his thick dark hair, and somehow it just adds to his appeal. He's wearing a watch that's worth an entire year's salary, yet his clothes seem simple. Expensive, but simple. This man oozes intrigue and desire... but it isn't his utter sexiness that's got me interested, nor is it the fact that he looks like a dark-haired version of the actor that plays Thor. It's the sorrow I see in his eyes. It matches mine perfectly.

"You seem to have had quite the day yourself," I tell him after he orders us both drinks. Much to my surprise, he orders himself a soda. I expected him to be a beer type of guy. Thor turns to me, and I smile to myself at the nickname. It clearly isn't his real name, but somehow it suits him perfectly.

"Try a bad few months, Ley. You have no idea."

I look into his eyes, noting the pain and exhaustion. "Aren't all those burdens you're carrying heavy? How do you feel about putting that weight down for a moment or two?"

He looks startled, his eyes finding mine. For a moment, we sit there together, looking into each other's eyes. I wonder if he's anything like me, constantly pretending, playing the role everyone expects us to play. Does he long for a moment of truthfulness, a single moment in which we can rid ourselves of the masks and revel in the pain we keep hidden?

"They weigh down on me heavier with every breath I take, Ley."

I nod and tear my gaze away, focusing my attention on my glass. Something about this man has my heart racing. The walls I keep up are shaking around him, and I can't tell if it's simply the night I've had, or if it's got something to do with him. Perhaps it's a combination of both; a matter of one broken soul recognizing another.

I take a sip of my drink, gulping more down than I'd intended in an effort to dismiss the way his gaze feels on my skin. He isn't even touching me, yet it feels like he's caressing me.

"Will you tell me about your shitty day?" he asks.

I shake my head. "I'd really rather not. You wanna tell me about yours?"

Thor chuckles and shakes his head. "Nah. I'm with you. Let's just blame Mercury being in retrograde. That's what all you Millennials do these days, isn't it?"

I burst out laughing and glance at him in surprise. "Okay, Boomer," I tell him. "You clearly know Mercury is in retrograde right now, though, so what does that say about you, you Millennial-wannabe?"

He gasps in mock shock, making me laugh again. It's surprising that he managed to turn a somber night around so quickly. I was certain I'd end up calling Amara in tears, yet here I am, sharing a smile with a stranger.

"Do you even know what actually happens when Mercury goes intro retrograde?" he asks, an alluring smile on his face. My gaze drops to his lips, and for a moment I wonder what it'd be like to kiss him. I want to know how his stubble would feel against my skin, how my lips fit against his.

"Electronics go to shit, and things you buried in the past come back to haunt you."

He laughs. "Oh, God," he murmurs. "You're the superstitious sort, aren't you? You know what actually happens, Ley... *nothing*."

I frown at him, and he smiles.

"Mercury going into retrograde is an optical illusion. It doesn't actually happen. Mercury is closer to the sun than Earth is, so its orbital speed is faster. That's why it looks like it's going into retrograde a few times a year, but nothing actually happens."

I narrow my eyes and shake my heads. "Oh, no... you're the rational kind. We can't be friends, Thor."

He chuckles and shakes his head. "Hmm, I don't know. We both love astronomy, it seems, but just in different ways. Besides... you're right. We can't be friends. We're definitely going to become a whole lot more than that."

I don't think I've stopped smiling since we started talking, and a burst of giddiness rushes through me as a giggle escapes my lips. "That's a nice way to put it, but you're definitely not convincing me that Mercury isn't messing up my life. I've had email issues four times this week, Thor. *Four*. That's four times my usual average," I say, ignoring the rest of his words because he's making me feel a lot more flustered than I want to let on.

He laughs and leans his elbow on the bar, his attention fully on me. It's busy in the bar we're in, yet it feels like it's just the two of us. "I'll show you," he says, his gaze lingering. "I have a telescope in my truck. Let's go and take a look at your supernatural Mercury."

I hesitate, startled by his proposition. I'm hardly a prude, but I'm definitely cautious. Leaving a bar no one knows I'm in with a man I've never met before seems irresponsible.

"I promise that I'm not a murderer or a weirdo."

I bite down on my lip, hesitating. "I have pepper spray and my best friend has access to my location data. I'm going to ask her to check in with me every hour, and if I go missing, she will come for you. She's terrifying. Definitely not someone you want to mess with."

Thor nods and holds his hands up. "Consider me warned, Ley. I promise I won't kidnap you. I won't touch you unless you ask me to."

I pause in the middle of texting Amara, my cheeks heating. I can definitely see myself asking him to do things to me I've been missing out on for longer than I care to admit. Hell, I can barely remember the last time I slept with someone. It certainly wasn't memorable.

I turn back to my phone and finish texting my bestie my location and details of my impromptu date. I'm not surprised when she texts me back instantly, offering encouragement instead of warnings. She's been pushing me to 'put myself out there' for as long as I can remember. I have no doubt she'll have a thousand questions for me when I see her tomorrow.

"Okay," I murmur nervously. "Let's go see Mercury."

Thor nods and smiles as he looks away.

"What?" I ask, suspicious.

He shakes his head. "I really want to make a terrible joke about Uranus, but I worry I'll lose my chance with you."

I burst out laughing again as I hop off the bar stool. "Uranus, really?"

He shrugs. "Too late, huh?"

"Yup," I tell him, knowing full well that I'm lying. With the way he's making me smile, it's going to be hard for him to lose his shot with me — for tonight, at least. The look in his eyes tells me he knows it, too.

meant to chase your every ambition, smashing goals like it's nothing."

I can feel her gaze on me, but I keep my eyes on the road. There's something about this conversation that feels intimate, though on the surface it's anything but.

"Sometimes it's the simple things in life that we need most. When it comes down to it, all I want is happiness. Perhaps it's cliché to want a husband who's obsessed with me and kids to raise..." her voice trails off, and she shakes her head. "Never mind. Who would you be if you could be anyone? Who do you want to be tonight, Thor?"

I smile, my heart overflowing with something I haven't felt in years. Giddiness? Excitement? A combination of both, perhaps. "Tonight I just want to be the man that gets to love you. Tell me, Ley. How many kids do we have? How long have we been married? How did we meet?"

She smirks, her index finger drawing circles on my jeans. I can feel her warmth straight through the fabric, and it's absurd how much that brief touch affects me.

"We met in college, and we've been married for... um, three years? We've got two kids."

I nod, strangely enjoying the thought of that. You'd think that the thought of marriage would repulse me after all Alice and I have been through, but somehow I find myself wanting to play along with Ley.

"How about a boy and a girl?" I ask, my thoughts turning to my own kids. For one crazy moment, I wonder if Ley would ever want to be with a man who has two kids of his own. I haven't given much thought to what my future without Alice will look like, and not once did I consider that I might one day remarry, but Ley has got me wondering.

She nods. "That would be amazing!"

I grin at her and try to resist pushing for more, failing the moment the words leave my lips. "How would you feel about twins?"

She snaps her fingers and grins. "Perfect! Yes, Thor. We've got twins. I like it."

I chuckle at her enthusiasm. Everyone always thinks it's nice to have twins, but mine are menaces.

"All right, wife. Then I suppose we're running from our kids tonight, eager for some quality time."

I grab her hand and entwine our fingers, keeping our joined hands in my lap. I can't recall the last time I was this nervous merely holding a woman's hand. Her hands are small and soft against mine, and I can't help but wonder what the rest of her body feels like.

"We sure are," she murmurs, her voice soft. "My handsome astrologist husband insisted on showing me the stars tonight."

I grin at her and raise our joined hands to my lips, pressing a soft kiss to the back of her hand. "You think I'm handsome, huh?"

Ley bites down on her lip and looks away, a smile on her face. "You're alright," she mutters, and I chuckle.

"And you're gorgeous beyond words. I'm a lucky man. Can't believe I made you my wife."

She laughs, and I struggle to keep my eyes on the road. She's so fucking beautiful. I've never felt this spark with anyone, but fucking hell... what I'm feeling for her can't be called anything else.

"It's the accent for me," she says, her voice soft. "You're handsome as hell, but that accent? I can't resist it."

I smirk and shift in my seat, my shoulders straightening as I keep my eyes on the road. Perk of living in London for over twenty years. My accent is no longer truly American, but it also isn't really a strong British accent either. It's something right in between.

"Should I call you *love*?" I ask. Ley sighs happily, and I chuckle. "We don't really use the word love as much as most people here assume we do, you know?"

Ley shakes her head. "I don't care. I insist on being called love for the remainder of our marriage."

She gives me an indulgent smile, and my fucking heart... I swear to God, it skips a damn beat. I'll call her whatever the hell she wants me to call her if she'll smile at me like that.

"Whatever you want, love."

Ley leans back in her seat, relaxed and seemingly as happy as I am. "We're here," I tell her, parking in the middle of a wide field, part of private lands owned by my family. I'm glad it hasn't changed a bit. This is where Amara and I spent our school holidays playing around. If I look closely, I can see the treehouse Grandpa had us built in the distance. This place used to be our sanctuary, and it's one of the few places I've never shared with Alice.

I jump out of the truck and rush around to open Ley's door. She grabs my hand with a sweet smile on her face. "Thank you," she murmurs, her hands on my shoulders as I lift her into my arms, holding onto her longer than necessary before I put her down.

She looks around, her eyes widening when she notices the clear skies. "Wow."

I grin and look up, the two of us leaning against the truck. "There isn't as much light pollution here. It still isn't the same as being outside of the city, but it's a little better than being downtown."

She nods and turns to me. Her eyes are a multitude of brown shades, and I could spend hours losing myself in them.

"Ley, I have to tell you something. I... I may have misled you."

Five

ADRIAN

"You misled me?" she asks, her eyes widening. I see the confusion in her gaze and bite down on my lip.

I nod and run a hand through my hair, worried I'm letting her down. "You can't actually see Mercury at night. Because it's so close to the sun, you can only really see it in the morning, at dusk, or just after sunrise."

Ley sighs and shakes her head, a laugh escaping her lips. "You... you trickster! I should call you Loki, instead. How are you going to make this up to me? I don't forgive easily, you know?"

I grin at her, relieved that she isn't angry. "I suppose it's a good thing that I have our entire lives to earn your forgiveness, huh, wifey?"

She shakes her head and wags her finger. "Sounds like a cheap excuse or an attempt at procrastination. I won't fall for it."

I smile and wrap my fingers around her wrist, pulling her closer. She's startled, and her eyes widen just slightly as I bring her hand to my face, pressing a kiss to her palm. Her sharp intake of breath has my heart beating a little louder. I feel like a teenager all over again. "Very well, love. Tell me how to make it up to you."

Ley smiles, her breathing quicker than it was moments ago. Whatever this is between us, she's feeling it too. "Do you really have a telescope with you, or was that all deception, too?"

I chuckle and nod. "I do really have one with me. It goes almost everywhere I go."

She tilts her head in question, and I look away for a moment before speaking. "Staring at the stars reminds me of how insignificant we all are, how small our problems are. There's so much out there that we haven't even discovered yet. The universe is so vast, you know? It gives me perspective."

She nods and rises to her tiptoes to brush a strand of hair out of my face. "Perhaps so, but that doesn't mean that our problems and worries aren't valid, that they don't deserve our full attention."

Her fingertips trace over the side of my face, and I grab her hand, holding it against me. "You're right, of course. It just allows me a moment to step away, to see things from a distance."

Ley nods, and I have a feeling she truly understands. "All of that, and you don't believe the stars and planets can affect us."

I purse my lips to hold back my laughter. "Mercury is not fucking up your emails. Besides, didn't you say that Mercury Retrograde brings stuff from the past back into your future? But this, my love, is a new beginning."

I can't tear my eyes off her. She's tiny, probably no more than five feet tall, but she's stunning. I let my eyes trace over her long lashes, her small straight nose, and those lips... those lips of hers. Full, and perfectly kissable. I want to know how she tastes, but damn it, somehow I just don't want to fuck things up with her. Before we drove here I promised myself that this thing between us wouldn't last beyond tonight, but the thought of walking away from her already fills me with regret.

"Let's grab that telescope, shall we?"

Ley nods and takes a step away as though my words snapped

her out of the trance we were both in. I inhale deeply as I grab my equipment from the backseat, my heart racing. When was the last time I felt anything like this? What is happening to me?

"Come to think of it," she murmurs. "This is the perfect place to bury a body."

I burst out laughing and glance at her. "Your mind is a terrifying place," I tell her, and she grins menacingly. "I'm starting to wonder if I should've been the one that's worried."

"Only one way to find out," she says, winking at me.

This woman... what is it about her? I suppose it's the carefree and impulsive nature of our date. I don't remember the last time I wasn't weighed down by responsibility. She's making me feel free in a way I haven't in years.

"Come look," I tell her. Ley walks up to me, and I lower the telescope for her, readjusting it to make sure she's seeing what I want her to see.

She leans in to look through my telescope, and I shamelessly wrap my hands around her waist, holding her close. "Do you see three bright stars that almost form a straight line?"

She's silent for a moment, and then she nods. "I see it."

"That's Orion's belt. If you look to the top on Orion's left, you'll see Gemini."

Ley pulls away and turns, finding herself in my arms. I should step back, but I don't. If anything, I want her fully pressed against me.

Her eyes widen, and she falls silent for a moment. "That reminds me," she murmurs, her voice barely above a whisper. "What is your zodiac sign?"

I chuckle, not in the least surprised she'd ask me that. "Scorpio."

"Ugh," she says. "Jealous, possessive, and petty. I'm a Leo, so we're surprisingly compatible."

I smirk and bite down on my lip, enjoying the way that draws her gaze to my mouth. "Scorpios are also loyal, passionate, and determined. We always get what we want, love, and we never let go." I might not believe in zodiacs, but I'm aware of the basics.

Ley places her hands on my chest, hesitant, as though she wants to move them up but doesn't dare to. "And what do you want?"

My eyes drop to her lips and I swallow hard. "I want to kiss you, Ley."

"Then kiss me, husband dearest."

I lean in and cover her lips with mine, a sharp burst of desire going straight through me at the feel of her full, soft lips. Fucking hell. I need to know what her lips feel like wrapped around my cock.

Ley moans, her hands finding their way around my neck, and I lift her into my arms. Her legs wrap around my hips instinctively, and I don't doubt that she can feel how hard she's making me straight through my jeans.

I hold her up, my hands on her ass as she deepens our kiss, her tongue stroking mine. The way she moves her body against mine tells me she wants me just as badly, and there's something so magical about this moment, here in one of my favorite places.

Ley pulls away for a moment, her forehead resting against mine as we both catch our breath, the two of us lost in this moment.

"I want you," she whispers. "I need you, Thor. I don't think I've ever wanted anyone quite as badly."

I nod. "The feeling is mutual, love."

My lips come crashing back down on hers as I blindly walk us back toward the truck. I struggle to pull away from her to see where I'm going, and I breathe a sigh of relief when I've got her pressed up against the car.

"Let me open this," I murmur against her lips as I let down the tailgate before putting her down. I spread her legs wide open to stand between them, enjoying the way Ley's hands run over my body. She's as impatient as I am. She's honest with her feelings.

There are no games, no pretence. It's refreshing, and it's sexy as hell.

My lips move to her neck as I try to discover every single spot that makes her shiver.

"Oh God," she moans when I kiss her right below her ear, and I smile against her skin before doing it again. I start to suck on her neck, wanting to mark her as mine, but she pulls away. "Don't," she pleads. "Don't leave marks, Thor." For a moment, irrational anger surges through me at the thought of her having someone in her life she'd want to hide evidence of tonight from, but then she silences my fears. "My parents would kill me. They don't care how old I am, they won't stand for indecency."

I chuckle and nod, moving lower as her hand disappears underneath my t-shirt, my muscles tensing as her fingers trace over them. I watch her expression as she explores my body, and she smiles shyly before moving her lips back to mine, hiding herself from me while giving me her all.

I smile against her lips and kiss her while my hand finds its way underneath her dress. The tips of my fingers trace over her skin, higher and higher. I love the way she squirms against me, the way she rolls her hips impatiently.

I brush my thumb over her pussy, straight through her silky underwear, and I smile when I realize she's wet for me. Just when I think she can't get more perfect, she does.

"We don't have to go any further than this, Ley."

She pulls away from me and looks at me. "I've decided," she tells me. "This is how you're going to make up for lying to me about being able to see Mercury. You're going to make me forget about anything but you."

I smile and nod, my heart skipping a beat. "Yes, my darling wife."

Six

LEIA

My darling wife. Each time he calls me that, my heart beats a little faster. This little fantasy we're lost in is one I won't forget anytime soon.

Thor seats me at the edge of his truck and drops to his knees in front of me, his eyes on mine as he spreads my legs. He smirks when he pushes my dress up, his eyes portraying the desire he feels. I don't doubt for a second that he wants me as much as I want him. I wonder... does he feel this connection between us the way I do?

I gasp when he presses his lips on my inner thigh, kissing me softly. Thor glances at me after every few kisses, his gaze keeping me enthralled. It's like I'm all he can see. "I might not be able to leave any marks on your neck, but baby... I'm definitely leaving some here."

He lifts my leg up slightly and leans in, sucking down on my inner thigh, leaving countless small marks as he moves his way up. I groan and thread my hand through his thick dark hair, loving the show he's giving me. Watching him between my legs has me throbbing, desperate for more of him.

He smirks when the black lace thong I'm wearing comes into view, and I try to still my racing heart. He's so incredibly handsome... those strong cheekbones, straight nose, and his perfect lips. Not too full, not too thin. Perfection. Thor looks like he's a roman statue come to life, though he's far more muscular than any statue I've ever seen.

He kisses the lace fabric between my legs, and a moan escapes my lips, disrupting the silence around us. I'm instantly reminded that we're outside, my entire body tensing.

"There's no one around for miles, love. I'm going to make you scream my name tonight, and not a single soul will know. Your moans are mine. Your pleasure is mine, baby."

I nod, and Thor grins as he pushes my underwear aside. I gasp when he leans in and kisses my skin, taking his time to tease me. "I want you closer," I whisper, feeling self-conscious. He looks as though he struggles to pull away from me, a pleading gaze in his eyes as he looks up to me, but I shake my head. "Please."

There's something about him that makes me feel vulnerable. I can't watch him between my legs, feeling as exposed as I do. I want his body covering mine, his lips on mine. "Mark my words, love. Someday, I'm going to bury my face between your legs, and you're going to beg me to let you come on my face. It might not be tonight, but that time will come."

I smile at him, my heart hopeful even as desire rushes through me. I want this. I want more nights with Thor. I want more of this thing between us.

He rises to his feet and pushes against my shoulder, until he's got me flat on my back. I giggle as he leans over me, giving me exactly what I wanted. I don't hesitate to hook my leg around his hips to pull him closer, and he smirks at me as he keeps his lips just an inch from mine. Close, but just out of reach.

"God, it's like you walked straight out of my wildest

fantasies," he whispers, his lips brushing over mine with every word. "You're so fucking sexy."

He kisses me, and this time, his kiss is different. Slower, sexier. His body moves against mine, and I moan against his lips. I tug at his t-shirt, wanting it off, and Thor chuckles as he rises to his knees. His eyes are on mine as he lifts his t-shirt, exposing his abs, taking his time. He's broad and strong, and I want to see more. I want him naked.

I bite down on my lip as his body comes into view. Damn... he felt good against me, but he looks even better. The way I'm looking at him must please him, because he chuckles before lowering himself back down on me.

"Your turn," he tells me, and I lift my hips for him as he pulls my dress up and over my head, leaving me lying here in nothing but my black underwear.

"Fuck," he groans. "I'm probably the luckiest husband alive, love. You're fucking stunning."

I look away, suddenly feeling self-conscious. The breeze that dances over my skin just adds to my shyness, and I turn my head, my cheeks heating.

"None of that," Thor says as he leans in, his lips brushing over my neck. He kisses me right below my ear, making me shiver in the best way. He kisses me like that, until he's all I can think of.

I'm desperate for his touch by the time his hands reach my bra, and a soft sigh escapes my lips when he undoes my bra.

"I'm going to make sure I'm all you think about every damn time you close your eyes, Leia."

Seven

ADRIAN

I pull her bra away so that I've got her lying in the bed of my truck in nothing but her lace thong. It's just me and her underneath the stars, and it couldn't be more perfect. She looks at me, her eyes brimming with desire, and I swear I could come just by looking at her.

I rise to my knees and let my eyes roam over her body leisurely, committing every second of this moment to memory. I already know one night with her won't be enough. She's got me spellbound, and I haven't even fucked her yet.

"These have to go," I tell her, placing my hands on her hips, my thumbs brushing over her thong. Ley nods, and I smirk as I drag the fabric down, exposing her pussy. Fuck. She's so fucking smooth, I wish she'd let me bury my face between those thick thighs of hers. I need a fucking taste.

"Your turn," she murmurs once I've got her naked, and I nod.

I bring my hands to my hips to take my jeans and boxers off, but she shakes her head and rises to her knees. "Let me."

I inhale sharply when she kisses my neck, my eyes falling

closed for a moment. There's nowhere I'd rather be at this moment. Ley kisses my neck, her teeth grazing my ear, and I groan as I bury my hands into her hair. She's teasing me, and I doubt she realizes how badly she's affecting me. "If you keep doing that, I'm not going to last long, baby."

She chuckles, and I can't help but smile, too. "I have a feeling you won't disappoint," she tells me, her fingertips tracing over my erection. She cups my cock through the fabric of my boxer shorts and smirks at me.

"If your hair wasn't dark, you'd really look like Thor, you know?"

She bites down on her lips as she drags my boxers down, my cock springing free. I barely keep from moaning when she palms my erection, holding it tightly, pumping up and down. Her fucking touch sets me on fire.

"Nope," I tell her. "I can't do this."

I grab her hair and kiss her harshly, lying her down, my body covering hers. The way she moans against my lips drives me insane. Just the sound of her is nearly enough to make me lose my damn mind.

I reach between us, my fingers finding their way between her legs. "Tell me how badly you want to come for me, wifey."

"You know I want it," she says, her tone pleading.

I smirk and brush my thumb over her clit, enjoying the way she moves her hips against me. Everything about her is so honest. There's no holding back, no games. It's clear she wants me, and the way she rides my fucking hand has my cock throbbing. I desperately need to be inside her, but not before I watch her come for me.

I push a finger into her, stroking her g-spot, and the way her eyes widen has me chuckling in victory. She looks fucking incredible lying here, her body on display for me. She's a work of art, and tonight, she's all mine.

"You're teasing me," she warns.

I smirk as I add my thumb to her clit, lowering my lips to hers to silence her moans. Her pussy is so fucking hot, so tight. I have no idea how my cock will fit inside her when she's sucking up my finger like that.

"Thor," she moans, opening up for me. My tongue brushes over hers, and the way she kisses me... fuck. That mouth of hers. She kisses me like she's sucking my goddamn cock, and I can't get enough of her.

"Please. Please, Thor."

"You want to come for me?"

She nods, her hands threading through my hair. Her nails brush over my scalp, her touch desperate and frantic.

"Then come for me, wifey."

And she does. Her eyes fall closed and I'm fucking enthralled. She looks like she's experiencing pure fucking bliss, and for a moment I wish I'd waited to make her come until I'm deep inside her, so I could join her in this moment.

She smiles at me lazily when she opens her eyes, her gaze roaming over my body. "You're the best husband I ever could've asked for," she tells me, grinning.

I tear open a condom and roll it on, my eyes never leaving hers. "And you're about to show me how much of a good wife you are, aren't you?"

I grab her ankles and push her legs over her shoulders. "I've wanted to fuck you like this from the moment I walked into the bar and saw you wearing these heels."

I push the tip of my cock into her, and another moan escapes her lips. "So fucking tight, baby. How am I supposed to fit my cock inside you, huh?"

She's fucking tiny. Five feet at most, but I have no doubt she can take me just fine. "Oh God, Thor," she moans. "I can't."

I push in further and shake my head. "You can, baby. Look at you, taking my cock like the good girl you are."

She groans when I'm halfway inside her and shakes her head. "Too tight," she murmurs. "I want you so badly, but I can't do it. It doesn't fit."

I chuckle and push in deeper. "You're doing so well, baby." I look down and watch my cock disappear into her hot pussy. I lower myself on top of her, pushing her legs further against her, until my cock is all the way inside her. "Such a good fucking girl."

She moans loudly and reaches for me, her hands threading through my hair. She pulls me closer roughly, and I kiss her, giving into my need for her.

I fuck her roughly, thrusting deep and hard, until I've got her screaming my name. "Oh God, Thor," she moans, and it's fucking music to my ears. It's just me and her, surrounded by the smell of freshly cut grass and a soft breeze.

I pull away to look at her when I get close, wanting more of her. I'm deep inside her, but it isn't enough. This woman... I want every piece of her.

"I'm going to come," I warn her, and she nods, her eyes glazed over with lust. I look into her eyes as I empty deep inside her, pleasure unlike anything I've ever felt before slamming through me.

All my strength leaves me, and I collapse on top of her. She lowers her legs and wraps them around me as I bury my face in her neck, needing a moment to catch my breath. "That can't have been real," I tell her, and she laughs.

"That's pretty much exactly how I felt. I think you ruined orgasms for me, Thor."

"It's all part of my evil plan," I explain. "Now that I've made you come that hard, no one else will ever compare. Every time you close your eyes and touch yourself, it's me you'll think of."

She chuckles and hugs me tightly. "You've got me hooked, huh?"

I nod and kiss her neck, my heart heavy. I don't want tonight to end, but I know it has to. I might be joking about getting her hooked, but the one battling an emerging addiction is me. I already need more of her, and my cock hasn't even softened yet.

I turn us over and take care of the condom before pulling her into my arms, my eyes on the stars above her. Ley has her head on my chest and her leg hooked over my hip, and I don't think I've ever felt quite this much at peace.

"Did I make you feel a bit better?" I ask. When I saw her sitting in that bar, she was shrouded in sadness. Even if it's just for a moment, I wanted to carry her burdens for her. "I know you said you didn't want to talk, but I can't stop thinking about the sadness I saw in your eyes. I just want you to know that I'm willing to listen. Sometimes, there's nothing better than talking to a stranger."

Ley shifts in my arms and nods. "It isn't something I dare admit, not even to myself." She hesitates, burying her face in my neck before she continues. "But somehow I just feel so comfortable with you."

I wrap my arms around her, holding her tightly as I wait for her to speak, if that's what she wants.

"My sister just had a baby a few days ago. I'm so happy for her, but I want what she's got. The chances of me ever having a child are slim to none. The doctors told me the chances of me ever conceiving are lower than one percent. That's why I wanted to indulge in that fantasy with you tonight. For just one night, I wanted to pretend that I'm just a normal girl, happily married with children of my own. I'll never have that."

My heart fucking shatters. I never would've suspected this at all. She just seemed so happy indulging in our little fantasy. I feel like a fucking asshole all of a sudden. I've got twins that I love more than anything, and though my family might be falling apart, I know I'd never give them up for the world. I can't imagine a world without them. I bite down on my lip and inhale shakily, vowing to hug them tightly when I get home.

"One percent is still a chance, Ley. I'll admit that I don't really believe in fate, but if it's meant for you, perhaps it'll happen one day. If it doesn't, then there's still some guy out there that would be the luckiest man in the world if he gets to call you his wife."

The mere thought of her with someone else has me tightening my grip on her. I will have to let her go, and someday, someone else is going to make her smile the way I did tonight. I can't stand the idea. Hell, my fucking heart aches at the thought of it.

"Tell me about your day," she murmurs, her nose brushing against my neck as she presses a soft kiss against my skin.

I can't tell her about the kids. It doesn't feel right to admit that the twins we fantasized about actually exist — not when she wants kids more than anything else. I can't do that to her. "It's nothing," I tell her. "I just had a few really dreadful weeks at work, but I pretty much forgot about it the moment I saw you."

I pull her closer and press a kiss to her forehead. "Someday, I'll show you Mercury," I tell her, hoping I get to keep that promise. The time isn't right for us, but I don't think I can let her go.

Eight

LEIA

"Your mom called me last night, asking where you were," Amara says, snapping me out of my daydreams about Thor. She smirks and turns back to the sex toy she's building in our lab.

I groan and run a hand through my hair. "No matter what I do or say, she won't stop treating me like a child. I assume you covered for me?"

Amara grins and winks at me. "Course I did. Told her you were at the lab and couldn't be disturbed because you were on a deadline you totally forgot about."

I smirk at her and shake my head. "Thanks, babe. Sorry about that."

Amara shrugs. "I love your mom. We had a nice little chat when she realized she wouldn't be getting you on the phone. She invited me over for family dinner tomorrow. She's making dal for me."

I gag. "I hate lentils. Why the hell does that need to be your favorite food? Because of you, I have to eat it every damn week."

Amara flips her hair and smiles, acting like the spoiled brat my mom turned her into. Over the years, Amara has become part of my family. Honestly, some days I swear my mom loves her more than she loves me.

"So, tell me about your date," Amara says, her tone coaxing.

I can see the excitement in her eyes and bite back my smile. I suppose it *has* been a really long time since I went on a date. "It was amazing. I just..." I sigh happily and lean forward, memories of last night replaying in my mind.

"I'm going to need more details, babe."

I chuckle and hesitate for a split-second before telling her every single detail. There's no way I would've been able to keep anything from her, after all. Not for very long, at least.

Amara listens, her expression betraying her giddiness. I love that about her. She wants me to be happy with such selfless voracity. By the time I finish telling her my story, she's got stars in her eyes.

"You're going to marry him. That fantasy is definitely coming true. I have a feeling about it," she tells me, and I burst out laughing, my heart skipping a beat. I wish. I doubt marriage is in the cards for me, but I'd love to spend more time with Thor.

"He hasn't texted me since last night. He drove me home and dropped me one block away. Didn't even blink an eye when I told him my family is crazy. For a minute, I thought he wasn't going to give me his number, but I channeled my inner Amara and outright asked him for it. He gave himself a missed call using my phone, but I'm not sure... I think he might actually not contact me."

Amara frowns and shakes her head. "How could he not? Your night together sounds absolutely perfect. I can't imagine him not wanting more of that."

I bite down on my lip and push down my worries. I was certain he wanted more too, but the way he looked at me before he kissed me goodbye... there was something finite about it.

"Text him," Amara says, crossing her arms. "Just something

simple. Something you'd send to a friend. Just see how he responds."

I shake my head. "I'm not sure that's a good idea."

"You can either get it over with, or torture yourself with waiting, and the countless scenarios that I'm certain are running through your mind. Forget the whole playing hard-to-get bullshit, Ley. When you have a connection like the one you described, that doesn't matter. He doesn't sound like the kind of guy that'd want to play games."

I nod and grab my phone, staring at it in fear. It's crazy how much power this little device holds over me. I glance back at Amara, who is looking at me with a confident smile, and I inhale deeply before unlocking my phone. I type out a text and show it to Amara.

Hi, this is Ley. Just wanted to send you a quick text to thank you for last night. You turned a somewhat somber night into a delightful one :)

"Sounds good," she says. "Send it."

I look at her, true terror coursing through me as I press send. My heart is racing and my hands are clammy, all over one measly little text. I jump when I receive an almost instant reply.

Hi! I think I had a missed call from you late last night too. I was home all night like a sad sap, so I think you might have the wrong number.

My hands start to tremble as my heart drops, a deep ache settling in my chest. He gave me the wrong number?

"What is it?" Amara asks, a hint of concern in her voice. She grabs my phone from me and reads the text, freezing as she undoubtedly comes to the same conclusion I did. "That asshole."

I take my phone back from her, disbelief urging me to send one more text. I can't believe he'd give me the wrong number. Not after the night we had.

This isn't Thor?

Once again, the reply comes almost instantly.

I'm no Norse God, though many women have told me I look just like one (okay fine, only my mom thinks so). Sorry, Ley. My name is Lex.

I put my phone down, my heart constricting painfully. He really gave me the wrong number. Why would he do that? Why not refuse to give me his number in the first place? Why not just tell me honestly that it was just a one-night stand to him? My thoughts drift back to last night. He told me he'd show me Mercury someday. He never once gave me any indication that we'd never see each other again after last night. If anything, he led me to believe quite the opposite.

I sink down in my seat, feeling like a complete fool. I should've known better. Good things aren't meant for me. I didn't even expect it to go beyond last night. Not truly. Yet somehow, I can't push away the intense sadness I feel.

"Ley, I'm so sorry," Amara whispers. "He's such an asshole. I can't believe he'd do that to you. Based on what you told me, I definitely didn't expect that. Do you think it might just have been an accident?"

I shake my head. "No. If he wanted to be sure he had my number, he would've checked his phone to make sure he truly had a missed call from me. He'd have made sure he had my number. He typed the digits into my phone himself."

Amara wraps an arm around me, and I lean into her. It's strange to feel so heartbroken when I barely even know Thor. I don't even know his real name, and he doesn't know mine. I should've known better.

"Aria can probably find him, if you want? She's brilliant. If it involves data, there's nothing she can't dig up. There isn't that much to go on, but I reckon Aria can still track him down, somehow. Should I call her and ask for a favor?"

For a moment, I consider saying yes. Aria, Amara's boyfriend's sister, is a brilliant programmer, but my pride saves me from saying yes. "No. If he wanted to be found, he'd have given me his real number. This isn't an accident, Amara."

She looks at me, my pain mirrored in her eyes. I sigh and stare up at the ceiling. It was just one night, so why does it hurt so much? I guess it's because I truly let myself feel something for the first time in years. For a few hours, I let myself believe I could have everything we were fantasizing about, that I could have a husband like Thor, that the happiness I felt last night could last.

That's where I went wrong. I used up all of my good luck when I survived against all the odds. I shouldn't be expecting more out of life.

"It's okay, babe," I tell Amara, knowing she's worried. "There are plenty of fish in the sea, right? He's just one guy. It was a bit of fun, but I doubt I'll even remember him in a month. It is what it is."

Amara nods, but I suspect she knows I'm lying to both her and myself.

college girlfriend for years now. The elusive billionaire cousin that specialised in robotics, just like she did. The one that inspired Amara's career path, the one she's always looked up to. The cousin who lives in London and has two kids. Twins. A boy and a girl.

He freezes when he sees me, his eyes widening. Noah shakes his hand, but his attention is on me.

It's been two years, but all of a sudden, the pain feels fresh. My heart squeezes painfully and I inhale shakily, trying to calm my racing heart. I wasn't just a one-night-stand. I was an affair while his wife was at home with the two kids he pretended to have with me.

I turn around and walk away, needing a moment to compose myself. For so long, I've wondered what it might be like to run into him again someday. For a little while, I deluded myself into believing that fate would bring us back together. I was convinced that what we had was so special that the Gods would make our paths cross when the time was right. I must've been crazy.

I was stuck on the memory of who I thought he was when I never even truly knew him. The worst part is that I realized it, but I kept allowing myself to live in a fantasy of my own making. I rush toward a quiet part of the garden the wedding is being held in, needing some space. A deep ache settles in my stomach as my heart constricts, my breathing becoming labored. I'm on the verge of having a full-blown panic attack or bursting into hysterical tears. If my lungs could support both actions, I'm quite certain I'd be doing both.

"Ley!"

I tense at the sound of his voice, hating the way it sends a shiver through me. I force myself to pull it together, to smile through the pain like I've done so many times before. I've never struggled to keep up pretenses, but tonight I worry the cracks in my carefully constructed mask will make my whole facade fall apart.

I swallow hard and force a smile onto my face before turning toward him. Seeing him feels like being punched in the stomach. He's every bit as handsome as he was that night. More so, in the tuxedo he's wearing. His deep blue eyes meet mine, his gaze pleading.

"Ley," he repeats, his voice soft. He looks at me the same way he did that night, and some of the guilt I carry falls away. I didn't imagine this. I didn't warp my memories of him to make them better than they were. He truly is looking at me like I'm all he can see. There's real emotion in his eyes, just like there was that night. How does he do that? How does he fool me with such ease, and how many women have come before me, after me? How many times has he cheated on his wife?

"Adrian, is it?" I ask, grateful for the polite tone of my voice. Somehow, I manage to sound unaffected, and he tenses, his gaze roaming over my face, almost as though he's searching for something.

"Ley. I—" he runs a hand through his hair, a tortured expression on his face, and I can't help but wonder why he's the one that looks pained when it's my heart that's breaking. I suppose it's because he's worried I'll talk and expose what he did. I doubt he ever expected to run into me again.

I stare at him, refusing to give him an easy way out. I'm many things, but I'm not immoral. I'm not a home wrecker. I'm not the other woman.

"You what?" I ask, forcing him to finish his sentence.

"I... I'm happy to see you again. How have you been?"

How have I been? Is he joking?

"How are *you*? How are your wife and kids?"

He flinches, and I grit my teeth. I want to ask him if his wife knows he goes around fucking other women when he's overseas. I want to know if he thought of me at all once he got back home to her. Am I just one woman out of many?

I look away, a thought occurring to me. His wife might be here. It's Amara's wedding, and he's her first cousin. The kids that stood behind him earlier looked like him, so it's reasonable to assume his wife is here too.

"It isn't... it isn't like that, Ley. I'm divorced."

I look up, startled. "Were you divorced when you slept with me?"

Thor tenses, the guilty look in his eyes betraying him. "Let me explain," he pleads. "It isn't what you think."

I inhale sharply, the pain in my chest making me lightheaded for a moment. As I look at him, I can feel my heart physically aching. I suppose that's why they call it heartbreak. The feeling goes straight from my heart right down to my stomach, a sense of hopelessness taking me captive.

"This isn't the time or place for it, Thor. Today is my best friend's wedding day, and that's all I want to focus on. Besides, it was just a one-night-stand. It doesn't matter."

I turn and walk away from the man that used to be part of my favorite memories. Within seconds, the same memories I treasured turned into a source of endless pain, and I only have myself to thank for it.

I take one lingering look at him and turn to walk away. The moment I realized he gave me the wrong number, I should've known. I should've forgotten about him right there and then. I should've forced him out of my thoughts.

That's the most painful part of regret. It's a hurt of its own. It festers, turning all it touches into ashes.

Ten

ADRIAN

I lean back in the hallway of our new house, unable to stop thinking of her when I should be exploring our new home. Leia. Her name is Leia. I've heard of her before. The few times I spoke to Amara, she'd mention her best friend with the lovable family Amara wishes she could be part of. The girl that has starred in my every fantasy for the last two years is my younger cousin's best friend.

"Dad?"

I tense and paste a smile onto my face as I turn toward my son. The last two years haven't been easy on the kids. They have to come first. I can't let the feelings Leia awakened in me take over. Ever since I saw her, I've been meaning to find her and explain myself. When I saw the pain in her eyes, I wanted to ask her to forgive me, but I know I don't deserve it.

"What's up, Colt?" I ask, my tone gentle.

He stares at me, his blue eyes unwavering. My son is far more perceptive than a ten-year-old should be, and he's often affected by my mood. If I'm even remotely sad, he will be, too. I can't figure out how he does it, but no matter how I try to hide my feelings from him, he always mirrors me.

"Can I pick out my room?"

I nod and glance around the fully furnished house, courtesy of my grandfather. It's a modern house that's far larger and newer than what we had in London. The large windows and the excessive amount of light coming in are my favorite features so far. That, and the security guards that come with the house. Not only is it in a gated community, it's also heavily guarded. Since I can't always be with the kids, knowing they're safe sets me at ease.

It's isn't the house I'd have picked for us, since I prefer older houses, but this feels like a fresh start. I easily could've found something myself, but part of the reason I wanted to move back here was so I could rely on my family more. I need to give them a chance to be there for me. They've never let me down before, but I have to be willing to receive their help. This house is a good first step for both my grandfather and me.

Colton takes his sister's hand and pulls her up the stairs with him. Colton seems to be handling the move well, but Lucy has barely spoken a word since her mother left. Alice and me separating has forced them to grow up quicker than I wish they did. I've tried my hardest to shield them from everything that's going on, but it's been near impossible.

The longer our divorce proceedings took, the more toxic Alice's behavior became. When she asked for a divorce, she swore she wouldn't involve the kids. I wish she'd kept her word.

I sigh as I follow the sound of Lucy's voice up the stairs, pausing in the hallway. It sounds like Colton is chatting up a storm in an effort to get his sister to join in on his excitement, and he seems to be succeeding. It's been so long since I heard the kids chitchat in such a carefree way. I lean back against the wall and let my eyes fall closed, a smile tipping up the edges of my lips.

A fresh start is exactly what we need. The home Colton and Lucy grew up in is filled with painful memories. I just hope I'm doing the right thing. I don't doubt that it isn't going to be easy.

The new house is exciting now, but that'll wear off. Once it does, I'll be left with twins who will be missing everything they've ever known. I hope I can make up for the loss of their mother's presence in their lives. I just hope I'm enough.

"Can I have this room, Colt?" Lucy asks, her voice so sweet that it hurts my heart.

"No way! This room is bigger than the other one!"

"*Please.* Look, you can see the birdhouse from here. You don't even like birds. You're just going to play Minecraft all day, anyway."

I purse my lips to hold back my laughter and tip my face up toward the ceiling. My sweet daughter is right. Colton is obsessed with that game. I've tried my hardest to take an interest so I can play with him, but I don't get it.

I wait and listen, curious what Colton will say, though I'm quite certain I know how he'll respond. "Okay, fine," he huffs, and I smirk. My little man can't deny his sister anything. Hell, I'm a fool for her, too. One sweet smile, and Colt and I give her our hearts on a silver platter.

I'm so glad they've got each other. No matter what my kids go through, they go through it together. People often say that twins are different, and it's true. They have a connection unlike anything I've ever seen before, right down to one of them knowing when the other is hurt. I've stopped trying to understand it and just count myself lucky for being their dad.

When I'm certain the kids are okay, I push away from the wall to find my bedroom. It's the only room in the house I furnished myself, and truthfully, it's strange having a room to myself, one that isn't to Alice's taste. I pause in the doorway, taking in the dark mahogany furniture, the entire room done up in black and browns. My eyes pause on the California King bed and my thoughts immediately turn to Ley and the fantasy we indulged in. Seeing her at Amara's wedding unsettled me far more than I expected. She wasn't meant to be more than a one-night-stand, but walking away from her was one of the hardest things I've ever had to do. I know I did the right thing for the kids, but I can't help but wonder what would've happened if I'd given her my number. I've thought of her so often since that night, and several times I was tempted to come back and hunt her down, even if it was just to have one more taste of her.

I think back to the pain and disappointment I saw in her eyes. I should've explained myself, but it wouldn't change anything. I still can't have her. My focus needs to be on the kids. I can't give Leia all of me. I can't introduce a woman into the kids' lives, and I can't date the way she'd want to. I can't treat her the way she should be treated, and I refuse to give her half a man when she deserves the world.

I run a hand through my hair, my heart heavy with regret. I wish I could have a chance with her. I love my kids more than anything, but a part of me wishes I could be the man she wants. Leia wants the type of love that builds slowly. She wants to date, get married, and then try for a baby. The way she described her dreams to me made it obvious she's the traditional kind.

Despite that, I can't help but wonder what she'd think of the kids. Would she accept me and my twins, even though she might deserve better? For a few moments, I let myself daydream about a reality where I could be with her.

I've wanted more of her from the moment I drove away, knowing I gave her the wrong number. I left her behind, yet fate brought her back to me. I'm not a superstitious man, but I can't dismiss this. I smile as I think back to her obsession with Mercury Retrograde, and I can't help but wonder what she thinks of us running into each other again.

I sit down on my bed and stare out the window, my heart hopeful. I might not be able to be with her, but if she'll let me, I can finally show her Mercury. If she'll let me, I'd want nothing more than to spend a bit more time with her. I don't know what it is about her, or what it was about that night, but I crave her presence. I can only hope she feels the same way.

Eleven

LEIA

I stare at Professor Larson, the words not quite registering. "Leia?" he says, his tone gentle. "I promise that it's going to be fine. I'm spending all of next week discussing your research and dissertation with Professor Astor. Don't you worry. Even though I'm retiring, I'll still be available for any questions you might have, but I really don't think you'll need me. Professor Astor is a brilliant young man. He's going to do an excellent job at supervising you, and he's published several papers that are in line with your research. He might well be a better fit for you than I ever was."

"No," I say, my ears buzzing. "No. I don't want to work with him." My heart starts to race at the thought of having to see him every few days, and not in a good way. My breathing becomes a little quicker as panic threatens to overtake me, and I struggle to stay in control. He can't become my advisor. I can handle seeing him every once in a while at occasions Amara might host, but I don't want to have to work with him.

Professor Larson smiles at me gently. He's been my PhD advisor for years now, and he didn't even tell me he was planning to retire. Even worse, Thor is replacing him? It can't be. This cannot be happening to me.

"Professor Astor will be able to provide you with any support you need, Leia. I promise you. None of the other faculty staff are a good fit for your subject. I stayed as long as I did because there was no one to replace me, but now there is."

I shake my head. "You don't understand," I tell him, scrambling to come up with an excuse. "He's... he's my best friend's cousin. It would be inappropriate."

Professor Larson crosses his arms and smiles at me. "What is the name of this college?" he asks me, and I grimace.

"Astor College."

He nods. "Your best friend's family owns this entire school. By that logic, either of you attending here would be inappropriate. We have rigid systems in place to prevent nepotism. You're still going to have to defend your dissertation yourself, Leia. Let Professor Astor help you. He's a good man, and his academic record is impressive. Besides, he's powerful. *Really* powerful. Adrian Astor isn't just Harold Astor's grandson, he's also made a fortune integrating machine learning with robotic prosthetics. The man is a genius. Having him in your corner would change your entire career. You're both in biotech, and the two of you working together could lead to unprecedented changes in the industry. Being associated with him could open up doors for you that I can't. He can shield you from some of the biases in the industry."

I hear the words he isn't saying. I'm a woman in a man's field, and I'm a woman of color, at that. Having Adrian Astor's name associated with mine would protect me from some of the bias and discrimination I often face. I get it, but I don't have to like it. Why is it that no matter how hard I work, it's never enough? Why do I need protection at all? Why can't my work speak for itself? What does my gender or ethnicity matter?

I nod, defeated. Professor Larson will not budge, and he's probably right. I can't think of another professor that would be a good fit. I looked up Adrian Astor the moment I realized who he was, and his research is impressive. It's not my exact subject since I focus on robotics in reproductive surgery, while he's more of a generalist, but he's likely to be a good advisor.

I'm lost in thought as I walk through the corridor, feeling conflicted. How could this happen to me? I spent two years thinking about this man, and now he suddenly invades every aspect of my life?

I can't stomach the thought of seeing him on a weekly basis, but there's no getting out of this. I always believed in fate, but this feels a lot like the cruel results of bad karma.

Twelve

ADRIAN

I stare at the file with details on the PhD student I'll be supervising. Leia Sital. Not only is she my little cousin's best friend, she's my student too. Getting involved with Leia in any way wouldn't just put my relationship with Amara at risk, it would also put my career and Leia's PhD at stake.

I sit back in my seat, my eyes on the framed certificates hanging on my wall. I shouldn't even be thinking of being with her. Besides, she didn't exactly look happy to see me, and I can't say I blame her. We spent one perfect night together, and I ghosted her.

Leia and I were never meant to last beyond that one night, yet I can't get my mind off her. I felt lost when I returned to London, and every day I regretted not giving her my phone number. A few times, I got so desperate to see her one more time, that I contemplated coming up with an excuse to go see Grandpa, just so I'd have a reason to return to the States.

Each time I got close to booking a flight, something would

happen with the kids, reminding me that I can't get involved with anyone while the kids are going through so much.

I tense when I hear a soft knock on my door and straighten my suit jacket before pulling on my tie. "Come in!"

The door opens, and Leia walks in, her expression carefully blank. "Professor Astor," she says, nodding politely. I wonder what she thought when she realized I'd become her professor. The blank look on her face tells me she was aware long before she walked in here. Was she at least a little bit excited to see me again?

I drink her in, letting my eyes roam over her face. She's still as beautiful as she was two years ago. "Please, take a seat."

She nods and takes the seat opposite me, the two of us alone for the first time in years. I wonder if she ever thought of me. Did she dream of our night together as often as I did?

"I'm sorry, Ley."

She looks up then, a flash of hurt in her eyes, and then it's gone. "I'm here because you're replacing my doctoral advisor. Is that correct?"

I nod, at a loss for words. She's shutting me down, and I'm unsure what to do. "Leia... look, we're going to have to work together. You're an adjunct professor, my teaching assistant, and I'll be your advisor for the remainder of your PhD. We can't avoid each other, and we're both adults. Wouldn't you rather start off with a clean slate?"

She looks at me, and I wonder what she's thinking. She's nearly impossible to read today, and it unsettles me. I'm not sure what I expected... I guess I hoped that despite the disappointment I'm sure I caused, she'd still think back on our time together somewhat fondly. It certainly still is one of my favorite memories.

"You're right, Professor Astor. However, I would argue that there isn't much to say. Let's agree to move forward as though today is the first time we're meeting each other."

I clench my jaw and look away for a moment, before turning back to her. "You want me to pretend that night never happened?

Like I didn't have your body underneath mine, your moans in my ear, and my—"

"*Yes!*" she cuts me off. "I want you to do exactly that. It was a one-night-stand, Professor, and it was years ago. I barely remember it, and I'm certain it's the same for you. There's no need to make things awkward between us, is there?"

She can barely remember our night together? That's bullshit. I stare at her, trying to figure out if she's lying to me or not, but there isn't a single hint of nerves on her face. To her, our night together is just a distant memory, a night of fun.

Hell, she's still a student. She's the only woman I've slept with in years, but it probably isn't the same for her. I stare down at her files and nod. "Tell me about your dissertation subject," I say, giving in.

I glance at her, unable to resist temptation. I've thought of her so often since I walked away from her, but I should've known better. A woman like Leia is far too good for a divorcee with two kids. I knew that when I gave her the wrong number, so I shouldn't be surprised to hear she moved on. I peek at her ring finger, relief rushing through me when I find it empty. At least she isn't married.

Leia nods and starts to run me through the prototype she built for minimally invasive surgical techniques that are becoming more and more common in gynecologic surgery, and it takes all of me not to stare at her. I already knew she was brilliant... I just didn't realize just how much so. It's one thing to write a dissertation, it's something else entirely to build an entire prototype to support your research. If I'm not mistaken, this has everything to do with the health issues she faces herself. I can see why this subject is so important to her, and why her research has taken her this long to complete.

I run a hand through my hair and rise from my seat, unable to contain my agitation. "You'll be teaching two of your own classes, and I'll expect you to resume your role as TA, so you'll be doing a lot of the grading for classes I teach."

Leia looks at me, her gaze searching. "Yes, that's completely fine by me. I want to go into teaching eventually, so I don't actually mind my adjunct professor role. If anything, I've sought it out. I don't even really mind grading."

I look at her and walk around my desk. Leia rises from her seat, and my eyes roam over her body. "Professor Astor?" she asks, her voice trembling slightly.

"Call me Thor."

This time, I notice the flash of anger in her eyes. Her shoulders tense and she lifts her head to look at me. She's so fucking tiny. I want to wrap my hands around her waist and lift her onto my desk. I want a taste of her.

"I think not," she snaps.

"Why?" I ask, pausing in front of her. She barely reaches my chest, yet she looks intimidating as hell staring me down like that. Intimidating, and beautiful as fuck. "I've told my other PhDs to call me by my name too."

"Your name isn't Thor."

"Then call me Adrian."

"I think I'll stick with Professor Astor."

I smile down at her. She could've taken a step away, but she hasn't. "Fine. I love the way you make it sound anyway."

Her lips part, as though in outrage, and I chuckle. I can't help it. I shouldn't be teasing her, but I don't want to be just her professor. I want to be more to her. I have no right to want anything from her, but I'm only human. There isn't much I want out of life — my entire world revolves around the twins. She's the only thing I've ever wanted for myself since they came into the world. Just her. I know I'll never have her, but I want these moments with her. I want to shock her out of the prim persona she's displaying. I want to tease out the Leia I used to know. I'm a selfish asshole for wanting to, but I do. I want her.

"Ley... I can't make up for what happened, but I was serious when I said I wanted a clean slate. That doesn't mean that I want to forget about our night together. It certainly doesn't mean that I want you to forgive me, because I know I don't deserve that... but we'll be working together, and maybe we could be friendly to each other, you know? Hostility and distance aren't going to help either of us, not when we'll be working together so closely."

"You want to be... friends?" Leia asks, taking a step away from me. Is that pain I'm seeing in her expression?

"No," I tell her. "I want a whole lot more than that, but friendship is all that can exist between us while you're one of my students. I might be a selfish asshole, but I won't put your doctorate at risk."

Leia's eyes widen, and she bites down on her lip. I swallow hard at the memories that assault me. Her taking my cock, her legs pushed over her shoulders. Those lips of hers on mine. Her lips on my neck as I stared up at the sky. This woman... there's no way she barely remembers our night together.

"I don't want to."

I blink in surprise, and Leia crosses her arms.

"I don't want to be friends with you, Professor Astor. I want you to do your job, and I'll do mine."

She's putting distance between us, and I can't blame her. I only have myself to blame for this.

"Understood," I tell her, but I don't get it. I know I wasn't the only one who felt that spark between us. I'm desperate to have her in my life in any shape or form, yet she can't wait to walk away.

Thirteen

&

ADRIAN

"Are you excited about starting school, sweetheart?" I ask Lucy. She looks up from the book she's reading and nods, but the excitement I was expecting is lacking. She's been like this ever since Alice moved out, and I'm worried. We were so certain she'd grow accustomed to Alice's absence, but she hasn't. For months after the divorce came through, Alice and I continued to live together, because we were worried about Lucy. Even now, I worry bringing her to the States was a bad call.

"Are you excited to see your great-gramps?"

She nods again, a small smile lighting up her face. It isn't like the laughter I'd taken for granted, but it's more than she's given me all day.

"What about you, my little man?" I ask Colt.

"Yup, I'm excited, Dad. You think the kids here play Minecraft too?"

I bite back a smile. "Yeah, I'm pretty sure they do. Don't forget the rules, though. No Minecraft if you haven't done your homework."

I already know I'm going to have to watch him. This kid is addicted to his games, but I'm admittedly quite glad he's got that. He's stayed in touch with his friends back home through it, and it's made the move a lot easier on him than it has been on Lucy.

The doorbell rings, and I grin. "I think your great-gramps and Grandma Charlotte are here," I tell them as I walk toward the door.

"Adrian!" my auntie Charlotte says, wrapping me in a tight hug. "I'm so glad to see you. It feels like it's been forever since you were home."

I smile and hug her back, the smell of her hair still the same as it was when we were kids. She might only be Amara's mother, but she feels like mine, too. She's never just been my aunt to me, and she's always treated me like her own son. "Missed you, Aunt Char."

She pulls away and turns toward the kids, smothering them the way she did me. This. This is exactly what my kids need. When Alice told me she didn't want custody, I knew I'd have to move closer to my family. It wasn't an easy choice to make, but seeing Lucy smiling at Aunt Char sets my heart at ease.

"How'd the move go, my boy?" Grandpa asks, offering me his hand.

I nod. "As well as it could've gone. The house is perfect. It doesn't really feel like nearly two weeks have passed already."

"That was all your aunt," Grandpa tells me. "She furnished it all for you, and she even made sure you'd have whatever you might need for the kids. Pretty sure she was comparing different first-aid kits for a whole day at one point."

I glance back at my aunt with a grateful heart. "Honestly, I'm not sure I can do this without you guys. It's been harder than I expected."

Grandpa places his hand on my shoulder and smiles. "You don't have to do this without us, kiddo. We're all right here, and we're all happy to help. Once Amara is back from her honeymoon, you'll struggle to keep her away from the kids."

I frown at the thought of Amara. I wonder if she knows about Ley and me. I doubt it. If she did, she'd probably have cursed me to hell and back already. I look forward to finally spending some time with my little cousin, but man, do I dread it too.

Perhaps... perhaps I could explain everything to Amara, and with some luck, the story might make its way back to Leia. I shake my head and run a hand through my hair. I'm losing my mind. Leia made it clear she wants nothing to do with me, and I should be grateful for it. I don't need any complications in my life right now.

"You'll be joining Astor Corporation?" Grandpa asks as we walk through the house, and I nod.

"I will, but I also want to keep teaching."

He walks into my home office and looks around, nodding to himself. "It's going to be hard, Adrian. Both jobs are time-consuming, unless you choose to lecture without doing any research for a while. I'll give you three years to wrap up your teaching career. I know you're not ready to say goodbye to it yet, but eventually you must."

I run a hand through my hair and nod. I knew I'd have to step up as Grandpa's successor when I moved here. "I've already put my research on hold for the time being. Interesting how much you get away with being an Astor at Astor College."

Grandpa smirks. "You've spent too much time away. It'll be good for you to be back home. You lost sight of who you are over there. You're an Astor, Adrian. About damn time you start acting like one. You don't need Alice to raise the kids. Not when you've got us, and the best help money can buy."

"That's just it, Gramps. I don't want the kids to be raised by nannies. I want to be there for them. The requirements I asked for still hold true."

Grandpa nods. "Very well. I've already notified building security that the kids will be joining you some afternoons. The next few months will be hard for you all."

I nod. "I know."

"Adrian?" Aunt Charlotte calls. I walk back to the living room and smile when I find Colton sitting next to her. He's usually shy around strangers, but I suppose the video chats throughout the years have helped. Lucy, on the other hand, is still staring down at one of her books. Her reading comprehension is way beyond her age, but I worry she's using reading as a coping mechanism. It's not uncommon for her to grab a book when people are around, and I'm not sure what to do about it.

"Yes, Aunt Char?"

"I'm in the process of hiring you a housekeeper and a nanny. I've personally selected everyone that'll be working with you, and they've all been screened. The housekeeper will start tomorrow, and your nanny will be starting on Sunday, so you have some time to get to know her and see how she interacts with the kids. She'll only work half days, starting with school pickup until you come home. Her hours are pretty flexible, and if you want her to work early mornings too, I'm sure we can make that happen."

I nod, uncomfortable with the thought of a stranger doing everything that Alice once did. Alice used to be a stay-at-home mum. We had a housekeeper, but Alice was still always there if the kids needed her. I don't like this one bit, but I really need the help.

"Understood. If I don't like her..."

"You will. But on the off chance that you don't, I've got a few more lined up. As it is, I'll be hiring two nannies, so there's always someone available."

I nod, glad that my aunt is arranging all of this for me. I'm not sure where I'd be without her.

"Thank you, Aunt Char. Everything you've done for us... honestly, you're amazing."

She smiles at me and shakes her head. "Don't be silly, my boy. You've brought me two kids to spoil. This is the least I can do."

She wraps her arm around Colton, and he giggles as she presses a kiss on his cheek. She and I both glance at Lucy, but my daughter doesn't even look up from her book. I'm worried. My working hours are about to increase, and we're about to introduce two strangers into our lives. I don't know how she's going to cope. I worry it's all too much change.

While I wish I could, I can't be a mother. Lucy and Alice always had a special bond, and I can't replace that. I'm doing all I can, but with each passing day, I wonder if I'm doing the right thing for my kids. I'm terrified that I'm failing them.

Fourteen

LEIA

I pause on the square in front of Astor College, my eyes on the black helicopter approaching us. Campus security starts to cordon the area off, and I move to the side, confused as to what's happening.

"It's Professor Astor, isn't it?" I hear a girl ask. "Typical of the Astor family. I heard he's started to work for Astor Corporation in addition to being a professor here. I barely manage to make it to all of my classes. I can't imagine doing more than one job."

Another girl laughs, the fake sound grating on me. "It's *Adrian Astor*. He's on another level. He's always worked hard, ever since he was young. It's good to have him back."

I turn around, glancing at them as discreetly as I can. I recognize one of the girls as someone Amara always makes small talk with but secretly hates. If I'm not mistaken, she's a family friend of the Astors.

"It sounds like you know him," someone else remarks, and she smiles, clearly enjoying the attention her connection to Thor is giving her.

"Of course I do. He's working on a deal with my father. We're having dinner tomorrow evening."

I take her in, my eyes roaming over her long blonde hair, not a single strand out of place. Her face looks perfect too, the type of perfection that isn't natural. Somehow, the thought of Thor having dinner with her doesn't sit well with me.

The helicopter lands, and the murmurs around me increase when Thor steps out wearing a three-piece suit that looks annoyingly good on him. He seems so unapproachable, so different to my memories of him. He glances at his watch before turning and heading toward the college's entrance, seemingly in a rush.

The blonde who'd just been speaking about him rushes after him, and I watch as she catches up to him. My heart squeezes painfully when he smiles at her and slows his steps to walk in line with her. Who is she?

I grit my teeth as I walk into the college, my mood turning sour. I was already not looking forward to attending my weekly meeting with him, but now I want to see him even less. I round the corner leading to his office and tense when I see him standing with that same girl, her hand on his arm. She's smiling up at him, and he's grinning back at her. What could possibly be so funny?

I should probably give him a moment to finish up his conversation, especially since our meeting isn't due to start for another five minutes, but I just don't feel like it.

"Professor Astor." My voice is sharp, irritation leaking into it despite my best attempts to hide it, and he looks up. His gaze roams over my body, moving over the beige blouse I'm wearing, down to my pencil skirt, before lingering on my silver shoes. They've got a large rhinestone bow at the front, and they're probably one of my favorite pairs. He smirks as his gaze travels back up my body, and I bite down on my lip, instantly nervous. Is he checking me out?

"Leia," he says, pulling back his sleeve to check his watch. "You're right on time. Please follow me."

He turns back to the girl in front of him and smiles apologetically. "I have a meeting, but it was good to see you."

She grins, her fingers brushing over his arm. "I'll see you tomorrow night."

He nods and walks past her, leaving me to follow him to his office. So she wasn't bullshitting then. She's really seeing him tomorrow night. What for? Is he going on a date? The thought of that infuriates me. He ghosted me, but now he can suddenly date?

He sighs as he unlocks his office door and holds the door open for me. I force a polite smile onto my face as I walk past him, catching a whiff of the same aftershave he was wearing years ago. Just the smell of it has a rush of desire spreading through my body, and I suck down on my lower lip in annoyance.

"Please, take a seat."

I nod and sit down opposite him, trying my hardest to keep my eyes off him. He looks tired, but still as handsome as he was then. I still remember the way my fingers trailed over his cheekbones, the way his lips felt against mine. It's strange to be sitting opposite him. Never in a million years could I have imagined that one day, the man who haunted my dreams would be sitting opposite me as my dissertation advisor. It's strange to have him become part of so many aspects of my life, and each time we meet, he seems different.

At Amara's wedding, he seemed insistent on talking to me about that night, but he's nothing but professional this time, and somehow I find myself feeling... *disappointed*. I don't want to listen to any of his excuses, but oddly enough, I don't want to be just another one of his students either.

"I didn't prepare for this meeting," he says, smiling apologetically. "I was running late this morning. I apologize."

I frown, realization dawning. He arrived by helicopter because he was running late for *this* meeting? Surely not?

"That's quite all right, Professor. I've already ran you through my research, so the primary objective of this meeting is to discuss the changes I want to make based on recently published findings."

He nods and indicates for me to continue. "The study released last week indicated that reproductive outcomes when utilizing robotic surgery appear similar to alternative approaches. But simultaneously, when using robotic surgery we're seeing a requirement for specialized training, increased costs and longer use of operating rooms. This study basically says that there's no real point in utilizing robotic surgery when costs of labor, training and facilities increase."

Thor looks at me, and something about his gaze unsettles me. He still looks at me as though I'm the only girl in the world, and I can't help but wonder if the girl I saw him with earlier felt the same way. I feel stupid, and I'm surprisingly upset with myself.

"I'd like to make a change to my dissertation. I'd like to implement machine learning into the robotic surgery equipment I'm designing. Right now, we can't control costs. That'll come with time, as is always the case with innovation. I can make the greatest impact by improving the tools we use. I'd like to focus on creating equipment that learns from each operation, so that reproductive outcomes when using my equipment increases versus manual surgery."

He nods and runs a hand through his hair. "That won't be easy, and it'll be quite the adjustment to your dissertation, but it's possible. I'll give you access to all of my research, both published and unpublished. That will give you a head start."

I look at him in surprise. "You'd really do that?"

He smiles at me sweetly and nods. "Of course I would. I'd like to see you succeed, Leia. If you can accomplish what you've set out to do, it could make a huge difference to the biotech industry. But don't forget, all you need for now is a good concept. It doesn't have to be perfect. Once you have something worth publishing, you'll not only have your doctorate, but you'll also have a good starting point to gain funding for the ideas you have."

I nod. That was my exact thinking too. This dissertation is only just the beginning of what I want to accomplish. I hear what he's saying too. I can't be a perfectionist when it comes to this. If I want to make a real impact, I need to finish my doctorate and find funding for my research.

I grin at him, relieved I came to this meeting after all. I've been feeling out of it, unsure how to handle being one of his students, but he's acted professionally throughout this meeting, leaving me feeling like an idiot for expecting anything else from him. "Thank you, Professor Astor."

He nods and leans back in his seat. "Leia," he says, his voice soft. The way he says my name has my heart skipping a beat, and I swallow hard.

"That girl just now... her name is Eleanor Williams. I've got a meeting with her father tomorrow evening because I'm attempting to acquire his company, and it appears she's attending alongside him. That's all it is."

I tense, trying my best to hide the surprise I feel. "Why are you telling me this?" I ask, even as relief rushes over me. This entire time, my heart has felt heavy. Just those few words took away the jealousy I'd been battling. Did he realize how I felt?

Thor rises from his seat and runs a hand through his thick dark hair. It's slightly longer now, and it looks surprisingly good on him. "No reason," he says, smiling. "I need to head back to Astor Corporation. I'll send you the research you might need, but don't hesitate to ask if you need anything else."

I stand up and nod, my thoughts reeling. "You... did you come in just to have this meeting with me?"

His eyes trail over my face, lingering on my lips for a moment before moving back up to my eyes. "Yes," he admits, before gesturing to the door. My heart is in disarray as I follow him.

"By the way, Leia," he says, turning back to me. His eyes drop down to my shoes, and he bites down on his lip for a moment before smirking. "I love these shoes you're wearing today. They look great. Looks like you have a thing for unique shoes, huh? These remind me of your sunflower shoes."

I stare at him, wide-eyed. He remembers the shoes I wore that night? "I... um, yeah," I mutter eventually, brushing past him and into the corridor. I look back at him, feeling conflicted. "Thanks for today, Professor Astor."

He stares at me, his gaze unreadable. "Anytime, Leia."

I walk away, but I can feel his eyes on me every step of the way.

Fifteen

LEIA

"I can't trust anyone else with VVIP clients, Ley," my sister says. "Please tell me you can take on this client."

I nod absentmindedly, a niggling feeling that I've been ignoring trying to come to the surface as I glance around Asha's office. My mind is still on Thor, and every thought leads back to him. I wonder if I should've let him give me an explanation. It wouldn't make anything right, but perhaps it would give me the closure I so desperately crave. It bothers me that he was so perfectly professional during our meeting, and it makes no sense. Isn't that exactly why I wanted? "Do you know more about who the client is?" I ask.

I've been working part-time as a nanny for Asha's business for years now. Initially, it was just because I wanted to help her out with her new business, but over time it's become something I do because it soothes my soul. I might never have children of my own, but this way, I still get to play a motherly role. I'm aware it's somewhat pathetic, but I've long learned to let myself do what makes me happy without judging myself for it.

"No. I don't have a file for the family. They insist on briefing you in person, but they came with a dozen referrals, and they're paying triple our usual rate."

Asha asked me to take on a special client shortly before Amara's wedding, and at the time I didn't think much of it. It's not uncommon for us to have celebrities or royalty as clients, but I have a feeling this is going to be different. I have a sinking feeling it's going to be *him*. My rotten luck would make it so.

Besides, the Astor family is known for how far out of their way they go to maintain their privacy. Not giving us any information is exactly the kind of thing they'd do, lest our files leak.

I'm barely coping with having him as my professor, I can't work for him too. I can't face his kids after what we did, and I can't be in his home day in and day out, not with the history we share.

For a moment, I consider telling my sister that she should find someone else, but I can see how stressed out she already is. Besides, I have no excuse whatsoever. I've been reassuring her for weeks that I'd take on this client for her, and I can't back out at the last minute. She knows I only teach in the morning, which falls outside of the client's requested working hours, so I can't even use that as an excuse.

"Don't worry," I tell her. "It's going to be okay. I've handled some of our worst clients with ease, haven't I?"

Asha nods, but her gaze lingers on my face. "Are you okay?" she asks suddenly, and I tense, surprised.

"Of course. Why?"

She stares at me and shakes her head. "I'm not sure. You seem off, somehow. You've been quiet for a few days now. Is it because Amara got married? It won't change anything between you two, you know? You won't lose your best friend. If anything, Noah probably feels like the third wheel between you two."

I smile at her words. She's right. Poor Noah does seem like the third wheel between Amara and me. They're on their honeymoon, but she's texted me every single day. I internally apologize to my best friend and seize the excuse Asha is handing me.

"Yeah, you're probably right," I tell her. "It's still weird, though. I miss her already."

Asha looks away, the hint of sorrow in her eyes telling me where her thoughts are leading her. "You should really date someone, you know? Mom is definitely going to start introducing you to the sons of her friends soon. You'll be getting *rishtas* coming your way if you don't find a man yourself."

I roll my eyes and flip my hair over my shoulder at the mention of arranged marriage proposals. "Not everyone wants to get married, you know? Some of us enjoy our freedom."

My sister crosses her arms and stares me down. "Do you? Do you enjoy your freedom? Because all I see is you working yourself to the bone without enjoying your youth. Hell, have one-night-stands every single night if you want. Go partying, get drunk. I'll cover for you, Ley. Just don't hide from life. Don't isolate yourself because you're scared of being vulnerable."

I glare at my sister, her words hitting me where it hurts. "Did you ever stop to think that I enjoy being my myself? I don't enjoy partying, Asha. I never did."

"Fine," she snaps. "But you're hiding behind those romance novels you read. You're clearly reading them because you're looking for a connection, for emotions and experiences you lack in real life. That's what escapism is, Leia. We get to lose ourselves in a world of make-belief... but you? You're so ridiculously beautiful, so talented, so smart, and so incredibly kind. Everyone sees it but you. Put yourself out there, Leia, I beg of you. Give happiness a chance to find you. Please."

My heart clenches painfully, and I push down the pain, leeching its force to fuel my anger. "You're one to talk," I say through gritted teeth. "Escapism?" I ask. "How about you stop trying to live vicariously through me and focus on your own supposed happiness instead? You accuse me of working myself to the bone, but what is it you're doing? You spend more hours here than you do at home. When's the last time you even went on a date with your husband? You're projecting. Stop telling me what I should be doing when you don't even have your own life together."

I regret the words the second they leave my lips, but it's too late. Tears spring into Asha's eyes, and my heart starts to ache for a different reason.

"Leia... I care about you, okay? Of course, my life isn't perfect. Life never is. No marriage is perfect, but I can assure you mine is filled with love, trust, and loyalty. Sure, having kids has been harder on us than we expected, but we're dealing with it. We're adapting, and we're growing. That's what couples do. Is it really so horrible that I want you to experience the thrill of falling in love and being with someone who completes you? Is it so bad that I want you to be happy?"

I look away, guilt rendering me speechless. I can feel my throat closing up and swallow hard in an effort to remain in control of my emotions. I know she wants what's best for me, but I'm not like her. I don't envision my future the way she does. I'm perfectly happy losing myself in books and movies. When I think of my future, I don't see myself married. I gave up on that dream when I was diagnosed as a teenager. I saw what my family went through when I was sick, and I can't ever make anyone else go through it too. I'm in remission, and there's no guarantee it'll remain that way. I prefer to be alone. That way, no one has to suffer alongside me. That way, I won't deprive anyone of anything.

"Leia, you're not broken," Asha whispers, and I look up sharply. "I see the fear and the longing in your expression, sis. You might lie to yourself, but you'll never be able to lie to me. Lash out at me all you want, Leia, but I'll never stop pushing you to reach for what I know you want. Deep down in that locked down heart of yours, I know my words are resounding. Maybe if I repeat it often enough, you'll start to believe it too. Leia, you're not broken. You deserve happiness, just like anyone else does. You are enough as you are."

A tear drops down my cheek, startling me. I wipe it away angrily and look away, my lower lip trembling. I swallow down my tears, refusing to look at my sister. I know she means well. I know she does. "Asha," I whisper. "Please. Just leave me be."

She shakes her head and walks up to me. "I won't. If you won't fight for yourself, I'll do it for you. That's what big sisters do."

She places her hand on my shoulder and squeezes briefly before pulling away. Asha walks away, and the moment she closes her office door behind her, I burst into tears.

Sixteen

LEIA

I stare up at the unfamiliar mansion while a security guard checks my ID, my nerves getting the best of me. I couldn't sleep last night, my thoughts running wild. I can feel it in my bones. The house I'm about to walk into... it'll be his. It isn't even just a house. This is something else. I've worked in expensive houses before, but none of them had this level of security.

Though I try to deny it, Thor has been on my mind from the moment I saw him at Amara's wedding. Even more so since the meeting I had with him. But it's more than that. I can't quite explain it, but it feels like I'm on the cusp of a major pivoting point in my life, and I have a feeling it's got everything to do with Adrian Astor.

I'm trembling as I walk up to the door, surprised when it opens before I even reach it. "Leia!" My eyes widen when Amara's mother waves at me, a wide grin on her face. "Come in, darling!"

Pressure rises to my head and my breathing shortens as I try to comprehend what's going on. Of course. Amara and Adrian are cousins. It makes sense that Charlotte would be here, but I still can't wrap my head around it.

"Charlotte," I say, my voice wavering.

She hugs me tightly before pulling me into the house. "I'm so glad you're here. For a little while, it seemed like your sister was going to refuse to send you. I didn't want anyone other than you looking after the kids."

She ushers me into the house, and I look around nervously. The inside of the house looks every bit as magnificent as the outside does. It's huge, and it's all marble and expensive art. I should've said no. When I suspected it'd be the Astors behind the hiring request, I should've declined. I should've come up with any excuse at all.

I can't do this. I can't be around his kids, not without remembering the betrayal I unknowingly had a hand in.

Charlotte leads me to the kitchen, and I freeze when I see Thor leaning against the wall. His eyes widen when they land on me, and he pushes away from the wall, his entire body tense. "*Ley?*" he asks, almost as though he's in disbelief. Even though I now finally know his name, he'll always be Thor to me.

"Oh good, you two have already met," Charlotte says, wrapping her arm around me. "Adrian, Leia will be your nanny. She's highly trained and has years of experience. She's also pretty much family, and there isn't anyone I trust more with the kids."

"No," he says. "Not her."

I flinch, a stab of pain going straight through my heart. "I agree," I tell Charlotte. "This is not a good idea. I think you should find someone else."

I try to turn away, but Charlotte's grip on me is tight. "And why is that?" she asks, her eyes moving between the two of us.

Thor and I look at each other, neither of us sure what to say. There's so much left unspoken between us, that neither of us can even quantify our relationship.

"We... we don't get along well," I say eventually.

Charlotte looks at me that way my mom sometimes does, as

though she's trying to assess how truthful I'm being. "Hmm... how could that be? You two have only just met, haven't you? How could you possibly have fallen out at Amara's wedding?"

My cheeks heat, and I count my blessings that my face doesn't usually turn rosy like Amara's does. "I... well, we had an argument. I don't think it's wise for us to work together. I'll find you a replacement, Charlotte. I'll personally vet them and make sure you're assigned the most qualified nanny that Asha employs, okay?"

"No," she says, her nose tipped up stubbornly, her expression identical to Amara when she's being stubborn. "No one else will do. You're family, Leia. What the kids need right now is someone who will care for them the way I know you will. I don't trust anyone else."

I look down, unable to deny her when it's clear my agreement means a lot to her. I bite down on my lip and look up at Thor, only to find that his eyes are already on me. I can't reject Charlotte's request, but he can.

"Fine," he says.

What? *Fine?*

"If the kids like her, she can stay. If she can make Lucy hug her before the day is over, she's got the job."

Charlotte's grip on my shoulder turns stiff, and I turn to look at her. Her smile is frosty, and I'd hate to be on the receiving end of the look she's throwing Thor's way.

"Very well," she says, before glancing back at me. "Let me introduce you to the kids before we do anything else. I've already prepared their schedules for you. Absolutely anything you need should already be prepared, and I'm always only a phone call away, but first, we'd better get you all acquainted."

I nod and follow her, oddly nervous. I can't quite make sense of my feelings. I'm feeling so incredibly conflicted. On the one hand, I hate being around Thor, but on the other, I don't want to let Charlotte down. She's always treated me like family, and she's never asked anything of me before. Besides, it's not like she's asking me for a favor. She's paying an obscene amount of money to employ me.

We walk into the living room and I notice that the girl tenses from her spot on the sofa, but she doesn't look up from her book. The boy, on the other hand, tosses me a quick smile before turning back to his game.

"Kids, this is Leia. She's auntie Amara's best friend."

That gets the girl's attention, and she looks up, her expression disarmed. I guess she has a sweet spot for Amara, huh? When she catches me looking at her, she hides behind her book, and I bite back a smile.

"Hi Leia," the boy says, without looking away from the screen.

"Lucy," Charlotte says, nodding at the girl on the sofa, "and Colton."

I nod and walk up to them to sit between them. Lucy tenses, but Colton barely glances at me. "Hmm, Roblox, huh?"

His eyes widen, and when he smiles at me, my heart softens. He looks just like his dad, but with such pure innocence in his smile. "You've heard of Roblox?"

I nod. "You're playing Adopt Me?"

The little guy's mouth falls open. "What? You too?!"

"Yup. Send me a friend request so we can play together."

"No way," he says, as he goes to the search bar. "What's your username? I should've known you were cool when Grandma Charlotte said you're Auntie Amara's best friend."

I smirk at Colton, realizing he's rapidly stealing my heart. "It's PrincessLeia2814."

He sends me a friend request, and then his attention is back on his game, but I don't mind it. There's no resistance on Colton's end. It's Lucy I'll have to win over. But then again... if I fail to make her hug me, then I get to walk out of this job, and I won't have to explain it to Asha.

I glance at Lucy, wondering who will replace me. Will the next nanny care about the way she's using her books as a shield? Will they see through it? Lucy has her walls up way higher than a ten-year-old should have.

"You're reading *The Girl Who Drank The Moon*?" I ask. "Which part did you get to? I loved that story!"

She glances at me over her book, her gaze quietly assessing me. "You've read this?"

I nod. "Yep, I read it with my niece. I loved the story so much I had to read it again. I almost never re-read a book, but I just really loved this one."

She hesitates, and I breathe a sigh of relief when she speaks. "I've only just gotten to the part where Xun feeds the baby moonlight."

"Oh, you're going to love this story! It's just so exciting to find someone who's about to experience a story you love, you know? I can't wait to hear what you think of it."

Lucy lowers her book and looks at me, a genuine smile on her face. "I know what you mean. I feel that way every time I recommend a book to my friends. They never read them, though."

"Yeah, not everyone is into reading, but honestly, it's their loss."

Lucy nods and picks her book up again, and I once again try to take a peek at the pages, trying my hardest to remember the story. "There's this book called *Furthermore* that was also really cool. I think you might like that too. I think I actually have a copy at home if you want to borrow it."

"Oh, I haven't heard of it. I should look it up."

I nod and take another peek at her book. "Do you... did you want to read this with me?" she asks.

My eyes widen, and I clasp my hand together. "Oh really? Can I?"

Lucy purses her lips, hesitating, but then she nods. I don't hesitate to scoot closer to her, and she holds her book out for me so I can read alongside her.

I chuckle when she and I both gasp at the same time, and before I realize it, we start to take turns turning the pages. There's something so sweet about this moment. I once used to be her. When life got tough, and even my own body failed me, I turned to books. I'd escape into worlds unlike my own, where I could be a magical heroine, where I'd be loved, and where there was no pain. I suspect that Lucy is doing the same thing.

"Homework, Lucy," Thor interrupts, and I glance at my watch to find half an hour has gone by without me even realizing it.

I rise from the sofa, hesitating. I know I shouldn't, but for a second I consider asking her for a hug. I bite down on my lip and shake my head slightly, dismissing the idea. Though I know I'd enjoy spending time with these two, I don't think it's a wise call. What I need most right now is distance from Thor. I won't have that if I become his children's nanny. There'd be no escaping him.

"I need to go now, Lucy. I'll make sure to give the book I mentioned to Charlotte, so she can give it to you."

Lucy looks up, and for a moment, I recognize the disappointment I see in her eyes. She's lonely, just like I used to be at her age. It breaks my heart, but I can't be the one to take away her pain. God, I might well be part of the reason she's so lonely. Was her father's infidelity the reason her parents split up? The mere thought of having caused this sweet child any pain kills me.

I swallow hard and turn away. I need to get out of here. "Bye Colton!" I shout, and he yanks his headset off, offering me a cute lopsided smile, and my heart skips a beat.

I hope whoever gets to take care of them does it with all the love I wish I could give them. I'll personally screen our employees to ensure they're assigned the best of the best. It's the least I can do.

My heart feels heavy as I grab my bag, and my guilt only increases when my eyes meet Thor's.

"Can I have a word with you, Leia? In private."

I'm inclined to reject his request, but there's nothing but professionalism in his eyes, so I nod and follow him.

Seventeen

ADRIAN

Leia is quiet as she follows me to my home office, and truthfully, I'm not sure what to say either. All I know is that my daughter loves her. It might not be clear to anyone but me, but she does.

"Have a seat," I tell Leia, gesturing toward the chair opposite my desk. I'm feeling conflicted as I walk around my desk and sit down opposite her. We're both tense, and there's so much left unspoken. We've only just gotten a handle on working together at Astor College, and having her in my home is disorienting.

"When did you become a nanny?"

She stares at me, clearly attempting to assess whether I'm asking her this for personal or professional reasons. "It's been nearly seven years. The company I work for is owned by my sister, and I initially joined to help her through the start-up phase, but I soon fell in love with the work."

I nod. "How have you been able to combine your education with your work?"

Leia straightens in her seat, her walls vanishing, replaced by the professionalism I'd expect of my children's nanny. I look into her eyes, memories flooding my mind. I still remember the way her eyes widened when I kissed her thighs, the way she gasped when I placed my lips right below her ear. I can't look at her without wanting her. I shouldn't hire her. I can't have her in my home for hours every day. I can barely deal with being her professor.

"The role is always diverse. During my undergrad, I only worked as a stand-in nanny. Our firm usually contracts two nannies, so there's always someone available for the family if one of us falls away. My working day as a nanny would often start once the kids are off school, so I'd use the time they were at school to finish my educational work. I've never had a problem combining the two, since my nanny hours have never been more than four hours a day."

How many bloody hours has she been working if you include her PhD? And for how long? It sounds like she's been working herself to the bone for years now. "What are your qualifications?"

"All nannies at our firm are trained in everything you might need, but primarily in habit building, motor skill development, cognitive skills, emotional and moral growth, nutrition, and behavior management. Of course, we're also trained in emergency care and child safety, sir."

"Sir?" I repeat, leaning back in my seat. I like the way that sounds on her lips. She looks so serious sitting opposite me, and I can't help but feel conflicted as hell. I still want her as badly as I did two years ago, but just as I knew then, I know I can't pursue her.

Leia looks away, clearly flustered, and my heart warms. I sigh and run a hand through my hair, trying my hardest to get a handle on my emotions. "Normally, you'd be the last person I'd want around my kids, considering our history, but Lucy likes you," I say eventually. "Colton has been okay, but Lucy has had a hard time recently. I think you might be good for her."

Leia turns back to me, her surprise evident. "Oh," she murmurs, her voice barely above a whisper.

"I would like to hire you, Leia, but before I do so, we need to talk. Really talk." I wouldn't even consider it if I even remotely suspected Leia had any ulterior motives. It's clear to me that she'd rather stay away from me, yet despite our issues, she treated Lucy with such care. She's the kind of person I can trust with my kids, and it's rare for me to feel that way.

Leia crosses her arms and looks out the window, and I stare at her. Her long dark hair drapes over her, and I wish I could thread my hair through it, my fingers grazing over her scalp, before I yank her closer. I grit my teeth and look away. I've never wanted anyone as much as I want her.

"I don't think we should work together. It's bad enough that we have to see each other so much because of my doctorate," she says.

"There's no getting out of us seeing each other, so what difference does it make?"

She looks startled, and then she nods. "I suppose that's true."

I exhale a breath I didn't even know I was holding. I shouldn't want her around my kids, but damn it, I do. Seeing her sitting there with Lucy, the two of them reading together... fuck. It just felt so right when for months, I've felt like I'm walking a fucking tightrope, like I'm one wrong step away from crashing down.

"I would like you to take the job as the kids' nanny, but regardless, we're going to be working closely together. I prefer to clear the air between us, if you will allow me. We can only evade the topic for so long."

She looks at me, her guard slipping back in place. She tenses, but she nods.

"That night two years ago? My ex-wife and I had already signed our divorce papers, but it just hadn't been processed yet. What should've been a straightforward filing ended up being a drawn out battle."

She looks surprised, and her shoulders slump. Ley... I have no doubt a million terrible thoughts ran through her mind when she saw the kids.

"Alice and I... the divorce came out of nowhere, which is what made it so much harder on the kids. They, and I, thought we were such a happy family. To say I was surprised when Alice asked for a divorce is an understatement."

Leia looks down at her hands, her expression hidden from me. I'm not sure what she's thinking, but I do know that I need to be honest with her. If she's going to be around my children, I can't have anything standing between us. I won't expose them to any more turmoil.

"That's the reason I walked away after that night, Leia. I won't lie to you and pretend it meant nothing to me, because that's not even remotely what it was. Being with you, having that night underneath the stars in one of my favorite places, it was magical. It was exactly what I needed after a couple of really shitty months. You made me feel like myself again, and you made me smile when my days had been filled with misery. That one night has been seared in my mind from the moment I walked away, and several times I regretted not giving you the right number, but in the end, I think I made the right call. I was going back to England, and the kids had been through enough. I was about to ask them to move to the States with me, and their entire lives would be uprooted. I couldn't introduce a new woman into their lives, and I certainly couldn't date you the way you deserve to. I give my kids most of me, Leia, and most days, I've got nothing left to give. I don't have time to date, even if I wanted to. That's why I walked away. It wasn't anything you did, and it wasn't because that night didn't mean anything to me. It was just the wrong place and the wrong time."

She nods, her expression guarded. "I get it, Thor. I do. It was just a one-night-stand, and I get that. What I don't understand is why you wouldn't just tell me that. Why would you go out of your way to give me the wrong number? Why not just be honest with me?"

I look away, my heart aching. Just hearing her call me Thor evokes memories of holding her in my arms. Would she believe me if I told her that night was probably the last time I truly felt happy? "I don't know," I tell her honestly. "I guess it's because I was considering giving you the right number until the very last second. Because I hadn't made up my mind until you asked me for my number. I wish I had a better excuse for you, Leia, but I don't."

Leia nods and wraps her arms around herself. "I understand," she says. "I appreciate your honesty."

"You and I..."

"I know," she says. "If we're working together in two different settings, there's absolutely no way we could get involved with each other — and honestly, I don't want to. I'm not interested in rehashing any part of our past, however brief it may have been. You needn't worry about me. I can promise you I'll always be professional. That night won't repeat itself."

It isn't her I'm worried about. It's me. She might be able to stay away from me, and to her what we had might just be a one-night-stand, but it's not the same for me. Even just having her sitting opposite me is too much. I want her closer. I want to beg for her forgiveness and kiss her until she tells me it's okay. This woman... she's a threat to my fucking sanity, and she doesn't even know it.

"In that case," I say, rising from my seat. "I look forward to working with you."

Leia rises and shakes my hand, our eyes meeting for a moment before she looks away. Yeah, I'm fucking done for.

Eighteen

Leia

I'm used to being a nanny for rich families, but it feels different this time. The expensive car Charlotte arranged for me just makes me anxious. Somehow, it feels like the stakes are higher now. This car isn't a make or model I know of, it's been custom built for Adrian Astor's kids, and driving it makes me anxious. I can't even imagine how expensive it must be. Do his kids really need that level of security?

I'm hyper alert as I walk up to the school, following their protocols on auto-pilot. I've had other kids that attended this school, so while they're familiar with me, they can't release Colton and Lucy to me without identification and clearance checks.

I know I'm well on time, yet I can't resist checking my watch. The last thing I want to do is keep the kids waiting on their very first day at school. Five minutes. Perfect timing.

I nod at several of the other nannies that I recognize, a few of them my colleagues. Most are in uniforms, and I'm glad Thor didn't ask me to wear one. Changing always added some time to my workday, and somehow it feels like that would just make the divide between Thor and me bigger. That shouldn't matter to me, but it does.

"Leia!" Colton says, his eyes wide with surprise.

I grin as I wave him over. "Didn't your dad tell you I'd be picking you up?"

Colton shakes his head, his excitement evident. "No, but he probably thinks he did. That happens a lot to Dad."

I smile and place my hand on his shoulder as we wait for Lucy to come out. "I'll be picking you up every day now. Your dad hired me as your nanny."

"Cool," he says. "We can play Fortnite together. Have you ever played that?"

I chuckle and nod. "Coincidentally, I have. I've got two nephews your age, and it's all they do. I had to learn or be the boring aunt, you know? No way was I going to let them call me boring!"

"Smart," Colton says, throwing me a lopsided grin. "But I don't believe you're any good."

I shrug. "I guess you're about to find out."

Lucy pauses in the doorway when she sees us, looking just as surprised as Colton did. "Leia?" she says, her tone reserved.

I nod. "Hi Lucy. How was school?"

She falls silent and stares at me for a moment. "Good."

I nod as I lead them to the car. Lucy doesn't say a word, and I can't figure out if she isn't happy to see me, or if she just didn't have a good day at school. I really hope she wasn't expecting Thor to show up, because I can imagine that'd have her filled with disappointment.

Thankfully, Colton doesn't stop talking once we get into the car, recounting every second of his day. "The girls all think my British accent is cool. The people here are weird, though. They call trousers pants. Don't they know that pants are, like, your underwear?"

I burst out laughing at the bewilderment in his voice. "Yes, there are quite a few differences between how the British say some things, and how Americans say them. Most of them I think you'll be familiar with thanks to your games, but others might be new to you. How about I make a list for you with common differences, so it's a bit easier for you?"

"Yeah," Colton says. "That'd be nice. Thanks, Leia."

I'm oddly nervous as we walk into the house. I've been working as a nanny for years, and even though all families are different, the job is mostly the same. Somehow, it just feels different this time. I'm scared of making mistakes, and though I shouldn't, I want the kids to like me.

"Lenora!" Colton says, greeting the housekeeper. "Did you miss me?"

I bite back a smile as Colton charms the woman who must be in her mid-fifties. I have no doubt he's after snacks, but we've been given strict instructions not to give the kids any. From what I understand, Thor doesn't like having a housekeeper, so she only comes in for a few hours during the day to cook for the family and tidy the house, and then she comes back to make dinner. It fits in with his personality, I suppose. He doesn't seem like the type to want live-in staff.

"Come on," I tell them. "Lenora made you a delicious lunch. Let's have some food before we do homework."

I glance around the huge kitchen equipped with every bit of tech they might need — most of which I suspect Thor doesn't even use. This house looks like a small replica of Amara's grandfather's house. It's modern and obviously expensive, and it doesn't really seem to suit Thor. But then again, I don't really know him as well as I thought I did.

"Ugh," Colton says, throwing his arms up in exasperation. This kid is a handful, but in the very best way. "I thought you said we were going to play Fortnite."

I nod and wag my finger at him. "I did, but I didn't say when. The quicker you finish your homework, the longer we get to play."

"Aaargh," he says, running his hands through his hair, and I try my hardest not to smile. I wonder if he takes after Thor.

Lucy is quiet and sits down for lunch without a single complaint. I have a feeling that winning her over will not be easy. A primary part of my job is to make sure she's adjusting well, but I can't do that if she won't let me in.

The afternoon passes by quickly, and I manage to prepare for my classes while the kids do their homework. They're not unruly kids, but they both seem lonely. It's going to take time for them to become truly comfortable around me.

Lucy sits up on the sofa when Adrian walks in, and he smiles at her. "Hi, sweetie," he says, opening his arms wide. She rises reluctantly and hugs him seemingly hesitantly, but I see the happy smile on her face. She hasn't smiled like that all day. There's something so endearing about seeing Thor with his daughter. He loves her so fiercely that it's hard for me to stay angry at him. I get why he did what he did two years ago and don't actually hold it against him, but that doesn't make it hurt any less.

Colton doesn't even look up from his game when Adrian ruffles his hair, and Thor shakes his head to himself.

"Follow me, Leia," he says, and I tense. "I'd like to hear about your first workday."

I'm instantly nervous. It's odd to have different parts of my life intersect in a way they never have before. He's my professor and my boss, but he's also the man that made me forget everything but him as he laid me down underneath the stars. It's becoming harder and harder to pretend that I don't remember, that I don't still want him as badly as I did then. It takes all of me to remain professional, and each time he smiles at me, I want to give in.

My heart hammers in my chest when he walks up the stairs, and I bite down on my lip when he walks straight into what I assume is his bedroom. Though none of the rooms in this house are off-limits to me, his room is one I never expected to enter.

I pause in the doorway and take his room in. It's in contrast with his ultra-modern house. His bedroom is done up in dark wooden tones. It's masculine and every bit as luxurious, but it has a lot more character than the rest of the house. My eyes fall to his bed, and images of the two of us flash through my mind.

Adrian places his briefcase on his bed and turns to me as he pulls his tie loose. "How were they?"

I watch as he unbuttons his shirt, letting it fall open. Damn him. Why does he still look as good as he did two years ago? For a while I was hoping that my memories of him were glorified, but the glimpse he's giving me of his abs tells me otherwise.

Does he realize how intimate this is? He's treating me like I'm his wife, chatting with me after a long day at work. I frown and cross my arms, a sudden thought occurring to me. "Do you take all of your employees into your bedroom like this?"

He pauses for a moment before pulling his shirt off. "No. Just you, Ley."

I blink in surprise, my cheeks heating rapidly. I don't know where to look when he's standing in front of me in those suit trousers, his torso bare. Does he realize what he's doing to me? "I... they were fine. Lucy wasn't very talkative, and I'm not sure what she thinks of me as her nanny. She didn't seem happy to see me, and I can't tell how school is going because she won't tell me. I gave her the book I promised her last time, but other than a polite thank you, I didn't get any other responses from her."

He nods and runs a hand through his hair, messing it up. It reminds me of the way I grabbed his hair, his lips pressed against my neck, and I force myself to look away. Two years, and the memories are still so vivid. I breathe a sigh of relief when he pulls on a t-shirt. I hate that I still find him so attractive.

"She wasn't like that before the divorce. She used to be as cheerful as Colton is. To be honest, between the two of them, he was the quiet one. I'm worried about her, but I'm not sure what to do. I was hoping she might like you, that having a nanny would make her miss her mother less."

I shake my head. "A nanny can't replace a mother, Professor."

"Don't call me that when we're at home."

"Then what would you like me to call you?"

"Adrian or Thor. It's up to you."

I look down at my shoes and purse my lips. I need boundaries between us if I'm going to survive him one more time. Though I don't want to, he makes me waver in my convictions every time I see him. "I can't. We have a strict no-fraternization rule at Asha's firm."

He crosses his arms, drawing attention to his biceps, and I force myself to look him in the eye. "I'm making it a requirement," he says, his voice stern.

I sigh and push a strand of hair behind my ear. "Mr. Astor," I say, trying my hardest to stay professional. "I'm not here to socialize with you. I'm here as your children's nanny, because I truly believe I can make a difference when it comes to them. I have no interest in reminiscing with you, nor do I want to act overly familiar with you."

He grits his teeth and stares me down. "I dare say there's no way for you to become any more intimately acquainted with me, Leia. If you can take my cock and beg for more, you can call me by my name. Let's not pretend that didn't happen."

My lips fall open in shock, a flash of anger blinding me for a moment. I straighten my shoulders and fish my phone out of my pocket.

"Very well, Adrian," I snap, handing him my phone. "Come to think of it, you should give me your phone number in case of emergency. The only point of contact I have right now is Charlotte, but it seems appropriate to have your phone number too. Try to give me the right number this time, will you?"

He types his phone number in angrily, and this time he waits for his phone to ring before hanging up. I snatch my phone out of his hands the moment he's done and walk away, letting his bedroom door slam closed out of spite.

I promised myself I'd be professional around him, yet the moment our conversation turned even remotely personal, I lost my composure. I need to do better.

Nineteen

LEIA

"You're upset," Lex says, startling me out of my thoughts. Every time I try to focus, my thoughts turn to Thor and the way I snapped at him last night. All he asked was that I call him by his name at home, and I overreacted. I'm not sure why I can't control my emotions around him, and I hate it. It's been two years, so why am I still so affected by him? "Want me to rough someone up for you?" Lex adds.

I grin and shake my head as I put my coffee cup down. As usual, we're in the coffee shop on campus, and though I'm supposed to be writing my dissertation, I can barely focus today. "Why do you always choose violence, huh?"

Lex shrugs. "There's nothing I won't do for you. You're basically my best friend."

I roll my eyes. "That's because I'm literally your only friend."

"Yeah, so you're my best friend by default. *Congratulations.* I know I'm yours too. Someone should really tell Amara."

I chuckle at the thought of Lex telling Amara that he's taken her spot as my best friend. They're both territorial as hell, and I think I'd bet on Amara in this instance.

"Seriously, Ley. Tell me what's going on. You've been quiet all morning. Actually, you haven't really been yourself in a while now."

I blink in surprise. I didn't think he'd noticed that, considering that we usually sit here quietly, studying together. I wasn't even consciously aware of it myself, but I have been sad.

"Do you remember how we met?"

Lex nods. "You texted me because some jackass gave you the wrong number."

I nod. "Said jackass reappeared in my life a few weeks ago. It was unexpected as it is, but now he just seems to be everywhere, and I... I don't know."

Lex's eyes widen. "No shit? Thor appeared?"

I nod. "I didn't expect it. He's just... everywhere. When I first ran into him, I had every intention of just pretending I didn't remember him, but that's going to be hard to do."

"Who is he?"

I shake my head. Lex and I are both students here. I can't tell him I slept with our professor. I trust him fully, but I'd better err on the side of caution. After all, Thor is my dissertation advisor. If word got out, I could lose everything I've ever worked for. All it takes is some inappropriate jokes for an investigation to be launched.

"It's nothing. Honestly, I don't want to talk about it."

Lex leans on his elbow and moves closer to me, his face inches from mine. "It's not nothing, Leia. You're upset. I suppose seeing him brought back the memories. Strangely enough, I've always been grateful to this guy for bringing you into my life, but I hate to see you hurting. I'm surprised he left such an impact on you, you know?"

I nod. "Yeah, me too. I know it was just one night, but have you ever met anyone you just felt an instant connection with? It feels like you've known each other forever, and you're just so at ease. Your heart just feels so full. Have you ever experienced anything like that?"

He shakes his head and looks away, but there's a hint of torment in his eyes, a fleeting memory. "No, I've never experienced a *genuine* connection, and I probably never will."

I bite down on my lip and grimace. I keep forgetting that he'll be in an arranged marriage. From what I understand, his engagement will be decided upon by his grandmother, not long from now. It's strange, because it's something that's not all that uncommon in my culture, but it appears the ultra-rich still do it too.

Lex clears his throat. "I'm glad you experienced that, though. If you felt that way, why aren't you happy to see him now? Did he at least give you a good explanation?"

I shake my head. "Yeah, I guess. Even so, there's no way we can be together."

Lex purses his lips and stares me down. "And why is that?"

I gulp and look down at my coffee cup. I'm a terrible liar, but I absolutely do not want to tell Lex about Professor Astor. "He's... unavailable." It isn't exactly a lie, because the kids do make him entirely unavailable, but not quite in the way I'm making it sound.

Lex tightens his grip on his coffee cup, his jaws clenched and his eyes filled with barely restrained rage. "That fucking asshole. Tell me who he is, Leia. I'll have a word with him."

I grin and shake my head. "You'll have a word, huh? With what? Your mouth or your fists?"

He smiles humorlessly. "I'll make sure the message gets across just fine."

I roll my eyes and place my hand over his. "I love you," I tell him honestly. Lex is the brother I never had, and I suppose I have Thor to thank for it.

He grabs my hand and raises it to his lips, kissing the back of my hand. "I love you too, sweet girl."

A chill suddenly runs down my spine and I tense, my body

aware of him before I am. *"Leia,"* Thor says, standing a few steps away from our table. How long has he been standing there? The look in his eyes has my heart dropping. Blood rushes to my ears, and everything falls away, until all I can hear is my own pulse.

Lex looks up in surprise and entwines our hands. *"Adrian Astor,"* he says, smiling. "Or is it Professor Astor now?"

I'm at a loss. What do I do? Do I pull my hand away? Lex and I have only ever had a platonic relationship, but I know what this looks like. Though I don't owe Thor anything, I still feel guilty and embarrassed.

Thor drags his gaze away to look at Lex, his gaze pausing on our joined hands. *"Lexington Windsor,"* he snaps. "You've grown up, huh? The last time I saw you, you were still wetting your bed."

Lex tightens his grip on my hand and clenches his jaw in annoyance. "And you look positively ancient," he replies. "Guess your fuckboy days are over, huh?"

"You two know each other?" I ask, shocked.

Both men turn to me, the two of them looking equally annoyed. "Our families are business partners and old friends."

I nod. "Ah, code for *we're both filthy rich and therefore move in the same circles*, huh?"

Lex looks away in embarrassment. For some reason, his family's wealth has always embarrassed him.

"How do you two know each other?" Lex asks, and I tense before remembering that we have a legitimate reason to greet each other.

"Professor Astor is my PhD advisor. He replaced Professor Larson."

It unnerves me that Thor is just standing here, staring at us. I'm still embarrassed at the way I snapped at him when he asked me to call him by his name at home, and this situation with Lex just increases my nerves. I try to free my hand out of Lex's grip as discreetly as I can, but he's holding on tightly. I'm not sure what I'm supposed to say, and I'm worried Lex will see straight through me. He's always been very perceptive, and I don't want him to realize that Professor Astor is Thor.

"Leia," Thor says, his voice harsh. "Come with me. There are a few things I need to discuss with you ahead of next week's classes."

I glance up at him, his blue eyes dark with something I can't quite name. Is it anger? Jealousy, perhaps? Surely not.

"Of course, Professor Astor." I have a feeling that disobeying him isn't a good idea right now. I'm not sure what it is about him, but it's almost like I can feel his anger radiate off him.

I'm quiet as I pack my bag and smile at Lex apologetically. Thankfully, he doesn't look suspicious, but I can never be too sure with Lex.

"I'll see you next week," I murmur.

"I'll call you tonight," he tells me, and I frown. He rarely calls me. We text occasionally, but we don't usually call each other. Thor tenses next to me and turns to walk away.

"Right. Sure. Speak to you then!" I rush after Thor, unsure what's going on. Both men are acting weird, and I'm worried. Worried that Lex is onto me. Worried that Thor misunderstood what he just saw. I shouldn't care what he thinks, but I do.

He's quiet as we walk to his office, and he doesn't say a word as he holds the door open for me. I walk in on shaky legs, my heart thumping.

The door closes behind us, and I tense. I haven't done anything wrong, yet I feel like I have.

I watch him as he walks around his desk and pulls out disinfectant wipes. "Come here," he snaps, and I jump. "Now, Leia."

I do as he says, and he grabs my hand tenderly as he wipes every inch of my skin. "What... what are you doing?" I whisper.

"Getting rid of every trace of him."

What? "Don't be ridiculous. Lex is just a friend."

"Friends don't hold hands the way you did. Tell me, Ley. Are you seeing him? The Windsor boy, really?"

He looks at me, his gaze intense. I still remember that fire in his eyes. He looked at me with the same kind of possessiveness two years ago. Thor's gaze drops to my lips, where it lingers, before I snap out of it.

I pull my hand away, rationality finally taking over. "It is, quite frankly, none of your business who I touch."

He looks at me, his expression so pained that my heart starts to ache. "Not him," he says, his voice soft. "Not someone I know. Please, Leia."

My eyes widen as he takes a step away and turns around, his hand running through his hair. I haven't seen him look this vulnerable since he walked back into my life.

I can't do this. I can't. For the second time this week, I find myself walking away moments after I'm alone with him.

For two years, I wondered if he ever thought of me, if he ever regretted walking away from me.

I have my answers now.

And I can't do anything with them.

Twenty

LEIA

My heart is pounding as I park in front of my house. Amara told me she'd join for our weekly family dinner tonight, and it'll be the first time I'll see her since she left for her honeymoon. She knows just how upset I was when Thor gave me the wrong number, and I've never lied to her before, nor have I ever kept anything from her. How do I tell her that the man I was so heartbroken over is her *cousin*?

I'm nervous when I walk in and try to hide it, but Asha throws me a concerned look, and her concern only worsens when I try to force a smile.

Mom holds her phone to her ear, and I cringe at the sound of her shouting. I don't even have to ask her who's she on the phone to. If she's shouting like that, she's making a phone call to India. For some reason that I'll never understand, my parents always shout when they're on the phone to anyone in India. It's almost like they think their voice won't travel all the way to India unless they scream. It's weird, because my mother is highly intelligent, yet she always does this. I shake my head as I walk past her, hoping she won't make me talk to family members that I barely remember.

"You're back!" I say, grinning at Amara.

She jumps up from the sofa and rushes up to me, squeezing me so tightly she nearly lifts me off the floor. "Oh my God, I missed you so much, Ley!"

"I kinda figured as much, since you were texting me practically every hour while you were supposed to be on your honeymoon."

She smiles happily. "It was amazing, but I really wish I could've experienced it with you too. We have to go to Fiji together."

"Sure. I'll just tell the hot doc that his wife is going on holiday without him," I say, walking into the kitchen to wash my hands. "Come to think of it, where is your dear husband?"

Amara follows me and shrugs. "He's at home. These family dinners have always kind of been our thing. Me getting married shouldn't change that."

I stare at her in surprise, my heart warming. "Love you," I tell her.

"Love you more," she replies as she leads me to the dining table, where my mother has already set the table. "I've so been looking forward to this."

I side-eye her and shake my head. "Did you come to see me, or did you come for the food?"

She smiles guiltily and shrugs. "Both?"

"Leave her alone," Mom says, admonishing me, and I hold my hands up in defeat.

"Look, Amara. I made your favorite," she says, pushing a plate of freshly baked cassava her way.

Amara squeals excitedly. "I'm secretly your favorite daughter, aren't I, Auntie?"

Asha and I both roll our eyes. "*Secretly*," we both repeat mockingly, almost in unison.

"I love all you girls equally," Mom says, and Asha and I both shake our heads. The truth is that neither of us minds the way Mom treats Amara. I'm just glad she gets to experience a few moments of motherly love, because her own mother wasn't exactly affectionate when Amara was growing up. Charlotte is better now, but she's still nothing like my mom.

"So, Amara," Mom says. "Your husband, does he have any doctor friends you can introduce Leia to?"

I freeze and let my eyes fall closed. Damn it. I should've expected that. "Look at her, Leia," Mom says. "She married a doctor. Meanwhile, you aren't even dating anyone."

I swear, Asian parents. I wasn't allowed to date anyone when I was younger, so where exactly am I supposed to conjure a husband from?

"Amara has also already finished her doctorate. What are you doing, huh?"

I glance at Asha, who sends me a sympathetic look. "Mom, leave her alone. She's so busy with work and school. Isn't that what you always told us to focus on?" Asha says.

"Yes, because that's what I'm supposed to say. I expected her to sneak around like you did and find a boyfriend, but she never did."

I burst out laughing, and Asha looks mortified, which only adds to my amusement. I glance at Rohan, but he just smiles to himself as he feeds their two-year-old daughter, Nalini, while Asha has their four-year-old son, Rohit, in her lap.

"Leia will find someone when she's ready," Dad says, and I smile at him in gratitude. "But by that time, I might be in my grave."

My smile drops. "Seriously, Dad?"

"Patient, I am not," he replies, doing his best Yoda impression, and I groan.

"Devi's son is still single. He's a lawyer, and he seems like a nice boy. Devi told me they're looking for a girl for him now. Why don't you meet up with him?" Mom asks.

Devi's son, Lakshman, is also a piece of shit that's cheated on every single girl he's ever been with. His parents pretend not to know about his girlfriends, but we *all* know. No, thanks. I'm also not at all interested in an arranged match. If I ever get married, I want it to be because I fell so madly and deeply in love that I can't see a life without that person, and despite my flaws, they'd feel the same.

It's not like I can have kids anyway. What's the point of getting married for anything but love? And if it's an arranged match, it won't take long for everyone to start gossiping about my fertility issues, since it isn't something we can keep from anyone who proposes a match.

"Actually, Leia," Amara says. "I think Noah might have a friend I could set you up with."

I glance at her, unsure if she's trying to save me from this situation or if she's being serious. "Yeah, sounds great," I tell her, figuring I can just cancel later, anyway.

"Such a good friend," Mom says, nodding at her, and I look up at the ceiling in frustration.

Thankfully, dinner is relatively quiet after that, my parents' attention stolen by their two grandchildren. The second I can, I escape to my bedroom, Amara hot on my heels.

"I hate it when they're like that to you," she says as she closes the door behind her.

"Aren't you used to it yet?"

"I am, but I still don't like it."

I shake my head. "My dad won't even let me move out, arguing that my sister didn't move out until she got married either, yet somehow I'm supposed to date? Can you imagine if I don't come home one night when they know I went on a date? All hell would break loose."

She sits down next to me and pulls her feet up, making herself comfortable on my bed. "When we were on our honeymoon, Noah mentioned something about our wedding day that I didn't notice because of all the excitement. Apparently, you were really shocked to see my cousin, Adrian."

My eyes widen a fraction, my heart skipping a beat. "How was your honeymoon, anyway? Did Noah sex you up?"

She narrows her eyes at me. "I've told you every detail about my honeymoon, almost in real time. You're changing the subject."

I look away, my nerves getting the best of me. "He... he's *Thor*."

Amara stares at me in disbelief. "*What?*"

I nod. "He told me his divorce papers had already been signed then, but yeah... it's him."

Amara sits back and nods, her shock evident. "Adrian, really?"

I nod. "Apparently Thor is a play on your last name, Astor. I can't believe I missed that. You guys don't look super similar, but still."

"What are you going to do?" she asks.

I shake my head. "Nothing. He's got Lucy and Colton, and they're still adjusting. He can't introduce any further changes into their lives. Besides, he's my PhD advisor. I can't get involved with him, not until I finish my PhD. It was so many years ago, Amara. It was just a one-night-stand. Now we're just... I don't even know what we are now." I think back to the way he wiped my hands clean after Lex held my hand, and my heart skips a beat.

"You've met Lucy and Colton?" Leia asks, her voice high-pitched.

I hesitate before elaborating. "Your mother hired me as their nanny."

"Wow, way to go, Mom," she says, her shock making way for that calculated look I've grown accustomed to. The one that spells nothing but trouble. "Leia, for as long as I've known you, you've believed in fate. How could this not be fate? Life is forcing you together in so many different ways for a reason."

I blink in surprise. That's not what I expected her to say. "Amara, he's my professor. He's got kids. It's not as simple as us being able to date and just seeing what happens. There are too many risks, too many hearts that could end up broken."

She nods. "I know, Leia. But there are also so many broken

hearts that could be made whole. It's what you do, babe. You're the glue that holds everything and everyone together, even if it means you're irreparably damaged because of it. For once, let someone hold you together. Let him do for you what he did two years ago. If you could spend every single night experiencing what you did two years ago, wouldn't that be amazing? Adrian is one of the best people I know. He's hardworking, and he's always been there for me, even if I called him in the middle of the night. He's loyal to a fault, and the way he loves his children is something else. He's a good man, Leia."

The hope I feel makes me uncomfortable, and I can't help but look away. "I mean, the sex was good, but he's just a guy, Amara. I'm over it."

"No, you're not. Tell yourself whatever you want, but at least think about it. I get it, it's hard. You know how tough it was for Noah and I to choose each other in the end. It felt like the whole world was against us, like everyone in our lives conspired to keep us apart, but in the end, I'd still choose him. Despite the pain and the difficulties we went through to get where we are, I'd choose him. I'd do it all over again. I have a feeling you and Adrian will be the same. Some things are worth fighting for, Leia, no matter the odds."

Her words haunt me for the rest of the night, and by the time my head hits my pillow, I'm filled with cautious hope.

Twenty-One

ADRIAN

I come home to a quiet house and run a hand through my hair as I walk through the hallway. I'm exhausted. Grandpa wasn't joking when he said he expected me to join Astor Corporation. Our assets are so vast that I'm struggling to keep track of all the different subsidiaries we own. There's a media division, a hedge fund we own, and then there's the college and so many other moving parts. I won't be able to hold on to my teaching job for long if he keeps demanding such long hours from me.

He said he'd give me three years, but it's pretty evident I can't do both jobs — not if I want to ensure that I have quality time to spend with the kids.

I loosen my tie as I walk into the living room, pausing when I see Leia lying on the sofa, fast asleep, papers she's been grading scattered all over the coffee table. I walk up to her quietly and kneel beside her, taking a moment to just watch her. Her long lashes flutter slightly, her chest rising and falling slowly. She's been so defensive around me, rarely letting her guard down. She's either acting hyper professional around me, or we find ourselves arguing.

There's been no in-between, and I miss her. I miss the girl I used to know. It's a fucking treat to see her like this, without those walls raised high to protect her.

It's clear that I hurt her when I walked away from the night we spent together, yet despite that, she's been taking care of my children without a single complaint. Tonight isn't the first night I'm home late, and she's never once said anything about it. She could've used my children to hurt me the way I hurt her, but it never even crossed her mind. I never would've hired her if I thought she was that kind of person, but I suppose part of me was still on guard.

I reach for her, gently brushing a strand of her hair out of her face. She's beautiful in more ways than one. I've met plenty of beautiful women — being an Astor means being surrounded by some of the most beautiful women in the world on a regular basis, but none of them are like Leia. None of them are just as beautiful inside.

Colton can't stop talking about how much he likes her, and she's been handling him with such ease, using the games he loves so much to motivate him. Even Lucy has been mentioning her lately. Just yesterday she asked me which books Leia might like, so she could buy her a present in return for the books Leia keeps bringing her.

It's not her job to nurture the children the way she does. All I hired her to do was pick them up from school and babysitting them, but she goes out of her way to ensure they don't miss me while I'm at work. I can't tell if that's something she would've done for anyone and if it might just be the service her firm provides everyone with, or if she's doing this for me. Maybe I'm a fool, but deep down, I'm hoping she still has feelings for me.

So far, she's given me no indication that she cares beyond being upset I ghosted her. I understand that she's mad about that, but what I want to know is if those feelings run deeper. Does she ever think of the night we spent together and want more?

My gaze drops to her lips and I inhale shakily. Some nights I still dream about her. I don't understand what it is about her. How could I possibly still be enchanted with her, when we only ever spent one night together?

Leia turns her head, her eyes fluttering open. She blinks in surprise when she sees me and freezes. "Thor," she whispers. My heart skips a beat at the sound of her voice. I love when she calls me Thor. It's intimate, and it reminds me of that night that haunts my dreams.

"Hey," I murmur. "You fell asleep."

She sits up and runs a hand through her long hair, looking a little flustered. I rise to my feet, unsure if I should explain why I was just staring at her or if I should just leave it alone.

"The kids are in bed," she tells me, and I nod. I figured as much. It's nearly ten in the evening. They're probably fast asleep.

"I should go."

Her body brushes against mine, and I grab her wrist, holding her in place. "Don't go." My voice is soft, my tone pleading, vulnerability I've been trying to hide making its way out.

Leia looks at me, the same need in her eyes. It isn't desire, it's something so much more than that. "I can't stay."

"Have a glass of wine with me," I plead. "I've had such a long day, and I know you have too."

I expect her to say no, but instead she stares at me for a moment, before nodding slightly, as though she's still undecided.

I smile at her and let go of her wrist. What I want to do is grab her hand and entwine our fingers, but instead I turn and walk to the kitchen, the sound of her footsteps following me.

She nods when I hold up a bottle of red, and I open it quietly. I doubt she realises just how expensive this bottle is, and I don't want her to know. I just want her to have the best of the best, quietly, without any pretense. I have no idea what I'm even asking of her. Companionship, perhaps?

Her hand trembles just slightly when she takes her glass from me, and a strange sense of heartbreak washes over me as I raise my glass to hers. How can I be hurting over something we never had? How is it that I see those same feelings reflected in her eyes?

She takes a sip, breaking our eye contact, as though the intensity is too much for her. I lean back against the counter while she takes a seat at the breakfast bar, the two of us keeping a sufficient amount of distance between us.

"If I ask you how you've been, would you answer me truthfully?"

She looks up then, regarding me for a moment, before nodding.

"Then tell me, Ley. How have you been?"

She smiles, but it doesn't reach her eyes. "It feels like mercury went into retrograde at some point, and it never went direct again. That probably makes no sense to you, does it? I feel like I'm always going through the motions because it's what I have to do, rarely truly feeling alive. To answer your question, I think I'm doing fine. Not good. Not great. Just... fine."

My heart clenches at her words and I look down at my glass. "Somehow, you've managed to perfectly capture how I feel too," I tell her, looking up to smile at her. "Except the mercury retrograde bit, that's all bullocks."

That earns me a chuckle from her, and it's crazy how much it lifts my mood. "If I offer, will you let me show you Mercury someday soon? I promised you I would, and I always told myself I'd keep that promise if I ever saw you again."

Her eyes darken, the expression in them changing, as though she too is remembering what else I promised her.

Mark my words, love. Someday, I'm going to bury my face between your legs, and you're going to beg me to let you come on my face. It might not be tonight, but that time will come.

I remember the words like I said them yesterday, and fuck, if she'd let me, I'd drop to my knees right now. Everything about us still feels the same way it did that night. I still feel that spellbinding spark, the desire, the connection. The way she's looking at me makes me wonder if she does too.

"Yes." It takes me a moment to remember what we were talking about, and her expression tells me she knows it. Leia smiles, and for the first time since she walked back into my life, it feels like we're okay, like we aren't at the cusp of another argument.

"I'll take you to see Mercury soon. Be prepared to have all your notions of Mercury going into retrograde dashed."

She chuckles, and bloody hell, the sound of it makes my heart skip a beat. I don't think I've ever just wanted to make a woman smile. Just sitting here with her, sharing a glass of wine after a long day, putting a smile on her face... it soothes my soul in ways it shouldn't.

"I never understood how a man who loves astronomy can so readily reject astrology. You know better than most that there's so much we still don't know about the universe."

"Oh, no." I shake my head. "Please don't tell me you believe in aliens too?"

She laughs and looks away. "You know what, if they ever come for you, I'm not saving you."

"I'll be sure to think of you when the blue aliens probe my butt."

She bursts out laughing, and I grin to myself. This... this is the Leia I missed. The one she's been hiding from me.

"No, seriously though. I get what you're saying. There really is a lot we don't know. I didn't use to believe in fate, but I'm not so sure anymore."

She looks into my eyes, her smile falling away. "Is that so?" she murmurs.

"How could I not believe in fate when the one that got away walked right back into my life?"

Her eyes widen and she looks away, clearly flustered. I watch as she throws back the rest of her wine and pushes her glass away.

"I really should get going," she tells me, her guard back in place.

I want to ask her to stay, but I can't. I won't. She's already given me more than I expected her to tonight, and for now, that's enough.

It's becoming clear to me though... she and I aren't over. Far from it.

Twenty-Two

ADRIAN

I enter the lecture hall and look around, surprised at how packed it is. From what I understand, Leia has been teaching for a few years now, and it makes me wonder why she's been procrastinating on the completion of her PhD. All she's got left to do is her dissertation, yet for years now, she's been teaching as an Adjunct Professor, taking on the required TA duties alongside her teaching role. Once she completes her PhD, she could join as full-time faculty staff, so why doesn't she? I suspect she suffers from fear of failure. I need to make her see that it's okay that her dissertation will never be perfect. It isn't meant to be. It should just be a starting point for future research she does, and that's sufficient.

I find an empty seat in the back and sit down. It's my job to guide her throughout her PhD, but from what I can tell from the files left behind by my predecessor, she doesn't need much guidance. Her dissertation subject is well-rounded, and though it's a tricky subject, it shouldn't take her as long to finish as it has. Leia Sital is a bit of a mystery to me. I want to know what makes her tick.

She moves from behind the wooden podium where she's connected her laptop to the screen behind her, and everyone falls silent.

"Welcome back to this class on Machine Design," she tells the students. "I see some unfamiliar faces, so I assume you've skipped my first few classes?" She stares a few students down, and the class falls silent. "For those of you who are new here, my name is Leia Sital, and I'll be teaching this class this semester."

I lean back and look at her, taking my time to enjoy the view. Usually when we're together, I have to restrain myself. I always have to make sure I don't stare at her too long, and though I often fail, I have to at least try to keep my eyes from roaming over her body. Sitting here, in relative obscurity, gives me an opportunity I otherwise never have.

I watch the woman that captivated me years ago the way I wish I could every day. Her ridiculously long hair is parted in the middle, half of it behind her, and half draping over her chest, straight down to her waist. Her lips are bright red today, and she's wearing a black pencil skirt with a white blouse. She looks perfectly respectable, yet I find her so fucking sexy, standing there in those high heels. She's wearing another pair of utterly unique heels today. This time, they're a studded silver color with red bottoms, and I'm surprised at how sexy I find them. I've never noticed shoes on a woman before, but I notice them on her.

If my life were different, could I have her? Could I have been the man that gets to love her, the one who shows her just how special she is, the one who gets to grow old with her?

I run a hand through my hair and shake my head. Fucking hell. I've never had these thoughts about Alice. We started dating whilst at university and everything just progressed so naturally for us. It was all so... comfortable.

Leia is anything but. She's passion and fire. She's everything my heart has always wanted, and everything I'd never dare reach for.

I watch as some of the boys nudge each other, and I can just about hear them whispering about how hot Leia is. It makes my fucking blood boil, and I struggle to keep my mouth shut. Hell, I can't even say anything, because I'd just been checking her out myself.

"Tell me what comes to mind when you think of mechanical behavior."

I watch as a guy in the front row raises his hand, and when Leia turns to him, she pauses in surprise before smiling in a way I haven't seen in years. It's an intimate knowing type of smile, and jealousy fucking guts me. Who is the guy she's looking at? He's clearly someone she knows. I lean in to take a closer look, annoyance slamming through me when I realize Lex Windsor is sitting in the front row, smiling at her.

"Yes?" she says, her tone playful. My stomach acts up, feeling all funny at the sound of her flirtatious voice, directed at someone other than me. I fucking hate it.

"Statics and dynamics?"

Leia nods. "Anyone else?"

I breathe a sigh of relief when she turns toward another student. "Robot arms," he says, and Leia chuckles.

"I suppose," she nods. "But think about those robot arms. What factors would you have to think of when creating them? Which factors would you test?"

She's a natural at teaching. She seems at ease in front of her class, and she's able to engage her students without too much effort. I suspected this would be the case, but as her advisor, I still had to see it for myself.

I want to do the best I can for her, but she genuinely doesn't seem to need any guidance. I should be happy about that, yet somehow I can't help but feel bitter. I want her to lean on me, and my role as her PhD advisor is the only capacity in which I can offer her support.

Leia's class flies by. It's rare for students to actually enjoy a class, but they really seem to. Leia announces an assignment that has to be handed in next week, eliciting a few groans from the crowd, but she takes it in stride.

The room slowly empties once class ends, but Lex doesn't leave with his classmates. Instead, he walks toward Leia, and I rise from my seat.

I walk down the steps, toward them, but neither of them notices me. Her eyes are on him, and it irritates me. "Leia," I say, my tone sharp.

She looks up, freezing when her eyes land on me. "Professor Astor."

"Good class, but there are a few things I'd like to discuss with you."

"Right. Of course, Professor."

I glance at my watch, not bothering to greet Lex. He's officially on my shit list. It irritates me that he's the same height and build as me. Clearly, she has a type.

"Follow me. I have some time before I have a class to teach."

Leia nods and turns toward Lex, smiling apologetically. "I'll call you later, Lex."

Leia walks past me, heading toward the exit, and I smirk at Lex before following her.

She's quiet as we walk to my office, the smile she was wearing for Lex nowhere to be seen. I'm nervous as I hold the door open for her. I don't necessarily have anything to discuss with her, I just wanted to get her away from that guy. I was so certain she felt what I did last night, yet here she is, flirting with fucking Lex Windsor.

"What's going on between you two? Are you dating him?" I ask as I close the door behind her and turn toward her.

Leia tenses and pauses in the middle of my office, turning back around to face me. "Who?"

She knows exactly who I'm talking about, but she's playing dumb. "Lex."

"Oh. He's also a PhD student."

"Then why was he in your class?"

"I... I'm not too sure. You'll have to ask *him*, Professor Astor."

I take a step forward, and Leia takes a step back, the two of us continuing our dance until her hips hit my desk. "I'm asking you. Who is he to you?"

"A friend," she says, her voice husky.

I place my hands on either of side of her, caging her in against my desk. "Do all your friends flirt with you the way he did?"

"I... what? He wasn't. Besides, even if he was, is it really any of your business, Professor Astor?"

I grit my teeth, annoyed. She's right, of course. "It's unprofessional. I don't want my PhD students involved in any petty drama or scandals. It's your responsibility to behave in a manner befitting the school." It's bullshit, and she probably knows it, but she doesn't say anything. She just looks into my eyes, as though she knows what I'm really thinking.

"Then what would you call what you're doing right now, Thor?"

I clench my jaw and look away. I'm usually so level-headed — it's one of those things Alice always hated about me. She always hated that she couldn't get a rise out of me, but it's different with Leia.

I pull away from her and run a hand through my hair, unable to suppress my frustration. When it comes to Leia, my mind and my heart are at odds. I keep convincing myself to stay away from her, but I can't make myself do it.

"You're ready to pick the kids up later?"

She nods, her expression softening. "Yes. Aren't I always?"

I look away, trying to come up with a reason to keep her here and failing. "I'm sorry," I tell her. "I was being unreasonable just now. When I saw him flirting with you... and the way you were smiling at him, I just..."

She leans back against my desk and smiles at me. "You what? You were jealous?"

I look down at my shoes and nod. I'm too old to be playing

games. I won't lie to her. "Yes, Leia. I was jealous. I shouldn't have acted on it, though. I apologize."

Her smile melts away and she shakes her head. "No, I get it. We have history, and there's no use pretending that we don't. You owe me one now. One free pass to act equally unreasonable."

I chuckle, surprised by her words. "Very well. You got it."

Leia walks past me and pauses by the door. "It can't happen again, Thor."

"Are you sure, Leia?"

She hesitates, but then she nods and walks away, the door falling closed behind her. I stare at it, my heart aching. What the fuck is happening to me?

Twenty-Three

LEIA

"What's wrong, Ley?" Colton asks. I smile at him and shake my head. The twins roped me into watching a movie after finishing their homework, and normally I would've enjoyed it, but today I can't focus.

"It's nothing," I say, even though I can't drag my eyes off the multiple texts Amara sent me.

Amara: *what's going on between you and Adrian?*

Amara: *Why was he spotted with Eleanor Williams last night? You know I hate that bitch.*

Amara: *I thought there was something between you guys? Didn't you tell me you two had a moment when you had that wine together?*

. . .

Leia: *what are you talking about?*

Amara sends me a link, and I pull up the gossip article from *The Herald*, a newspaper that somehow always knows the inside scoop on every socialite in town. There's a picture of Eleanor and Thor, his suit jacket draped over her shoulders as they walk together. The dress she's wearing makes it clear that they were on a date. There's no way she would've worn that to a business meeting. Lately he's asked me to work evenings, and he told me it was because he's been taking over a lot of work from his grandfather.

My heart squeezes tightly as I take in the way he's smiling at her in that photo. Why would he lie to me? Why not just tell me the truth, or just tell me nothing at all? I'm his nanny. He doesn't have to justify where he goes, so why bother lying?

I bite down on my lip harshly in an effort to suppress the pain I feel. Amara is right. I did think there was something between us that night when he asked me to stay and have some wine with him, but realistically, nothing really happened. He was being nice to me, and I pushed him away. I don't have the right to be mad after repeatedly rejecting his advances, but I am. I'm pissed off and hurt.

I scroll down, unable to help myself. I shouldn't read this article if just seeing the photo hurts this much, but I can't help myself.

Has Eleanor Williams taken Adrian Astor off the market already?

Dear readers of the Herald,

. . .

We have obtained exclusive footage or Adrian and Eleanor on a date last night. The pair went to Fleur, one of the high end and exclusive restaurants owned by Astor Corporation, and our sources tell us the two were cooped up in a private dining area for hours.

When they finally emerged, Eleanor was wearing Adrian's suit jacket. One can't help but wonder why that might be. Did the zipper on the back of her dress break in all the excitement? It was, after all, an uncharacteristically hot night. There's no way the beauty needed a jacket to keep her warm.

Adrian Astor is notorious for keeping his distance from women, yet in this photo, Eleanor is clearly holding his arm. Though the ladies at The Herald are heartbroken, we must admit that the two make a nice couple. The billionaire and the heiress are incredibly well-suited, and don't they look adorable together?

I click the article away and lock my phone, unsure what to say to Amara's endless texts. Jealousy unlike anything I've ever felt before consumes me, starting in the pit of my stomach and spreading until my heart aches so badly my breathing becomes uneven. I'm the one who said I wouldn't get involved with him, so why am I surprised he's dating someone else? I could try to convince myself that I'm just angry that he wasn't honest with me, but that isn't what it is. I'm hurt. It hurts that he's moving on when I can't.

I've been pushing him away because I know we can't be together, not when I'm his nanny and his student, but I'm selfish. I don't want him to be with anyone else. It's irrational, but I can't help it.

I sit up straight when I hear his footsteps in the hallway. Looks like he's home early today. I bite down on my lip in an attempt to get my emotions under control. If I face him now, I'm sure I'll lash out in pain and anger, and I have no right to do that.

"Dad!" Lucy says when he walks in. She jumps up and runs to him. "You're home already!"

He lifts her off her feet and twirls her around, hugging her tightly. "Yep. I missed you. It feels like we haven't spent much time together, doesn't it? I still have a lot of work to do, but I thought it would be nice to work at home so I get to see you."

She nods. "Colt and I already did our homework, so we can't work with you."

Thor chuckles, and the sound of it brings a different kind of ache to my chest. It's a painful kind of longing that I can't explain.

"That's okay, sweetheart. I'd be happy if you just read while I sit and work. How about that?"

She nods, but Colton groans. "I'm going to watch this movie with Leia!"

Thor looks our way, but I keep my eyes on the television. I should greet him, but I can't. It's irrational, and it's immature, but I can't face him. I'm too scared he'll see straight through me.

"Leia, could you follow me, please? I'd like to speak to you."

I tense and bite down on my lip as I nod and rise to my feet. I want to leave, but I can't come up with an excuse that would get me out of a brief conversation, and I'm not willing to come across as unprofessional just because avoiding seeing him right now would be easier for me.

Much to my surprise, Thor walks up the stairs, instead of toward his home office, and I follow him reluctantly.

He holds the door open, and I walk in, suddenly feeling vulnerable. Thor closes the door behind him and pulls his tie off. He lets it drop to the floor, seemingly lost in thought. He's staring out the window instead of looking at me, and I can't drag my gaze away as he takes his suit jacket off, placing it on the bed.

His hands move to the shirt he's wearing, and my heart skips a beat when he starts to unbutton it, more and more of his skin coming into view, until the shirt falls open. He pulls it off, and that too joins the jacket on his bed.

"What are you doing?" I murmur, my voice soft.

He looks at me then, his gaze intense. "Changing."

I clear my throat and nod. "Should I wait for you outside while you do that?"

He looks at me, his expression unreadable. I can't tell if he's angry, or if he's just unaffected, but something seems off.

"Why bother? It's not like there's any part of me you haven't seen yet."

I swallow hard as he undoes his suit trousers. He looks incredible, standing there like that, the sunlight illuminating his silhouette. The muscles on his arms are bigger and thicker than they used to be, and the sight of that v-line on his abs has me feeling flustered.

I'm mad at him, and I'm hurt, and every instinct in my body is telling me to walk up to him and show him just how angry I am. I want to grab his hair and kiss him. I want to leave kiss marks all over his chest, so any other woman he undresses in front of knows he's taken, and I want him to sink deep inside me and tell me that I'm his.

He pulls on gray sweats and a white t-shirt, before finally turning to me. "I will need you to watch the kids for me tomorrow night. I'll need you to be here all night."

I wrap my arms around myself as my heart clenches painfully, jealousy settling in my stomach, spreading slowly, until I'm barely thinking straight. He wants me to watch the kids overnight? He's not planning on coming home at all?

"I see," I murmur. "I'll make sure I'm here."

"Will you, now?" he asks, smiling humorlessly.

"Of course. That's my job, isn't it?"

He nods and runs a hand through his hair. "You won't ask me where I'm going, or who I'll be with?"

"I have a pretty good idea of who you'll be with," I snap, unable to help myself.

"No," he says. "You don't."

I shake my head and take a step away. "Since you're home now, I'll be leaving. I'll be here tomorrow."

"Leia," he says, sounding every bit as angry as I feel. What right does he have to be angry with me when he's the one fucking around?

I slam his door closed before rushing down the stairs. I try to keep my mind off him being with Eleanor, but I can't. All I can think about is everything I want, everything he's giving to someone else.

Twenty-Four

ADRIAN

"Is it true you were named after a princess?" Colton asks Leia. "One of my Fortnite friends says you are."

I lean back against the kitchen counter, realization dawning. "No way," I mutter. "Tell me you weren't named after Princess Leia?"

She looks up at me for a moment before looking away again. That's the first time she's even looked at me today at all. "I was. My father is a huge Star Wars fan. Honestly, I don't even know how my mother let him get away with it. I strongly suspect they initially decided on another name, and when my dad went to register me, he just put down whatever he wanted."

I chuckle, but she doesn't laugh with me. Instead, she turns to Colton. She's been avoiding me since I got home tonight, and I don't know what to make of it. When I came home yesterday, I wanted to explain to her that what she saw in The Herald wasn't what it looked like, but she didn't seem interested in listening at all. I shouldn't have provoked her by asking her to watch the kids tonight, but just once, I wanted to see her lose her cool over me. I expected her to question me, or to at least give me any indication that she's jealous, but she gave me nothing.

"Princess Leia isn't a real princess, Colt. She's a fictional character," she says.

"Fictional characters feel real, though," Lucy murmurs, looking up from her book. I wonder if Leia notices that Lucy has really warmed up to her. She used to read in her room, but now she'll read wherever Leia is, moving along with her from the sofa to the kitchen, and so forth. She still doesn't speak much, but I'm happy with the progress I'm seeing. In just a few weeks, these two have become closer than I expected them to be.

"Yeah, you're right. Who is your favorite princess?"

"Belle," she says dreamily. "I want her library."

Leia smiles then, her first real smile tonight. "Me too, Lucy. When I was growing up, one of my biggest wishes was to have that library. I'll take you to the college library someday soon, because it's the closest thing to it that I know of. Would you like that?"

Lucy lights up, but all she does is shrug. "I guess."

Leia looks a little defeated, and it takes all of me to keep my mouth shut. I want to tell her not to be discouraged, but I've decided that I won't interfere in the relationship between Leia and Lucy. It's something special, whether either of them realises it or not.

"Who is your favorite princess?" I ask Leia.

She looks at me, a hint of annoyance in her eyes. "I'm not sure," she says, looking away.

She's been standoffish with me, and while it isn't the jealousy I was expecting, it's something at least.

I straighten my t-shirt and smile at Lucy. "How do I look?" I ask her, provoking Leia further.

Leia's eyes run over my body, seemingly dispassionate, but I see the anger she tries to hide.

"You look cute, Dad."

"Cute? Is that good or bad?"

The look Lucy throws me is one that can only be described as pitiful. "It's... fine. You look fine."

"What do you think?" I ask Leia.

Leia glances at Lucy before turning back to me and nodding. "I agree. You look cute."

These two women... they're conspiring against me.

Leia grabs the papers she was grading at the breakfast bar and straightens them, keeping her hands busy. I noticed that's something she does when she's restless, but despite those thoughts going through her mind, she won't ask me where I'm going tonight. I wish she would.

"I think you look great, Dad. Is Uncle Silas bringing one of his cool cars? Do you think he'll take me for a ride around the block before you leave?"

Leia freezes, her eyes slowly moving toward me, and I smirk at the relief I see in her eyes.

"I don't know, buddy. If you ask him nicely, he'll probably let you."

"Cool," he says. "Take some pics for me, Leia. My friends will lose it. I should ask him to drive me to school one day."

I shake my head. Does this kid not realize that we're just as rich as my best friend is? The only reason we don't have supercars is because they aren't safe enough.

Colton jumps up and makes a run for it when the doorbell rings, and before long, I hear Silas's voice behind me. "I'll see you later," I tell Leia. "Once the kids are in bed, you're welcome to use any of the guest rooms and catch an early night too. I'm not sure what time I'll be back."

She nods, still looking flustered. "Have fun with your friend," she says hesitantly, and I nod, an indulgent smile on my face.

It's almost impossible to get Colton out of Silas's Ferrari, but eventually, we make it to the bar right outside his building. Colt doesn't know it, but the only reason Silas came to pick me up at all was so my son could mess around with his car for a bit. Silas is like that. Quiet, but with a heart of gold.

"That's her, isn't it? Your nanny? She's the girl you were obsessing over," he says the moment we sit down.

"How did you know?" I ask, but then I shake my head. Reading people is what Silas does. He runs the best and most expensive private security firm in this State. He probably knows exactly who Leia is. Hell, he probably knew the moment I hired her. He's always quietly looked out for my family and me.

"What are you going to do? You let her get away once, are you going to let her slip away again?"

"Damn, Silas. Buy me a fucking drink first, man. What's with the interrogation?"

He leans against the bar and smirks at me. "Someone has to ask you these questions, Thor. No one will do it but me. I always knew Alice wasn't for you. You never lost your mind over her, the way you did over Leia."

It's true. "She's one of my PhD students and she's my children's nanny. She's also Amara's best friend. She's as fucking off-limits as it gets."

Silas nods. "But she won't always be. Someday soon, she'll graduate. If the kids love her, then why wouldn't they love her as a stepmom too? Besides, let's be real, if you tell Amara you're making her best friend family, she'll be your biggest cheerleader."

"Fucking hell, Silas." This is the reason I've been dreading seeing him. He has this way of instilling hope in me that I have no business having. I know his words will be resounding through my mind for weeks to come. Would Leia wait for me? She's still a few months away from finishing her PhD. Would she want to be with me after she graduates? And if she does, will the kids be okay with it? Perhaps, by then, they'll have grown accustomed to having her in their lives.

It's hard to push down the joy the mental picture brings me, but I know I'm being unrealistic. While it'd be an ideal situation from my perspective, chances of Leia wanting to be involved with me are pretty slim. My night with her was filled with dreams of her own family, of a love that grew through the years. She wants to experience every step, starting with dating, moving into an engagement and at last, a wedding and everything that comes with that. If she were to be with me, she'd be forced to skip most steps, ending up with a family before she's even ready.

"I found her, you know. I found Alanna."

I turn toward Silas, my eyes wide. Other than Alice, he's the only person I ever told about Leia, and the only reason I felt comfortable doing so is because his story is somewhat similar to mine.

"How? Where?"

He looks away. "You won't fucking believe this, man. She was dating my asshole little brother."

I tense, my heart sinking. Silas's relationship with his half-brother has always been rocky, but this... "Did he target her intentionally?"

He looks at me and shakes his head. "I haven't found any evidence of it, but I have my suspicions."

Fuck. "If she's dating your brother..."

"Was," he corrects me. "Do you really think something like that would stop me? It's Alanna."

I chuckle and shake my head. "Right."

"It gets worse, though," he tells me.

I raise my brows in question. "She applied for a job at my firm, and I hired her."

I chuckle, laughing at his expense. "You're fucking kidding me."

"Nah man. Not only did she date my brother, she's my damn employee too."

"We're both fucked."

Silas nods. "Indeed, we are."

Twenty-Five

LEIA

I check up on the kids, making sure they're asleep before I head to the kitchen, my eyes dropping to the wine fridge.

My heart skips a beat as I remember the way Thor looked at me that day he offered me a glass of wine. I should've declined, but I couldn't, not when he looked at me like he needed a dose of me as much as I needed him. He's got me addicted to those little highs he makes me feel when he smiles at me, when everything fades away and it's just us, no matter how hard we try to pretend it isn't. I'm worried I've pushed him away too much, and I can't stop thinking about the photos I saw of him.

Now that I've gotten to know the kids, I completely understand why he chose to walk away from me two years ago. It was the right thing to do. The part that hurts is that our circumstances haven't changed. I see how much of himself he gives to his children. He doesn't have time for a woman in his life — not one that expects to become a permanent fixture, anyway. It hurts that he'll never be mine, and it kills me that for one night, he pretended Lucy and Colton were ours.

I bite down on my lip as I roam through the house restlessly. It's been nearly two months, and this house still doesn't feel like a home. Sure, there's the LEGO sets that Thor and Colton have been building, and there are dozens of Lucy's books strewn around the house, but there's still something lacking. We're getting there slowly, but we're not quite there yet. My fingers trail over the photo frames by the stairs, and I smile at the pictures of Thor with the twins. For a split second, I wonder what these photos would look like if I were in them, too.

I dismiss the thought and keep walking up the stairs. I'm restless tonight, unable to sit down or focus on anything. My thoughts are running wild, my heart longing for things that will never belong to me.

I pause in front of Thor's bedroom. It's perhaps the only room in this house that truly feels like his. I hesitate before pushing the door open. I know I'm invading his privacy, but I'm filled with this intense need to be surrounded by him.

I check my watch and bite down on my lips as I walk further into his room. He's got his telescope set up by the window, and memories of his hands on my waist come to mind. I smile as I think back to him showing me Orion's belt, and the way I turned around to find myself in his arms.

I sit down on his bed and brush my fingers over his pillow. I'm acting like a crazy stalker and I know it, but I can't help myself. Admitting that I want him will result in a broken heart, but here, all alone in the darkness... it doesn't matter how badly I need him.

I lie down on his bed and let my eyes fall closed, imagining myself waking up with him one day, his body against mine. I want to know if the way he touched me was truly as good as it is in my memories.

I sigh and let my hand roam over my body, wanting to rid myself of the desire I feel. My fingers trace over my breasts, down until I reach the hem of my dress. I'm so tempted to slip my finger underneath it, to make myself come surrounded by the subtle fragrance of Thor's aftershave.

"Leia."

I gasp, my eyes snapping open as I sit up in a rush, moving so quickly that my vision spins for a moment. Thor is standing in the hallway, watching me through the door I left ajar.

I swallow hard when he pushes the door open and closes it behind him, his eyes never leaving mine.

"I...I-I'm..."

He walks up to me and places his knee on his bed, his eyes trailing over my body. "You're right where I've always wanted you," he says, his voice low. "In my bed."

I swallow hard, unable to look away from him. He's loosened his tie and the top few buttons on his shirt are undone. Tonight, more than usual, he looks irresistible.

"Tell me, Leia. What were you thinking of as you were touching yourself in my bed?"

My cheeks heat and I bite down on my lip. "I wasn't touching myself," I whisper.

"Perhaps not, but you wanted to. Tell me, baby. Why did I come home to find you in my bed, when you fight this thing between us so hard? If you want my hands on you, all you have to do is tell me."

"I don't." My voice lacks conviction, and he smirks.

"No? Let me tell you what I'd do to you if you'd let me. I'd keep that promise I made two years ago. I'd have you sit at the edge of my bed, my hands on your knees as I kneel on the floor in front of you. I'd spread your legs and kiss your thigh, right where I know my lips would make you shiver. I'd move my way up, taking my time with you, until I've got you soaking wet before I've even kissed you where you want me most."

I squirm, my heart racing as I focus on the sound of his voice. I can't take this. He's torturing me, and he knows it.

"I'd kiss you right through the lace I know you're wearing, teasing you, knowing you want my tongue on your pussy, but I wouldn't give it to you. Not straight away, at least. I want you desperate for me, Leia. I want you ready to come with a single touch."

He joins me on the bed and lies down, placing his hands behind his head as he watches me, almost as though he doesn't trust that he can keep his hands to himself.

"I'd rip that thong straight off you, exposing your pussy. Do you have any idea how long I've wanted a taste of you?"

I'm breathing hard, trying my best to maintain my composure. I'm trying to tell myself that this is inappropriate, that he's drunk, and that I should leave... but I'm spellbound. I'm blinded by desire, by the need to hear that he wants me as badly as I want him.

"I'd kiss your pussy, right above where you want me, teasing you until I've got you begging, and then, only then, I'd give you what you want. Since this is a fantasy years in the making, I'd take my time circling my tongue around your clit, close, but keeping you squirming for more, until I've got you riding my face, making demands with your body."

My eyes roam over his body, the bulge in his jeans making it clear how badly he wants me. All it would take is me saying yes. I could have everything he's telling me about if just ask for it.

"I'd grab your hip with one hand and use the other to finger fuck you while you ride my face, forcing you to come on my tongue, over and over again, until you're begging me to stop, telling me you can't take any more."

He moves his hand down his body, until he's got it resting on his jeans. He watches me, his desire as blatant as mine. "It's not until I've got you so satisfied that you're not sure if you can take any more that I'd give you my cock, baby. You're the last woman I slept with, so the second I get anywhere near that pussy of yours, I'm fucking done for."

I gasp, my heart skipping a beat at his words, and he smiles at me, nodding. "Yeah, wifey. I'm so fucking obsessed with you, no one else could compare. You've ruined me. Utterly fucking ruined me."

Two years, and I'm the last person he slept with? An unfamiliar ache spreads from my chest through the rest of my body, a deep kind of need that far surpasses the desire I feel.

"Tell me you want me, Leia, and I'll make every single one of your fantasies come true. I know you're wet for me, baby. Tell me you feel this thing between us, and I'll make you come right fucking now."

I look into his eyes, every bit of logic falling away. He's my professor and my boss. I can't get involved with him. I barely survived losing him last time, there's no way I can recover a second time.

"I do," I whisper, unable to deny him. "I want you, Thor."

He sits up, disbelief crossing his eyes, as though he actually expected me to reject him. Sometimes I wonder how he sees himself. How could he think, for even a single moment, that I can resist him?

He reaches for me and cups my cheek, his thumb brushing over my lips. "Thank fuck," he growls, before leaning in.

"*Daddy?*"

The sound of Lucy's voice just outside the door rips us apart before our lips even meet, and he drops his forehead to mine. "No," he whispers, sounding pained. "Please, not now."

"Go," I whisper back. "I... I really need to leave, Thor. This... this is a bad idea."

He pulls away and rises to his feet beside the bed, his eyes flashing with frustration. "I'm going to put her to bed, and when I get back, you'd better still be here."

He walks away, and I think he knows as well as I do that I can't be here when he gets back. Things between us are already far messier than we ever should've allowed. He's my professor, for God's sake. What am I doing?

I slip out of his bedroom quietly, wondering if Lucy waking up when she did was a sign... one telling me to stop going down this slippery slope with Thor again.

Twenty-Six

LEIA

I hold my phone between my shoulder and my ear as I flip scroll through the case study that was released last night. Every time I get close to finalizing my dissertation, my research becomes near outdated. It's insane how fast the biotech industry moves. I want my dissertation to make a real impact, and I'm worried it won't be good enough. "I really can't," I tell Asha, barely paying attention to what she's saying.

I watch as Colton tries to google the answers to his homework instead of actually doing it, and I roll my eyes. I can't stay on the phone long, because Colt really can't be trusted.

"You have to," she warns. "I've already told Krishan that you'll be there, and Mom called me three times today to confirm you'll be going."

I groan and pinch the bridge of my nose. "Asha, I need to work late today. I can't go on a date."

Truthfully, I barely remember agreeing to go on this date at all. If she hadn't called me to confirm, I would've forgotten it.

"I'll call Emily. You two were hired as a pair, and she's never had to stand-in for you yet. She's not going to mind, even if it's late notice."

I bite down on my lip, unable to come up with an excuse. I don't want to go on a date, but going would make my family feel much more at ease. They're convinced I intend to remain single for the rest of my life, and they're not having it.

Maybe if things were different, I wouldn't have minded it so much, but after last night... I can't do it. Granted, nothing actually happened between Thor and me, but it just doesn't feel right. All day his words have been on replay in my mind. It wasn't just lust, it was so much more than that. It's hard to put my finger on it, but something shifted between us last night, and I'm worried he'd be hurt if he found out about tonight.

"I don't want to go," I tell my sister honestly. I run a hand through my hair, feeling conflicted. Last night Lucy interrupted us, and now it's Asha. I'm a big believer in signs, and these all seem like pretty obvious signs that I should be moving on, yet I'm ignoring each and every one of them.

"I know, Ley," Asha says. "But he's a nice guy, so just consider it meeting up with a friend. I just really think it'd make Mom and Dad feel better, you know?"

I sigh and nod. I know what she means. If I go on this date, then at least I won't have to hear them complain for a little while, since they'll feel like I'm at least trying.

"Okay," I give in. "I'll go, but never again. Don't even dream of setting me up ever again."

Asha exhales in relief. "You never know, Krishan might be the one, and I'll never have to."

"Doubtful." The guy is an accountant, and from everything I've heard about him so far, he seems as dull as dishwater.

I let my eyes fall closed as I listen to Asha make random small talk for a while, telling me to wear something nice, and God knows what else. By the time she hangs up, I'm hanging on by a thread.

"You're going on a date?" Lucy asks the moment I put my phone down.

"Seems like it."

"Is he your boyfriend?"

I shake my head, unsure how to even explain this to the kids. I don't even know what's going on myself. Honestly, most of the time I don't feel like I understand this whole adulting thing.

"Finish your homework," I tell them both. They nod, but for the rest of the day, they continue to question me about this date. What I'll wear, what his name is, where I'm going. They never run out of questions, and with each new one they think of, I'm reminded that they truly are Amara's niece and nephew.

I'm a nervous wreck by the time Thor gets home. I can't face him, not after last night. What would have happened if Lucy hadn't woken up when she did?

"Hey," he says. I throw a quick nervous smile his way and walk past him after bidding the kids goodnight, but he grabs my hand and stops me. "Ley?"

I pause and turn to face him. "Yeah?"

"Are we good?"

I nod. "Of course."

"Then why are you rushing off like that? You've barely spoken two words to me."

"I... um, I just need to go. I have somewhere to be."

He narrows his eyes at me, his gaze trained on my face.

"Where are you going?" he asks, his voice low, threatening.

"She's going on a date!" Colton shouts, and my eyes fall closed in mortification.

"The fuck you are," Thor growls. The possessiveness in his tone has me biting down on my lip hard. The way he looks at me... that's exactly how he looked at me last night.

"Thor," I murmur. "It's not like that."

"It's not a date?"

"No, it is, but this was before..."

"Then why are you still going?"

I sigh and run a hand through my hair, unsure what to say. He wouldn't understand, not truly. "It's essentially a favor to my sister. She arranged it, and it seems to mean a lot to her that I go."

He looks into my eyes, and for once, I can't read him at all. "Don't go," he says. "Don't, Leia."

"I have to."

"*Fine*," he snaps, and disappointment rushes over me. That's it? I look away, unsure why I expected him to fight me on this.

The two of us stand there, looking at each other, the air filled with unspoken words. "*Fine*," I repeat eventually.

He smiles at me humorlessly, anger radiating off him. I grit my teeth and walk away, knowing that my entire night is now ruined. For every second of the rest of the evening, I'm going to be second-guessing my decision, and I hate myself for it.

Twenty-Seven

LEIA

I smile at Krishan and try my best to focus on his story about the corporate fraud case he handled at his previous firm, but all I can think about is Thor. He looked upset when I left, and the pleading gaze in his eyes haunts me.

"That's honestly really cool," I tell him, feeling terrible about my inability to focus on him. He seems like a nice guy, maybe someone I actually would've liked if I'd never met Thor. I smile at him while I try to think of an excuse to leave early, but my smile melts away when I see Thor walking my way. What is he doing here?

"Leia."

Krishan looks up at Thor, and then back at me. I'm so at a loss for words that I can't even think of anything to say.

"Thanks for keeping my girl company," he tells Krishan, "but I've got it from here."

My face heats at those words and I look at Krishan with wide eyes, unsure if I should apologize or laugh off Thor's words. He merely smiles at me and nods. "He's not your boyfriend, is he?"

I shake my head. "No, not exactly."

"But he's something?"

Thor places his hand on my shoulder. "Damn right, we're something."

I smile nervously and tuck a strand of hair behind my ear. "I'm really sorry, Krishan."

He shakes his head, dismissing my apology as he rises from his seat. "That explains why I could barely keep your attention." He smiles sheepishly, and I try my hardest to smile back at him, but guilt prevents me from doing so.

I groan when Krishan walks away, and Thor takes his seat. "What the hell are you doing here?" I snap.

"I asked you nicely not to go on this date," he warns. "Since you wanted to go so badly, then we'll go."

My lips fall open in shock as I stare at him, taking in the possessiveness in his demeanor. Every time I'm alone with him, he shows me a different facet of himself. This part of him might well be my favorite, though I'd never admit it to him.

"You're insufferable."

"You're beautiful."

"What exactly do you think you're doing? Aren't you afraid of people seeing us together?"

"This?" he asks. "This is our weekly dissertation meeting."

A startled laugh escapes my lips and I shake my head. "You're shameless." He crashed my date and won't even outright admit he did. "How did you even know where I was?"

"It took Silas approximately seven minutes to track you down. Far too long, in my opinion."

I stare at him wide-eyed, a strange sense of satisfaction washing over me. He and I have been dancing around each other, neither of us truly admitting the way we feel. Today he's not holding back, and it exhilarates me.

Thor stares me down, his eyes flashing. "I told you not to leave my bed last night, and you did. Then I told you not to go on this damn date, and you fucking did. What did you think I'd do, Leia?

135

Sit at home while some asshole accountant gets to have dinner with you? No, baby. You admitted that you want me last night, and you don't get to take those words back."

"You're being a hypocrite. You went on a date just last week, but I can't do the same? You must be kidding me."

He smiles at me and leans in, his arms crossed. "Did, I, though? Did I go on a date? All I remember doing was having dinner with Roger Williams. I didn't even know his daughter would be there, and I didn't care she was. He heavily hinted that I should stay and have a drink with her after he left, so I stayed for one single drink. The girl managed to spill wine all over her dress and asked to borrow my jacket, so I gave it to her. If you'd just asked me about it, I would've told you everything. I have no interest in playing games with you, Leia. Ask me anything, and I'll always tell you the truth. You're the only one I want, and you know it. I'm done pretending it isn't true, especially now that I know you feel the same way."

I lean back in my seat, my thoughts reeling, but before I can say a word, a server appears with what appears to be the manager. "Good evening, Mr. Astor," he says. "It's so good to have you. If you'd told us you'd be here tonight, we would've ensured you'd have a better table. Please let me know if there's anything you need."

I've seen Amara be treated like this everywhere she goes, but Thor has always seemed different somehow. Perhaps because I usually only see him at home or at Astor College.

He smiles politely and holds up the wine menu. I watch him as he asks for recommendations and orders a bottle to match the food Krishan and I already ordered. He's so shameless. I have no doubt he has every intention of actually eating Krishan's dinner too.

His eyes find mine the second the server walks away, and the way he looks at me is different. I've gotten used to him being kind and reserved with me, but today he looks the way he did two years ago... like a man who knows exactly what he wants and isn't afraid to go after it.

And what he wants seems to be *me*.

"Our circumstances haven't changed," I tell him, my voice soft. "You still have children that desperately need you. I'm still your nanny and your student."

He nods. "I know, but I don't care anymore. I don't think you understand, Leia. I can't be without you anymore. I'm tired of feeling so fucking miserable, of having you within reach and being unable to touch you. I'm exhausted. I'm done wondering if you want me too, if maybe I could be the one to make you smile, the one to offer you a shoulder to lean on when you've had a rough day. I'm done with all of it."

My heart clenches and I bite down on my lip, a whirlwind of emotions rushing through me. His words ignite a spark within me, a desire so deep it'd have me weak in the knees if I wasn't sitting.

"Thor... I don't want to be your dirty little secret. You know we can't be together publicly. I'd be risking my PhD, and there's a high chance it'd disrupt the children's lives. They've only just gotten used to school and life here."

He falls silent then and looks away, frustration marring his features. "Time is all we need, Leia. If you ask me to wait for you, I will. I can wait till you finish your PhD, till the kids have a bit more stability. They're already smitten with you, and I think they'd accept us being together if we give them time."

I nod, my heart racing. "Then answer this question, Thor. Be honest with me. Do you see yourself marrying me someday? Would you ever want to have another child, even though you already have Lucy and Colton? Just because the chances of me ever having a child of my own are slim to none, doesn't mean I won't try. If you and I start dating, I need to know there's a future for us, one that aligns with what I envision for myself."

"Yes," he answers without hesitation. "Someday, I'm making you my wife. Yes, Leia. I want to have children with you. Am I crazy for wanting that after everything I just went through? Maybe, but maybe not. That fantasy we indulged in on our first date? I want that. All of it. If it's with you, I want it all."

I stare at him in shock, his words barely registering. This isn't what I expected him to say. I was so sure he'd tell me he never wants to get married again, and that Lucy and Colton are enough for him.

"Baby, if you want to, we can start trying straight away. I have no doubts when it comes to you. I *will* marry you — preferably as soon as you graduate."

"I..."

"Just say yes, Leia. Say you want the future we fantasized about. Tell me you'll give us a chance."

"I... I don't want to wait," I tell him honestly. "I'm tired of fighting this, too. Maybe this is the worst decision I'll ever make, but what if it's the best? I want to try with you, Thor."

He smiles, and it transforms his entire face. I'm falling for him all over again, and this time, there's no going back.

"Thor," I whisper, and he nods. "We have to keep this quiet until I finish my PhD. To be honest, I'm not sure how my family will feel about us being together, and that's something we'll have to discuss at some point, but for now... for now, I just want to be with you."

He reaches for my hand and entwines our fingers. "I'll do whatever you want me to do, so long as you tell me you're mine."

"I'm yours. Heart and soul."

He grins and lifts my hand to his lips. "Oh baby, make no mistake. It isn't just your heart and soul I want. I want your body too."

I burst out laughing, my heart skipping a beat. Is this really happening? It all feels so surreal. The last couple of weeks have been a whirlwind of broken hearts and longing. I hope that isn't how our story ends too.

Twenty-Eight

ADRIAN

"Thank you for the offer, Professor Isaacson, but I must decline. I always have dinner with my children. It's the only time of day that is always theirs. I'd never take that from them. I appreciate the offer, though."

She smiles at me and leans into me the way women do when they're trying to indicate interest. A few months ago, I would've felt flattered. Today, I'm nervous as hell. I can see Leia heading our way, her eyes trained on the hand Professor Isaacson placed on my arm, and she doesn't look happy. Last night I had to take her home after our date because I'd asked Silas to watch the kids for me, and it turned out to be a disaster. I didn't even get to kiss her goodnight because he let Colton eat so much candy that my boy was puking by the time I made it home.

"Oh, it's so rare to meet someone who has twins. How about we go to the zoo? I'd love to take them."

I shake my head and remove her hand from my arm. "My kids hate the zoo. My daughter thinks the forced captivity in zoos is inhumane, and several times, she's asked me to sign petitions that would stop new animals from being added to zoos. If she could have it her way, zoos would be turned into animal rehabilitation centers, where you can go see animals that are recovering from injuries. She has a lot of ideas, that one."

"Professor Astor," Leia says, her tone sharp.

I turn toward her, my expression calm even though my heart is racing. I'm just not interested in playing games with Leia. Even if I can't publicly be with her, I need her to know that she's the only one I want.

"I need to discuss the syllabus of the class you asked me to teach. I have some ideas for additional tests, and I'd like to hear your thoughts."

Additional tests? What? She's been teaching that class for months now, and she hasn't once asked me for feedback. My Princess is jealous, and I'm loving every second of it.

"He's busy," Professor Isaacson says, turning to stand right next to me, her arm brushing against mine. "We were just about to grab a coffee."

I watch Leia's expression carefully, noting the anger in her eyes. She hides it well, but watching her has become my favorite hobby. I've become a master at recognizing the amusement she hides when Colton makes an inappropriate joke, or the frustration she feels when Lucy won't respond to her attempts to engage her. What I haven't seen in her eyes before though, is anger. Leia doesn't really get angry. With the kids, at least, she has the patience of a saint. Just last week, she tutored Colton for two hours after she was meant to get off work, nipping every one of his budding tantrums in the bud without losing her patience once. So what is it that has her eyes flashing like that?

"Is that so, Professor Astor?" Leia asks, almost daring me to agree with Professor Isaacson, whose first name I can't even remember.

"No. Not at all," I reply, just a touch too quickly. "Why don't we head to my office, and I'll take a look at your proposed amendments."

Leia nods and walks past me, her entire body tense. Yeah, she's mad, and I have a feeling it's got a lot to do with Professor's Isaacson's blatant flirting. I shouldn't, but I get a perverse sense of satisfaction from it. For so long, I felt like I was the only one feeling frustrated. It feels good to know she feels the same way about me.

She seems impatient as I unlock the door, her anger rising when I take my time, and I bite back a smile. She doesn't even have any documents on her, so I'm pretty curious to see what she's going to come up with. It's obvious she just made up an excuse when she saw me with another woman.

I hold the door open for her and watch her closely as she walks in, noting the exact moment she realizes what she just did.

I lean back against my closed door, my eyes roaming over that tight skirt and her high heels. Today she's wearing bright red heels, and the heel itself is thin as hell, the color a gradient from red to pink. Whatever the hell that contraption is, she looks hot in it, and I'm instantly reminded of the way I fucked her in her heels so many years ago.

"The syllabus?" I ask, my brows raised.

She hesitates. "Yes," she snaps, walking over to my desk. I bite back a smile when she sits down in my seat and turns on my computer, without a single ounce of shame.

I push away from the wall and approach her, my eyes never leaving her. I can see her getting more nervous the closer I get, and by the time I'm standing beside her, half of her bravado has disappeared.

I lean in, my face far closer to hers than is appropriate, and type in my password. "It's Coltcy," I tell her. "That's my password."

She looks up, her expression disarmed. "Why would you tell me your password?"

"You sat down behind my desk like you own my office, so I thought I'd aid you in what I'm sure Lucy would call your boss moves. Besides, you're my girlfriend. I won't keep secrets from you."

She purses her lips, failing to hide her budding smile, and turns back toward the screen. Much to my surprise, she actually pulls up her class syllabus.

"So we're really doing this, huh?" I murmur.

"Doing what?" she asks, her voice husky.

"Pretending you didn't walk up to me because you didn't want to see me with Professor what's-her-name."

She looks up, her eyes flashing. "Fine," she admits. "I'm using half of my Free Pass."

I chuckle, remembering the way she gave herself a free pass after she caught me acting jealous after a class she taught. "Very well. Only half, huh?"

She nods. "I wasn't half as bad as you were."

"I wish you were."

Her lips fall open, and I smirk. "Thor," she admonishes.

"Come here."

Her eyes widen a fraction and I smirk as I pull her out of my seat, her body crashing against mine. "Our evening was cut short last night, and I never did get round to punishing you for going on a date with another man. How should I make you pay, Princess?" My eyes fall to her lips and I smirk. "I think I'll start with a kiss."

I thread my hand through her hair, my fingers grazing over her scalp before I wrap my fingers around her hair and yank her head up. She moans when my lips meet hers, her body melting against me. Fuck. Leia's hands slide up my chest, until she's got them wrapped around my neck, neither of us wanting any distance between us.

I deepen our kiss and turn us around, my lips never leaving hers as I lift her onto my desk, spreading her legs so I can stand between them. "Thor," she moans, the sound of her driving me fucking insane.

"You fucking crazy woman," I murmur, sucking down on her lower lip harshly. "Going on a fucking date with someone else."

She chuckles and leans back a little to look at me, her gaze provocative. "I think I like you being jealous. I might do it again. Should I ask Lex if he wants to have dinner with me?"

My lips fall open in shock and I shake my head. "The fucking audacity. You're going to get me arrested." She laughs then, and I groan. "You definitely need to be taught a lesson."

"Go on, Professor. Teach me a lesson."

I chuckle, my heart skipping a beat. I've never had this before. I've never had this much desire and happiness tangled all up in one. "Get on your knees, Princess."

She smiles but obeys, kneeling underneath my desk as I sit down in my chair and undo my belt buckle. I watch her, enjoying the desire and impatience in her eyes as she kneels between my legs. "You want my cock, don't you?"

She bites down on her lip and nods. She looks fucking hungry for me, and it does something to me. After a lifetime of playing games and keeping score, being with Leia is exhilarating.

A soft moan escapes her lips when I free my cock, and she reaches for me. "I forgot how big you are," she whispers.

"I'm about to remind you."

I thread my hand through her hair, my fingers grazing over her scalp before I ball my fist and grab a handful of her hair, pulling her face closer. "Suck my cock like the good girl you are, Princess." She opens up her mouth for me, and I watch as the tip of my cock disappears between her sexy lips. She swirls her tongue around the tip, teasing me, and I shake my head.

"Nah, baby. After what you did last night, I have no intention of being nice to you. I'd planned to make you come a handful of times before I ever even fucked you, but you haven't been the good girl you should've been for me. You're about to learn who the fuck you belong to."

I pull her head closer, watching her take more of my cock, careful to not push her too far. Her mouth is so fucking hot and tight, and I can barely take it. I'm not sure if she's the one being punished or me.

I freeze at the sound of knocking on my door, my eyes finding

Leia's. Before I can react, the door swings open, and Professor Isaacson walks in.

"Oh, good!" she says, pausing in front of my desk. "I was hoping Leia would be gone by now. That girl is so uptight. Honestly, she's so obsessed with her research and teaching, I was worried she'd talk about it for hours and I'd have to come save you from her."

I keep one hand in Leia's hair and use the other to play some music in an effort to hide any noise Leia might make. I glance down at her to find her staring at me, anger flashing through her eyes. Acoustic music starts to play from the speakers on my monitor, and I smirk as I pull her head closer again, bringing her lips back to my cock. She opens her mouth and slowly takes my cock back into her mouth, her tongue teasing me.

"Yeah, so uptight," I agree. "Smart girl, but I doubt she's any fun at parties."

That's got her sucking down on my cock hard, the suction almost too much for me. If she continues to torture me like that, I'm going to come in her mouth before she has any say over it.

"Oh, Leia doesn't attend parties," Professor Isaacson says, rolling her eyes. "That girl is always working or studying. I don't think she does anything else. Honestly, I'm surprised you were able to get rid of her so quickly."

I tighten my grip on Leia's hair and move her head up and down my cock slowly, making sure to keep as quiet as possible. "Yeah. She's a good girl, though. Such a good girl."

"So, about that coffee?" she says.

"Oh, Professor Isaacson," I say, shaking my head. "I wish I could, but I've got a class to teach in a bit. Rain check?"

Leia's teeth graze over my cock in warning, and I rotate my hips slightly, pushing deeper into her mouth. I can't risk her gagging on my cock right now, but fuck if I don't want to hit the back of her throat.

"Oh, call me Linda," she says, waving off my rejection. She grabs a sticky note off my desk and writes down her phone number. "This is my number," she tells me. "Call me anytime. It must be hard being a single dad. If you ever want to, you know, let loose... call me."

Leia pauses her movements, and I cough to hide my impatient groans. Linda smiles at me as she walks away, and I lean back in my seat when the door closes behind her. Fucking hell.

I stare down at my girlfriend, whose eyes are flashing with jealousy and irritation even as her mouth is filled with my cock. "I'm going to lock that door, and then I'm going to fuck you on this desk until you're so sore, you won't be able to go on another fucking date."

Twenty-Nine

LEIA

"*Call me, Professor Astor,*" I mimic as I rise to my feet. Thor locks the door and turns back to me, his cock still hard and demanding my attention.

"Look who's jealous now."

I cross my arms and stare him down. "So what if I am?"

He smirks and walks up to me, pausing in front of me with the biggest smile on his face. He wraps his hand around my neck, his thumb resting on my throat. "Then I guess I'd better appease you, wifey."

He leans in and kisses me, his touch gentler now. Thor's hands wrap around my waist, and he lifts me on top of his desk. "Tell me, baby... how can I make you feel better?" He sit down in his chair and spreads my legs. Thor looks up at me as he kisses the inside of my thigh, his teeth grazing over my skin before he sucks down, marking me. "How do I make you forget all about what's-her-name?"

I smile when he moves his lips to my other thigh and leaves a small mark there too, the way he did the first time we slept with each other.

His fingers brush over the soaking wet lace thong I'm wearing and he chuckles. "Of course you're already wet for me. Enjoyed sucking my cock, didn't you?"

I nod, not willing to hide anything from him. He pushes the fabric aside and slips two fingers into me, his thumb brushing over my clit. "Oh God," I moan, my eyes falling closed.

"No," he warns me. "I want your eyes on me, baby."

I bite down on my lip as he grabs my thighs and wraps them over his shoulders before leaning in. I gasp when his tongue strokes my clit, drawing circles around it, as though he wants me in agony. The combination of his fingers inside me and his tongue on my clit is too much, and I struggle to keep quiet.

"Adrian," I warn.

He pulls away just slightly, his fingers keeping up their rhythmic motion that has me descending into insanity. "Yes, Princess? Tell me."

"You know what I want."

He looks at me as his tongue finally brushes over my clit, slowly, teasingly. Just once, before he pulls away. "You want that? You want to come on my tongue?"

I nod, desperate for his touch.

"Beg."

I swallow hard and grab his hair. "Please, Thor. I need it. *Please* make me come on your tongue."

He sucks down on my clit, and it's almost enough to push me over. Almost. "Tell me you won't ever go on a date with anyone else again. Tell me you won't think of anyone but me, and I'll make you come."

"I swear. You're the only one for me. Only you, Thor."

He looks up at me, and my heart skips a beat. There isn't just possessiveness in his eyes. It's something deeper and darker than that. "Good girl," he growls, before giving me what I want.

His tongue drives me crazy, until wave after wave of pleasure washes over me, his name on my lips.

He leans back and watches me shatter for him, intense satisfaction lighting up his face. "I've wanted to taste your pussy for years. You taste like fucking sunshine and sin, like I knew you would. Soon, baby. Soon, I'm going to need you to sit on my fucking face."

I bite down on my lip, my pussy clenching at his words, and he smirks as he stands up, drawing my eyes to his cock. He leans in and wraps his hand around my neck, tipping my face up to kiss me, until he's got me breathless.

"Are you clean, Leia?"

I nod. "Good. So am I."

He looks into my eyes as he places his cock at the base of my pussy, pushing the tip in slightly. "Do you have any idea how long I've been dreaming of this pussy? It's still as tight as I remember."

I bite down on my lip harshly as he pushes in further. I feel so incredibly full, and it hurts a little, despite how wet I am. "Thor..."

He shakes his head and tightens his grip on my neck. "You can do this, baby. You can take all of it. We'll go slowly, okay?"

I nod, and he pushes in further, pausing again. He tilts his head and kisses me, slowly, his tongue tangling with mine leisurely until he's got me moaning.

"Are you sure you don't want to use protection?" I ask, a hint of fear in my chest.

"I'm sure."

He looks into my eyes, and it hits me then. He's serious about this, about us. "Do you realize what you're saying?"

Thor's hand moves from my neck to my hair, his fingertips grazing my scalp while his other hand cups my cheek. "Yes, Leia. Two years, I dreamed of you. I've always heard people say that when you know, you know. I finally get it. You and I were years in the making, and I'm ready."

He pushes into me all the way, and my eyes fall closed as a

pained groan escapes my lips. "Thor," I moan, and he kisses me as he stretches me out fully, letting me adjust for a moment before pulling back slowly.

"I want it all with you, Leia," he says, thrusting back into me, hard. "Every high, every low. I didn't believe in destiny until you walked into my life. If it exists, then it's you. You're my destiny."

He moves his hands to my legs and holds my thighs as he pulls back almost all the way, watching as his cock disappears back into my pussy. "I must be crazy," he murmurs, increasing the pace.

"We both are." Our relationship is moving too quickly. It's too much, too intense, and it's never felt more right.

He smiles as he tightens his grip on my hips and fucks me harder, tilting my hips up as he places his thumb back on my clit, watching me as he gets me closer and closer to another orgasm.

He groans when I come for him again and increases the force of his thrust, coming deep inside me seconds after I do. "Fuck, Leia. I'm fucking obsessed with you."

He drops his head to my shoulder and kisses my neck tenderly as we both try to catch our breath. "I'm late for a class," he tells me, and I burst out laughing.

"Professor Astor," I admonish. "You're so irresponsible."

He leans back and looks at me, a satisfied look in his eyes. "What can I say... my future wife is insatiable."

Future wife... the sound of that has my heart skipping a beat in excitement, yet it also terrifies me. He has no idea how many obstacles we'll face, but I do.

Thirty

LEIA

Lucy's phone buzzes, and I pull my gaze away from my dissertation research to look at her. She's sitting next to me at the dining table, the two of us having grown accustomed to our afternoons together. She and Colton will do their homework with me right here at the table, and if they get it all done to my satisfaction, Colton gets to play his games, while Lucy gets to read or watch TV for as many hours as she wants.

Usually her nose is buried in a book, but today she's barely looked up from her phone. "What's going on, Luce?" I ask, equal parts curious and concerned. I understand that the kids having their own phones was part of the divorce agreement, ensuring their mother could always reach them, but technology is scary these days. She could be talking to anyone, anywhere. I finally understand my mother's paranoia. What if she's chatting with some type of sick bastard who's pretending to be her age and is befriending her? I take a deep breath, trying my hardest to keep from overthinking. Damn it. When did I turn into my mother?

"Oh," she says, looking up, her cheeks rosy. My heart

hammers in my chest, part of me expecting the worst. "It's my mum."

I freeze, guilt slamming into me at the thought of Thor's ex-wife. The kids are still healing from the pain caused by the separation of their parents. The last thing I should be doing is lusting after their father. She looks so happy at the mention of her mother, and my stomach knots uncomfortably. If she knew what Thor and I did, she'd be heartbroken.

"She says she misses me. I'm trying to convince her to come see me, because Dad will never let me go to her. Definitely not while I have to go to school." She hesitates, and then she puts her phone down for a moment. "Would you... would you maybe talk to Dad for me? I know you work together at school too, and you seem to be friends. Maybe he'll listen to you? I'd ask uncle Silas, but he doesn't... well, he doesn't like Mum."

I look away, unsure what to say. "Lucy, I'm not sure it's my place to do that. This sounds like a family matter."

"But you're family, aren't you? You're nothing like the other nannies we've had. You actually care about us, and you're Dad's friend."

I sigh and lean in to brush her hair behind her ear. "I can't promise anything, Luce. I can mention it, but I'm not sure how your dad will react."

She nods and wraps her arms around herself. "He gets mad when we mention Mum. He thinks we don't notice, but we can tell."

"Yeah?" I murmur, unsure what to say to her. This is the first time she's really opening up to me about anything at all, and I don't want to dismiss her, but it feels inappropriate to be discussing her mother after I slept with her father. The memories of Thor's hand in my hair as he pushed his cock into my mouth is still fresh in my mind, and the guilt is almost too much to bare. The idea of their father moving on would hurt the kids endlessly, but it being me, someone they trust... I'm not sure they'd ever be okay with that.

"I just miss her," she whispers, her voice breaking. "I want her to come home. I want us to be happy again."

I wrap my arm around her, barely able to contain the remorse that threatens to overwhelm me. If Lucy ever found out about her father and me, she'd never forgive me. I have no doubt she'd feel intensely betrayed. How are we ever supposed to tell her? "Aren't you happy now, Lucy? We hang out together every day, and we have fun, don't we?"

She nods, but her sniffles betray her sorrow. I wrap my arms around her fully and hug her tightly. "It's not the same. I miss her so...so much." Her breathing changes, as though she's drowning in sobs that she's keeping inside, and I tighten my grip on her. "Colt has Dad, and their bond is different, but I had Mum."

I pat her hair gently as I try my hardest to keep my own tears at bay. How did I never realize just how badly she was hurting? She's never given me any indication that she misses her mother.

"I know it wouldn't be the same, but if you'd like to, you and I can go on a spa date? We could even invite auntie Amara too, if you want to? You're right, my love, Colton has your dad, and they play games and sports together, but you've got me. We're friends, aren't we?"

She pulls away to look at me, wiping furiously at her tears as though she's embarrassed she cried at all. She's such a strong little girl. I wish I'd done a better job. I wish she didn't feel the need to act so strong all the time. I should've been there for her. I should've realized she was hurting.

"Really?"

"Absolutely. We can go this weekend."

"You mean it?"

"Have I ever lied to you before, Lucy?"

She shakes her head and sniffs again. "Just you and me? You won't bring Colton or Dad?"

"Nope. It's girls-only! Would you like to invite Auntie Amara, or shall we just make it a private Lucy-Ley day?"

She hesitates, a shy smile on her face. "Lucy-Ley day," she whispers, and I chuckle, my heart overflowing.

"You got it, my love. I just need to ask your dad for permission, but I think he'll say yes." I rarely work weekends, since Thor likes to take care of them himself then, but I have a feeling he'll let me take Lucy for the day.

"I hope he says yes," she says, her tone hopeful, and I nod.

"He will."

I stroke her hair gently, running the tips of my fingers over it. "Luce, you know you can talk to me anytime, right? I'm very sorry that I didn't realize you missed your mom so much. I can never replace her, but if I'd known, I would've done my best to plan activities with you that you might miss."

She nods. "I know, Ley."

"Is there anything else you'd like to do with me?"

She hesitates, and then she nods. "Would you take me shopping? It's so awkward to go with Dad and Colt. I was going to ask Auntie Amara, but I want to go with you."

"Of course, my love. I haven't been shopping in ages. You can help me pick out a new pair of heels."

She chuckles. "Ley, your heels are crazy. I don't even know where you can buy some of the crazy ones you wear."

I shrug. "Sounds like a fun challenge to me."

Lucy laughs, and I breathe a sigh of relief. Her earlier sorrow is gone, but for how long? She clearly misses her mother, and I feel like an imposter. Like I'm trying to steal Thor's ex-wife's spot in everyone's lives. It makes me feel disgusted with myself.

I can't shake the feeling for the rest of the day. Just this morning, I'd been looking forward to Thor coming home. I'd been imagining us sneaking into one of the bedrooms together, even if it's just for a quick kiss. Now I can barely stomach the idea. The mere thought of causing the kids any more pain sickens me.

I check my watch when I hear Thor walk in, surprised at how quickly the day flew by. I managed to spend most of my afternoon overthinking things instead of working on my dissertation.

"Princess," he says as his eyes fall on me, and my heart skips a beat. His gaze roams over my body, and I bite back a smile.

"You're home earlier than I expected."

"Yeah," he murmurs. "I couldn't wait."

"Thor," I say, my tone hesitant. "Can we talk?"

He tenses and looks away, but not before I catch the frustration in his expression. He nods and tips his head toward his home office, and I follow him.

"This isn't quite the welcome I expected," he says as the door closes behind him.

I nod. "I know, but I..."

"You what? You had a change of heart? Don't tell me you regret what happened, Leia. Please."

I shake my head. "No... and yes. I spoke to Lucy today."

Thor's eyes widen, confusion crossing his eyes. "Okay," he says, indicating for me to continue.

"She told me she really misses her mother, and she wanted me to ask you if maybe her mother could come see her? From what I understand, they've been texting."

Thor leans against his desk and runs a hand through her hair. "What the fuck?" he murmurs, seemingly more to himself than to me. "Why the fuck does she want to see Lucy now? She didn't even fight for custody. When I told her I was taking the kids here, she didn't protest for a second. She even told me some distance would do us good, so why the fuck is she suddenly showing an interest?"

I shake my head, unsure what to say. "I can tell Lucy is hurting, Thor. She and I also discussed doing a spa day together, and I was wondering if that would be okay with you? Could I take her with me on Saturday? I know it isn't really my place, but I'd really like to."

He straightens, and the way he looks at me sends my heart into overdrive. "Of course you can, Leia. I just... with us being together, I want you to know that I don't have any expectations of you. I want as much as you're willing to give me, and I won't ask for any more than that. I don't expect you to take on Alice's role. I would never ask that of you."

I cross my arms, a hint of anger blooming in the pit of my stomach. "I'm not after her role, Thor. I care about Lucy. Don't mistake this for me having ulterior motives."

He smiles, unraveling my anger before it has a chance to take root. "I wish you did have ulterior motives, Princess."

My eyes widen and I look away, forcing myself not to read too much into his words. "Thor... we really should also talk about us. I care about Colton and Lucy, and I don't want them to be affected by what's going on between us. I'm not sure... maybe we shouldn't—"

"No," he cuts me off and walks toward me, his hands wrapping around my waist. "There's no way I'm letting you walk away again, Leia. What happens between you and me is a private matter, and we'll keep it that way." He cups my cheek, his thumb brushing over my lower lip. "There's a reason I didn't use protection, Leia. I want a future with you, the same one you envision for yourself. We'll keep our relationship private until we no longer can, but it certainly won't be forever."

I nod, a tender ache settling in my chest. Once the kids find out about us, everything will change, and not necessarily for the better. We're on a collision course, he and I. They're still healing from their parents' separation, and I don't want to be the reason they're hurt again. They might like me as their nanny, but I can't be sure they'd welcome me into their family.

And then there's my own family. Our cultures are too different, and the fact that he has kids from a previous marriage would be unacceptable to my parents.

I just hope that what we have is enough to weather the storm. I hope no one gets hurt.

Thirty-One

LEIA

I'm nervous as I unlock Thor's front door, memories of the way he kissed me goodnight before I left last night still fresh in my mind. The way Thor touched me, his possessiveness, the passion. God, I can't get enough of that man.

How am I supposed to spend a day with his daughter, acting as though I'm nothing but her nanny? How do I listen to her concerns and the pain she's experiencing as a result of her parents' divorce without feeling like a complete jerk for sleeping with her father, when she's still hoping her parents might reconcile?

The house is mostly quiet when I walk in, the only sounds coming from the kitchen. I pause in the doorway when I see Thor standing behind the stove in a white t-shirt and gray sweatpants that make his ass look perfectly grabbable.

I lean against the doorway and admire the view, a pang of longing going straight to my chest. I want this. I want lazy Saturday mornings and home-cooked breakfasts with him. I want to wake up with him and spend whole days doing nothing together.

I watch his side profile, my heart skipping a beat when he smiles. "See something you like?" he asks, his voice as sexy as everything else about him.

"Yeah, looks delicious," I tell him.

Thor chuckles and turns to look at me, his smile vanishing when he takes me in. I'm wearing a loose sun dress today, nothing overly fancy, but the look in his eyes makes me wonder whether what I see in the mirror might be different to what he sees when he looks at me.

"Oh yeah? Which part looks delicious?"

I grin and let my gaze roam over his body, enjoying the eye candy. "I like the eggs, but I'm more interested in the sausage."

He bursts out laughing, and I can't help but giggle too. "Hey, don't forget, you're the guy who joked about Uranus on our first date. You set a precedent for lame jokes, and you'll never live that down."

He smiles at me, his gaze filling with something deeper, something that makes my heart race in the weirdest way. I don't usually get nervous or flustered, yet that's exactly how I feel right now. "You look beautiful today," he says eventually. "I wish I didn't have to share you with Lucy. Is it weird to be jealous of my own daughter?"

I smile at him, shyness overcoming me. "No," I murmur. "But maybe I can hang back when I drop her home later... to make up for the gross crime I'm committing by not being yours today."

He chuckles and turns off the stove before walking up to me. "Oh baby," he whispers. "You're always mine. You have been from the moment I saw you sipping that cosmopolitan. You just didn't know it yet."

My heart skips a beat when he reaches me, his hand cupping my cheek gently before he leans in.

"What are you guys doing?"

I jump away from Thor, surprised to find Colton standing behind me, his eyes moving between his father and me. "Oh, Leia had something in her eye," Thor says, his tone nonchalant.

"That happens to me sometimes," Colton says, nodding in understanding, and I grimace. We really should know better than sneaking around when the kids are at home, but I was so lost in him for a moment that I forgot about everything that's at stake. Thor does that to me. He makes me forget about everything but him.

"Leia!" Lucy yells, rushing up to me with the biggest smile on her face. I open up my arms as she crashes into me and hug her tightly, my heart totally overflowing with tenderness. This is the first time I've seen her act her age, and it proves how much she needs today. It's strange how guilt and love for this little girl entwine, leaving me feeling helpless.

"Are you ready for today, sweetheart?" I ask.

She nods so furiously that I can't help but laugh. "I'm so excited, Ley!"

I hug her tightly and nod back at her. "Me too! Lucy-Ley day, here we come!" I squeal, neither of us aware of the glares the boys are sending us.

"I hope you don't have fun," Colton says, stabbing his fork into the omelet Thor made him, and I suppress my chuckle.

"That's a little mean, Colt," I tell him gently. "That hurts a little."

He looks guilty instantly, a look of panic crossing his face. "I'm sorry," he says, his voice soft.

"You can make it up to me by playing Minecraft with me after school on Monday."

He looks up, his eyes lit with excitement and relief, and then he nods. "Okay!"

"You ready to go, or do you want to have breakfast first? The spa I'm taking you to has a restaurant inside, so I was thinking it'd be nice to have an early lunch there, just you and I?"

Lucy nods and grabs my hand. "Yes! I'm not hungry. I'm too excited. I just want to go already, Ley."

"You got it, Luce."

I glance at Thor, wishing I could walk up to him and kiss him goodbye. It's the small things I want most with him. His eyes drop to my lips, and I watch his Adam's apple move as he drags his gaze away. I smile to myself in satisfaction. We might not be able to do these kind of things, but knowing he wants it as badly as I do sets me at ease.

"Let's go, Ley!" Lucy says, pulling on my hand, and I chuckle as I let her drag me out. I've never seen Lucy so excited before, and it brings me such joy to see her act like a child. I wish I'd asked her more questions about her old life, so I'd known what she misses most. I'll never replace her mother, but I should be able to take away at least some of the pain she feels. At least, I hope so.

"This spa is one that your auntie Amara introduced me to. I think it's going to be so much fun. They have the fluffiest robes, and they've got like a million saunas and pools we can try. They even have this really cool ice room. I booked us facials and manis too!"

"Really?" Lucy asks, her eyes wide. "Wow, Ley. I really can't wait!"

"Me neither," I tell her. Over the last few months, I've come to care about Lucy and Colton far more than I ever cared about any of the other kids I've taken care of. It's different with them, and I don't think it's necessarily because of Thor. They've both stolen my heart and filled a void I thought I'd always have to live with.

"Oh, and thank you for talking to Dad," Lucy says, her cheeks bright red. "He said that Mum can come see Colton and me, and I think it's thanks to you."

I tense, my grip on the steering wheel tightening. Thor's ex-wife is coming here? Why didn't he tell me? Insecurity takes root deep inside my heart, spreading its poisonous vines until unwanted thoughts are all that fill my mind. He said that the divorce was unexpected, leading me to believe that it never would have occurred if Alice hadn't asked for it.

I don't know how seeing her will impact him, and fear mingles with my insecurity, leaving me trembling. I can't help but wonder if at least some part of him still loves her. I know their divorce was a bitter one, but underneath all that pain, is there still love? "That's great, sweetheart," I tell Lucy. "Are you looking forward to seeing your mom again?"

She nods. "I can't wait to introduce you. I told her all about you, and she's excited to meet you too."

I smile at Lucy, praying I'm doing an adequate job of keeping my inner turmoil from her. The very last thing I want to do is meet Thor's ex-wife, but I have a sinking feeling that I won't be able to avoid it.

I bite down on my lip, scared of what the future might hold. I should've known not to be too happy. Every time I think happiness is within reach, it's taken from me abruptly and brutally. I'm hoping this time will be different, but admittedly, my hopes aren't very high.

Thirty-Two

ADRIAN

I check my watch for the tenth time in just as many minutes, impatient for my girls to get back home. How long can you possibly spend at a spa? They've been gone for hours. If Leia hadn't been texting me regularly, I'd be worried sick by now.

I sit up when I finally hear the sounds of giggles and excited chatter coming from the hallway, and I take a moment to just enjoy it. For a really long time, I was worried I'd never hear my little girl laugh the way she used to. I thought Alice and I forced her to grow up too quickly, and that her last remaining childhood years were lost.

If not for Leia, they might have been. Slowly but surely, she teased out the Lucy I thought I'd lost, and she did it so effortlessly. She never pushed, always providing Lucy with the support she needed, until one day, my daughter fell as hard for Leia as I did.

"Daddy," Lucy says as she walks in, and I open my arms up wide. She giggles as she rushes up to me and hugs me tightly.

"Sounds like you had a good day?" I murmur, my eyes on Leia who's leaning back against the wall, her smile as wide as Lucy's is.

Lucy nods and pulls away. "The best day, Dad." She holds her hands up for me. "Look, Leia and I got matching nail polish."

I glance at the light pink color and pretend to admire it, even though I know jack shit about nail polish, and this color barely looks different to her skin tone.

"Is it really matching?" I ask. "I'll have to see yours, Leia. How else can I compare?"

She pushes away from the wall and walks up to me, her hips swaying ever so slightly as she walks. She's a fucking siren, and I have a feeling she knows what she does to me when she looks at me that way.

Leia sits down next to us and holds her hand up for me. I grab it and hold it tenderly, my thumb brushing over the back of her hand. This is what she does to me. She makes me act like a fucking teenager, eager to just hold her hand.

"Beautiful," I murmur, my eyes on her.

"I know right!" Lucy says, and I grin, dragging my gaze back to my daughter.

"Did you eat dinner, love? You two are home a lot later than I expected."

Lucy and Leia both nod in unison. "Ley and I went on a posh date," Lucy tells me, before proceeding to tell me all about the fancy restaurant Leia took her to. She spoiled Lucy today, huh? I'd better make sure I adequately reward her for it.

Lucy yawns, and I smile as I brush her hair out of her face. "Go brush your teeth, sweetheart. I'll come tuck you in soon."

She nods and disappears through the door. Leia and I both listen for the sound of her footsteps on the stairs, and then she leans into me.

"I missed you," I tell her. "You're all I've been able to think about all day."

I thread my hand through her hair, my fingers grazing her scalp as I tip her head up. I kiss her leisurely, taking my time to drive her as crazy as I've felt all day. My attempts backfire, because within seconds, I'm hard as fuck for her.

"I missed you too," she whispers against my lips, before pulling away.

"I'm going to need you to show me just how much you missed me, Leia. Preferably all night long," I tell her before giving her another lingering kiss. "But first I'm going to put my little girl to bed."

She nods. "Meanwhile, I'll go make sure that Colt isn't secretly still gaming."

I chuckle as we both get up, and I can't help but wonder if she feels it too. We fit together so perfectly. I can see Leia truly becoming part of our family. Fuck. I can't wait to make her my wife. I've never felt that way before. I only ever married Alice because it was the next logical step, but there was no deep primal need to make her mine.

By the time the kids are in bed, I'm barely hanging onto my sanity. I'm so eager to have Leia to myself that I can barely think straight.

"Finally," I murmur as I pull her into my bedroom, pressing her against the door the second it closes behind us. I kiss her hungrily, impatiently. "I've been dying for you, baby," I murmur in between kisses. "I've wanted to kiss you since this morning."

She melts against me and looks up at me, a sweet smile on her face. "Me too. Watching you standing there in these damn sweatpants, teasing me like that. It's unfair."

I smirk and bite down on my lip, loving how honest she is with me about how much she wants me. There are never any games with Leia, and it's so fucking refreshing after years of marriage to a woman who continuously messed with my head.

Ley looks up at me, something in her eyes I can't quite place. It's not sorrow, but it's a pain of some sort.

"What's wrong, Princess?" I ask, my tone gentle. I tuck her hair behind her ear and cup her cheek, leaning in to kiss her forehead.

"Thor... Lucy told me her mother is coming to visit soon. I

know it isn't any of my business, but I just haven't been able to stop thinking about it."

I pull back a little to look at her, taking in the torment in her eyes, the insecurity. Fucking hell. I'm so fucking glad she chose to address her concerns instead of keeping her worries in, letting them fester.

"Anything that pertains to me is your business, Leia. Always. Don't ever doubt that."

She looks startled for a moment, and then the tension flows away from her body, her shoulders sagging in relief.

"I meant to tell you today, but honestly, the mere mention of my ex-wife puts me in a terrible mood, and we were just having a nice little moment this morning. I didn't want to ruin your day or my own, but I should've known Lucy would tell you. I never meant to keep it from you, Leia."

She nods, but her eyes are still filled with questions. I give her a moment, disappointment flooding me when I realize she won't ask anything more. Does she not feel like she has the right to? If she doesn't, then I'm to blame for that.

"After you told me what Lucy said to you, I sat down with the kids and talked to them about their mother. Both of them wanted to see her really badly, and I didn't even realize it. She's coming to see them in a few weeks, when they have some time off school."

"That's good," she says. "It'll be good for Lucy and Colton."

I nod at her and cup her cheek. "It will be, and while their mother is with them, you and I can go on as many dates as we want. I can't wait to spend all day in bed with you, Princess."

The way she looks at me puts me on edge. It feels like there's distance between us that wasn't there mere moments ago. "Do you still love her?"

I frown, surprised by her question. "No. *No*, Leia. I absolutely do not still love her. That's not something you'll ever have to worry about. Her visiting will not impact us at all. You have nothing to worry about, Princess. She and I are over."

"I can't help it, Thor. I just... I keep thinking how good it would be for the kids to have their parents together, how much happier they'd both be. And then my mind drifts back to you telling me that the divorce was so unexpected, and I just can't help but wonder. If she hadn't asked for a divorce, would you still be with her?"

I pull away from Leia, unsure what to tell her. "I honestly don't know, Leia. I don't see how it matters, because that isn't the case. What's the point in tormenting ourselves over what-ifs?"

"Your inability to answer my question speaks volumes," she says, wrapping her arms around herself. She looks so hurt, so heartbroken, and I hate that I did that to her.

"Leia, I won't ever lie to you. If she hadn't asked for a divorce, I would've done what's best for the kids. I would've stayed." Leia flinches, and I run a hand through my hair to keep from reaching for her. What she needs right now isn't physical comfort. She needs the truth. I won't have our relationship built on anything but honesty. "But I can also tell you that I stopped loving Alice long before she asked for a divorce, and she knew it. I think she realized it before I ever did. I hear the questions you aren't asking, my love, and the answer is no. No, you aren't a second choice. No, I would never choose her over you if given the chance. No, you won't lose me to her. No, her being here won't affect me in the way you're imagining."

Leia's eyes fill with tears, and I pull her toward me, capturing her in my embrace. "That day in my office when I told you that you're mine, I failed to make it clear that in return, I'm yours too. I've been yours from the moment you proclaimed yourself my wife on our very first date."

"Prove it," she whispers, rising to her tiptoes. I kiss her until she's moaning against my lips, her touch as needy as mine.

"Gladly, Princess. I have a feeling you're not easily convinced, though. I think this might take all night."

She laughs, and just like that, everything is right in my world again.

Thirty-Three

LEIA

"Krishan said your date was cut short," Asha says, her brows raised. I look at her, wide-eyed. Shit. I should've known it would get back to her. I take a big bite of the freshly made aloo paratha my mother made, taking my time chewing.

"We just weren't compatible," I say eventually.

Asha nods, but the look in her eyes tells me she isn't taking that for an answer. Krishan must have told her someone interrupted our date. What am I supposed to tell her?

Thankfully, Rohit and Nalini are keeping her busy enough for a while. If I'm lucky, they'll start acting up after dinner and she'll have to take them home.

I can't tell my sister that I'm dating the man that she asked me to work for. Not only would she fire me, she'd be so incredibly disappointed in me for breaking her no-fraternization policy. I can't quit either, though. Not now that I've established a bond with Lucy and Colton. If I quit now and reappear as their father's girlfriend, it'd be so much harder on us all.

"In other news," I announce proudly. "I'm almost ready to

hand in my dissertation, so I expect to finish my PhD next semester."

Dad grumbles, his version of acknowledgement, and Mom smiles. "Finally," she tells me. "You're not getting any younger, Leia. Once you're finished with school, we can start finding someone for you."

I groan, tempted to argue with her, but I leave it be. I get it. Education has always been important to my parents. In their eyes, it's a way of ensuring that our lives are easier than their own were. Most first-generation immigrants are like that, and I get it. It's one of the reasons I hid behind it for longer than I should have — as long as I'm studying, my parents don't feel the need to look into other areas of my life, such as marriage, which is probably their second highest priority.

Despite raising us to be strong and independent women, my parents still think it's important that we marry into good families that they approve of. Ideally someone that shares our culture and religion. Someone very unlike Adrian. I'm not sure if it's a relic of their own past, or if it's another way of ensuring that we're taken care of without forgetting our roots. I wish they realized that both Asha and I are perfectly capable of taking care of ourselves.

I breathe a sigh of relief when dinner wraps up without anyone asking me to go on any dates, and with no further talk of marriage. Just as I was hoping, the kids are tired and cranky, and Asha shoots me a look before taking them home, promising me that her interrogation about my date with Krishan is far from over.

I'm still thinking about a plausible excuse by the time I lay down in bed, my mind blank. With everything Thor said to him and the way he acted... I don't know. I can't tell Asha about us without losing my job, but I also can't keep quiet. Maybe, just maybe, she'll just let it go. Every once in a while, my sister surprises me by giving me the space I need, knowing I eventually come to her when I need her.

I sigh and turn in bed when my phone buzzes. I unlock it and grin when I realize Thor texted me.

Thor: *I'm outside your house, in the same spot I dropped you off at way back. Come see me for a minute.*

I sit up in shock. Oh no. This man... he really doesn't understand how my family works. If one of my neighbors sees him, I'm toast.

I slip out of bed quietly, my steps silent as I throw on a cardigan and slippers before sneaking out of the house. I can't even remember the last time I did that. I must've been a teenager the last time I sneaked out of the house like this.

I find Thor parked around the corner, in the same place he dropped me off at when he gave me the wrong phone number. Seeing him leaning against his car like that feels bittersweet.

"Hey."

"Princess," he says, reaching for me.

I jump away instinctively, and he frowns. "Um, how about we go for a drive?" I ask, my voice trembling.

He nods, his mood seemingly sinking further.

"What's going on?" he asks as he takes a left at the junction near my street. "Why are you acting so... shady?"

I laugh nervously and shake my head. "It's just... my neighbors are seriously so meddlesome. If they see me with you, my parents will know within an hour that I'm not home and that I was seen with a man no one recognized. It's... um, well, it's an Asian thing, I guess. It doesn't matter where I go, there's always someone who knows someone who knows my parents. It's weird, to be honest, and it's pretty hard to explain, but it's true."

He huffs, his expression telling me how displeased he is. I watch as he tightens his grip on the steering wheel, his shoulders tense.

"Thor, it isn't that I don't want to be seen with you," I murmur.

"I know, Ley," he says. "I know that, but I don't enjoy

sneaking around with you. I can't wait till the day you and I can just be together, out in the open."

"It's just a bit tricky, Thor. My parents are very traditional. My sister never even introduced my brother-in-law to us. We didn't find out they'd been dating until his parents showed up at our house asking for her hand. That's how traditional my family is. I get that you don't understand it, and I know how weird it sounds, but that's just how my family is, and as much as I can, I want to respect their traditions."

"You're right, Princess. I don't understand it, but I'm willing to learn. I've said it before, and I need you to know that I mean it. I'm going to marry you."

I hesitate and wrap my arms around myself. "My parents might not accept us being together. While I don't have a problem with it at all, they might not like that you're divorced and have children."

I don't even know how to bring up the fact that they won't like that he isn't Indian. Marriage is one of the ways through which we preserve our heritage, and they'll feel like part of that will be lost when I marry Adrian. Much to my surprise, he nods. "I understand. I know it won't be easy, but we'll win them over, Leia. I know we will."

"Thor, if they do accept us being together, they'll want us to have a full-blown Indian wedding."

He chuckles then. "Is that supposed to deter me, because honestly, baby... it sounds like fun."

I smile then, my heart set at ease. Most men would've run at the sound of what I just said, but I should've known he'd be different.

"I'm sorry I was moody with you just now," he says. "It's just all so new to me, and I really hate sneaking around with you. I want the world to know you're mine, and right now, that just isn't an option."

I nod and grab his hand. "I hate it too, babe."

He raises our joined hands to his lips and kisses the back of my hand. "I came to see you because you've seemed down the last couple of days, and I wanted to come cheer you up and reassure you about Alice visiting. I was planning to go and watch the stars with you and spend a romantic evening together. Instead, I just got into a strop myself."

I shake my head and grin at him. "Thank you," I tell him. "I didn't even think you'd noticed. With how much you've been working lately, it wouldn't surprise me if you hadn't."

Thor glances at me and shakes his head. "I notice every single thing about you, Leia. I always have."

He parks in the same spot he took me two years ago and looks at me. "You and I are going to be fine, Leia," he tells me. "I know you're worried about your family and Alice, amongst so many other worries... but I need you to believe in me. Have faith in us, Leia."

I smile at him. "You brought me to see the stars because you need some perspective?"

He nods. "You remember."

"I remember everything about you, Thor."

He leans in and kisses me, setting my restless heart at ease. I do have faith in us. I just hope that faith won't waver in the next couple of months.

Thirty-Four

LEIA

"So, when were you going to tell me?" Lex says.

I look up in surprise. Lex and I are seated outside today, our research laid out on one of the picnic tables behind the lab. I tip my face up and bask in the sun, letting it recharge me. The last couple of weeks have been crazy. "Tell you what?" I ask lazily.

"That Adrian Astor, *Professor Astor*, is Thor."

My eyes snap open, and I straighten, panic flooding me, followed by regret. Shit. My reaction instantly gave me away, and there's no way I can play this off now. "Um, what? That's ridiculous."

He leans on his elbow and smirks at me. "Is it? You told me Thor reappeared, and it just so happened to be at the same time that Adrian Astor moved back. Every time you two are together, he can't take his eyes off you. If another man so much as dares to approach you, he makes up some type of excuse to intervene."

I shake my head. "No, you're overthinking it. He's just looking out for me because I'm his cousin's best friend."

Lex chuckles. "Adrian Astor doesn't give a damn about

anyone but his kids. He wouldn't look out for you no matter how nicely Amara asked."

I cross my arms, my nerves getting the best of me. "He's my PhD advisor, Lex. It's his job to look out for me."

"Are you really telling me that's all it is?"

I nod, even though my confidence is shaky at best.

"Fine, let's put that to the test. He's walking our way right now, and he doesn't look very happy. I wonder what he'll do," he says, wrapping a strand of my hair around his finger as he leans in, "if I kissed your cheek?"

He sits up and leans in. His lips brushes over my cheek, the kiss chaste at best, the same kind I give Colton and Lucy.

"Leia!" Thor snaps.

I freeze and turn toward him, his murderous expression making my heart race. "There we go," Lex murmurs. "I guess I was right."

"Keep your fucking hands off her, Windsor," Thor says, but Lex merely chuckles.

"Or what?"

"Or she'll be the last thing you'll ever fucking touch."

I hold my hands up, aware we're gathering attention from the few tables surrounding us. "Calm down," I say, my voice soft and urgent. "Both of you."

"Leia," Thor says, keeping his eyes on Lex. "Grab your stuff."

Lex grins and throws me a look that screams I told you so, and I sigh, pure exasperation coursing through me. I'm tempted to snap at Thor, but doing so would only garner more attention, so I rise from my seat and pack up my documents, low key fuming inside.

"We will talk later," I tell Lex pointedly, but he just smiles unapologetically.

I'm tense as I follow Thor, his anger palpable. What was he thinking, approaching us like that? He knows how much we've got at stake.

The moment his office door closes behind him, I turn to face him, my anger overflowing. "What the hell did you think you were doing just now?" I snap.

"You're angry at *me*? Really? Why the fuck was he kissing you like that? Why is he always so fucking close to you? Every fucking time, Leia. Why are you always with him?"

I let my bag slip off my shoulder and lower it to the floor as I hang onto my last thread of patience.

Nope. Too late.

I walk up to him and press my index finger against his chest. "He's my friend, Thor, and you're being a total dick about it. I have a low tolerance for controlling behavior, so if you think you can tell me who I can or can't be friends with, you're sorely mistaken. You can honestly fuck right off if you think I can't have male friends."

He wraps his hand around my wrist and pulls me closer. "I couldn't care less if you have male friends, love. But you're sorely fucking mistaken if you think I'll let anyone touch my girl. It isn't fucking happening. He'd better keep his goddamn distance, because I've just about had it with him."

He tightens his grip on my wrist and threads his free hand through my hair, tipping my head up roughly. "You're mine," he says, his voice rough. "No one is touching you but me. Let me be really fucking clear about that, Leia. No. One. Touches. You."

He lowers his lips to mine, capturing my mouth roughly, his kiss punishing. He turns us around until he's got me pressed against the door, and I kiss him back with all I've got. Both of us are filled with frustration at having to keep our relationship secret, the pressures we face with his ex-wife visiting soon and having to face the kids and my family. It was only a matter of time before either of us snapped.

Thor wraps his hands around my waist and lifts me up so I can wrap my legs around him, and the feel of him has a moan escaping my lips. He pushes my dress up and yanks my underwear aside roughly as he pushes two fingers into me. "Of course you're already fucking wet. You want my cock, don't you, Princess?"

I suck down on his lower lip and nod. "Yes. It's been so long. Every time I get a second alone with you, we're interrupted, or we just don't have enough time together. Please, Thor. I just need you."

He smirks and strokes my clit with his thumb, eliciting a needy groan from me. "Tell me you'll be a good girl for me. Tell me you won't let any other man touch you. Tell me you're mine, and I'll fuck you right against this door, right now."

I glare at him, and he circles his thumb over my clit, not quite giving me what I want, but giving me enough to keep me needy and desperate.

"Say it, Leia."

"I'll be a good girl, Thor. I'm yours. *Only yours.* No one will ever touch me but you, I *promise.*"

He smirks and reaches underneath me to undo his belt. My eyes fall closed when his cock pushes against me, and I moan when he pushes into me.

Thor wraps his hand over my mouth and shakes his head. "Remember where we are, Princess," he says, and I look around at his office. There are probably so many students walking through the hallway right outside this door, and we really shouldn't be doing this, but neither of us can help ourselves.

He keeps one hand pressed over my lips while he supports me with the other as he fucks me against the door, his thrusts deep and hard, as needy and impatient as I feel.

He pulls out almost all the way, his eyes on mine as he slams back into me. "Mine," he growls, and I try my hardest to suppress a moan.

"This pussy," he says, pulling out again, "is mine." He thrusts into me hard, and I clench around him. The desire in his eyes, the way he's touching me, it's all too much.

"Every inch of you is mine, Leia. One day, I want you wearing nothing but my last name."

I moan against his hand, and he drops his forehead to mine. "Are you going to be quiet for me?"

I nod and he takes his hand off my mouth and grabs my ass, holding me tightly as he fucks me hard, his lips on mine. I try my hardest to suppress my moans, but I can't. I kiss him with all I've got, taking everything he's giving me.

I feel a sense of desperation today. My need for him is greater than it's ever been before, and I can't get enough. I need him inside me, as close as I can get him, and that still isn't enough to still the countless insecurities and worries that weigh me down.

He tears his lips off mine to look at me, his expression telling me that he's close. "I love you, Leia," he says, moments before coming deep inside me, his final thrust hard and demanding. He drops his forehead to mine and inhales shakily. "I love you," he repeats.

I tighten my grip on him, hugging him to me tightly as I rest my head on his shoulder, my lips pressed against his neck. "I love you too, Thor."

I do. Deeply and irrevocably.

Thirty-Five

LEIA

My phone buzzes just as I finally start to concentrate on formatting the list of current sources for my dissertation, and I look up in annoyance. My heart drops when I realize it's the kids' school.

"Hello?" My voice wavers, a thousand thoughts going through my mind. Did one of them get hurt? Are they sick? The school wouldn't call me unless something is wrong.

"Good afternoon, Ms. Sital. You're listed as Colton Astor's emergency contact, and we would like to request that you come in."

"Is everything okay?" I ask, my phone stuck between my ear and my shoulder as I frantically pack all my papers.

"I'm afraid Colton has been in a fight. He's not injured, but another student is."

"I'll be right there."

Colton getting in a fight? How could that be? I'm worried sick as I rush over to the school, and by the time I reach the principal's office, a thousand different scenarios have played through my mind.

I walk in to find Colton and Lucy standing in one corner, while a boy their age stands in the opposite corner, his eye badly bruised. That's definitely going to turn blue. What could've possibly happened for sweet Colton to do something like that?

"Ms. Sital," the principal says. I nod at him and glance at the woman sitting opposite the principal. The injured boy's mother, I assume.

She looks at me, her gaze appraising, as though she's trying to assess who I might be. "I won't stand for this," she screeches. "I assume you're the nanny? I want to speak to the kids' parents at once! You're crazy if you think you'll get away with harming my son!"

I glance at Colton and Lucy to check if they're okay. They both seem upset. Both of their eyes are red, their posture the same, both of their arms crossed. Thankfully, they seem physically fine.

I turn to the principal and raise my chin. "I would appreciate it if you could tell me what I was called in for."

"Did you not hear me?" the woman next to me screeches, and I glance at her in irritation.

"I'm not speaking to you," I tell her curtly, before turning back to the principal.

"I didn't come here for you to waste my time. Either start informing me why I was called in, or I'll be taking my kids home right now. Both of them seem upset, and either you or they will tell me why that is. Who is it going to be?"

The principal looks taken aback, but I couldn't care less. Not when I see tears in both Lucy and Colton's eyes. Every fiber of my being is telling me that they're hurt far more than they're letting on, and I won't sit here for a second longer than I need to.

"Am I correct to assume that you're the kids' nanny?" the principal asks.

I cross my arms and smile at him. "No. You're incorrect to be assuming anything at all. I was called in because I'm the kids' emergency contact, and I would like to know why."

The woman next to me huffs. "Of course she's the nanny," she says. "The kids look nothing like her."

I suppress the pain I feel at the statement, filing it away for later. She's right, they don't look like me, but they very much feel like mine, and right now, they're in my care. That's all that matters.

"During recess, Colton hit Mrs. Thom's son, Steve. From what I understand, it's because he was told that their nanny only shows them affection because she's paid to do so. Colton didn't take that well, and the two boys got into an altercation that escalated. Shortly after, Lucy joined in by grabbing the largest tree branch she could find and hitting Steve until teachers were able to separate them."

I purse my lips to keep from laughing. That's my girl. I must not hide my amusement well enough, because the lady next to me sits up and glares at me.

"Who was the instigator?" I ask the principal.

He shakes his head. "Colton says it was Steve, and Steve says it was Colton. At present, we are unsure, but the teachers are asking some of the other kids if they might have seen what happened."

"I'm going to sue you so hard you'll have to take them out of school. You'll never recover from this," the lady tells me. "I don't care who started the fight. I just care that my son was assaulted."

I turn to look at her and smile. "Were you present during recess?"

She falls silent, and I nod. I didn't think so.

"What about you?" I ask the principal.

He hesitates, but then he shakes his head. "No teachers were present during the argument itself. Not until they intervened to separate the kids."

I nod. "So this is all hearsay and you are unsure who the instigator was. What disciplinary action will you be taking?"

The principal's eyes widen just a fraction, but that's enough to tell me I've thrown him off. I'm not what he expected, as usual. "We'll be suspending Lucy and Colton for the rest of the week."

I nod. "Very well. What disciplinary action are you taking against the other child involved in the fight?"

He hesitates once more, and at this point, he's just pissing me off. If he thinks he can suspend my kids when it was another who bullied them in the first place, he's insane.

"My child was victimized! Why would they be taking disciplinary action against him?"

I lean back in my seat and face her. "My child has also been victimized. From what I understand, he's been bullied. Not to mention, that scratch on his cheek wasn't there this morning, and I doubt he put that on himself. Assault, you called it, didn't you? Indeed. It looks like Colton has been assaulted."

"We'll be suspending all three children," the principal eventually says.

"That's not what we discussed," crazy mom replies, but I merely nod.

I reach into my bag and pull out a business card, holding it up. "Since you're insistent on suing me, go ahead and do so. I will let the Astor legal team know to expect a call."

She tenses then. "Astor?" she asks.

I place the card down on the desk and slide it toward her. "Did I stutter?" I ask, entirely out of patience.

I rise from my seat, my jaws locked in anger as I glance at the principal. I won't forget how he sought to blame the kids the second this crazy bitch started to make trouble. He'll regret not doing his job.

"Let's go home," I tell Lucy and Colton.

They both jump out of their seats, both of them staring at the floor instead of looking me in the eye, and I sigh as I lead them out.

They're quiet as we walk through the desolate school, and I can't help but wonder if I handled that right. Today, more than ever, I wish I really was their mother. I had no right to respond the way I just did, but I have no regrets.

"Are you okay, Colton?" I ask when we reach the car.

He looks up at me, his eyes filled with tears, and I sink down to my knees in front of him.

"Are you hurt, sweetheart?"

He shakes his head. "Are you m-mad at me?" he asks, his voice breaking as tears fall from his eyes.

I wrap my arms around him and hug him tightly. "No, sweetheart. I'm not mad at you. I will never be mad at you before asking for all the facts, so I need you to tell me what happened, and I need you to be honest with me."

He wipes at his tears and sniffs loudly, trying to control his emotions and failing.

"Colt was bragging about how you play Minecraft with him, and Steve said you don't really love us, and that you only hang out with us because Dad pays you to do that."

Lucy sounds just as upset and Colton, her silent pleas for reassurance stabbing me right in the heart. "Your dad does pay me to watch you two," I tell her honestly. "But he doesn't pay me to play Minecraft with Colt, or to take you to the spa. He doesn't pay me to cuddle with you or read to you, nor does he pay me to stay with you once he's home. I do that because I enjoy spending time with you, because you two mean the world to me. Even if your dad fired me tomorrow, I'd still always be there for you. I'd still always love you. That would never change, you hear me? Even if someday, your dad and I don't get along, I would still want to hang out with you if he'd let me."

Lucy nods, a tear dropping down her cheek. "Come here," I say, opening up my arms to hug them both, one of the kids leaning on each shoulder. I hold them tightly, my heart breaking.

I hope Mrs. Thom does sue. I hope she gives me an excuse to make her pay for making them cry.

Thirty-Six

ADRIAN

I check my watch and sigh, disappointed that I wasn't able to make it home before dinner tonight. In addition to my work at the college, Grandpa has started to increase my working hours at his company. He's given me a lot of leeway since moving here, but it's clear he's running out of patience. He wants me to join the board sooner rather than later, and I'm running out of time and excuses. I'm going to have to suck it up and do my part as an Astor.

The house is oddly quiet as I walk in and I pause, standing in the hallway for a moment, just listening. Usually, I can hear Colton and Leia gaming around this time, and if they aren't doing that, the three of them are usually watching a movie. Tonight, everything is silent.

I walk in, surprised to find Leia sitting on the sofa by herself, staring into space. "Ley?"

She snaps out of her daze and looks at me, her expression concerned. "Hi," she says, forcing a smile.

I frown and take a good look at her. There's something about her expression that puts me on edge. She looks nervous. I have a feeling I know why.

"What's wrong?"

Leia's eyes widen as though she's startled, and she shakes her head. "There's something I need to tell you."

I nod and walk over to the sofa to sit next to her. "Where are the kids?"

"In bed."

"This early?" I glance at my watch again in confusion. "It's seven."

"Um," Ley murmurs. She hesitates and wraps her arms around herself protectively. "I should've told you about this immediately, and in not doing so, I failed you as your nanny."

She inhales deeply and looks down at her hands for a moment. "This afternoon, Colton and Lucy were involved in a fight, and I was called in. Rather than informing you at once, I took them home. The fight they got into had to do with me, and I struggled to find the right words to tell you what had happened, so instead, I stayed quiet, avoiding the conversation altogether. My behavior was unacceptable, and I would like to formally apologize."

I nod, relief washing over me at the realization that there isn't anything serious going on. "I wondered how long it would take you to tell me, and whether you would at all. The school emailed me a confirmation of their suspension."

She looks up in surprise. It seems the kids haven't told her that I've already spoken to them on the phone. They seemed fine, if not a bit embarrassed by the situation.

"Oh. Of course. Honestly, that's not all, Thor. I overstepped the boundaries of our working relationship, and I shouldn't have. I spent all day thinking about how I acted, and I had no right to make any decisions on your behalf. There's a chance the boy's mother might sue us as well. If that happens, please let me know, and I'll shoulder the costs. I'm the one that provoked her, after all."

I smile to myself and lean back against the sofa. I can pretty much imagine what went down. The kids got into trouble, and Leia's fierceness showed itself.

"Tell me what happened." The principal called me the second Leia left his office, complaining about her behavior, but she doesn't need to know that. Nor does she need to know that the school instantly lost a sizeable chunk of its donations.

She looks down at her hands, looking guilty. "Colton was talking about gaming with me, and some kid at school told Colton that I only hang out with him because you pay me to do so, and that I don't care about him. They got into a fight, and Colton punched the kid. Realizing her brother was in trouble, Lucy apparently found the biggest tree branch she could find and hit the boy, too."

I pinch my nose to keep from laughing. My little girl did *what*? I would've paid good money to see that.

"Right," I murmur. "How did you respond?"

She looks at me, regret marring her face. "I lost my shit," she says, and this time I do chuckle.

"Of course you did, Princess. Tell me what you said, and I'll handle it."

"I told them everything was just hearsay since they didn't have any witnesses, and I accused the boy Colt hit of assault because both boys claimed the other started the fight. I, well, I may have told the woman to just sue us. I even gave her your attorney's card."

I suck down on my lower lip to keep from smiling and nod. I wondered if she'd be honest with me. I trust her with my kids, and I'm happy my trust wasn't misplaced. She didn't lie to me, but I have a feeling she's omitting something.

"When it comes to the kids, you're always calm and collected, so why is it you lost it today?" It's the one thing I've had on my mind today. I didn't doubt that Leia handled the situation correctly, but I wondered why she snapped the way the principal told me she did.

"This is the part I feel most guilty about," she says. "I acted the way I did because I... well, it's because they were treating me like a nanny, when the way I feel about these kids is so much more than that. It wasn't right, and it was unprofessional. I had no right to behave that way, and if it caused you any embarrassment, I sincerely apologize, Thor. I really am very sorry. I don't know what I was thinking."

"You do," I say, my voice soft. "You do have that right, Leia. I see the way you love my kids, Princess. I know you only ever want what's best for them. You aren't just their nanny, Leia, and we both know it. The kids feel it too, or they wouldn't have gotten into that fight in the first place. Just because we can't formally define what you mean to them just yet, doesn't mean the relationship isn't there. You reacted the way any parental figure would have, and I'm grateful you were there to handle it. You never need to apologize for doing the right thing. You're only human, Ley. So long as you're doing your best, then that's all I can ask for."

Leia sniffs, a tear falling down her cheek, and my heart fucking shatters. "Baby," I whisper, taking her into my arms. "Don't cry, love. You did nothing wrong. The kids and I are so grateful we've got you."

"What are we doing, Thor?" she asks, her voice breaking. "All the lines are blurring and I'm so scared. I'm scared of making the wrong choices, of hurting them or you. I'm scared of my own heart breaking. What if you walk away, and I lose Lucy and Colt too? What if they find out about us and hate me? What about us? Will we survive if they fall apart?"

I stroke her back, my eyes falling closed. Truthfully, I've had a lot of the same worries. I pull away to look at her and cup her cheek, swiping away her tears with my thumbs.

"Look at me, Princess. Us being together comes with tremendous risks, but you know as well as I do that we were inevitable. Now I won't lie to you and tell you that the road ahead of us is easy, but if you're willing to give my kids and me a chance, I want nothing more than to try. Isn't that all we can do?"

My heart pounds as she looks at me. It kills me that I can't make her see how I feel about her. There's no doubt in my mind that we're going to be okay. The security and stability I feel with her despite everything we're risking is unreal, and it's something special. I hope she feels that too.

"I can see it, Ley. I can see us being a family. I can see you not leaving us at night. I can see myself going to bed with you, and making breakfast together on a lazy Sunday. I see us leaving the kids at Amara's house while we go on a weekend away, and I see us having quickies in the house while the kids do their homework. Everything I once swore off, I want with you. So long as you want that too, we'll be fine. This is just one of the phases we'll go through in life. When we've got the rest of our lives together, this isn't so bad, is it?"

I entwine our fingers and raise our joined hands to my lips, kissing the back of her hand gently, and she smiles at me. "Perspective," she murmurs, and I nod.

Leia tightens her grip on my hand, but I see the concern in her eyes. I have no doubt her worries are identical to mine. The kids are far from ready, and I'm not sure they ever will be.

Thirty-Seven

ADRIAN

"I can't believe you took us to a water park, Dad!" Colton says, his eyes wide with excitement.

I reach for his hand, but he doesn't even realize it. Instead, he runs up to Leia and grabs her free hand. Both of my children abandoned me in favor of Leia. "Wow. I'm not sure if I should be jealous or happy," I say, but the kids simply ignore me. Leia looks over her shoulder and sticks her tongue out at me, and I shake my head in amusement.

I watch the trio, their joined hands swinging back and forth, smiles on their faces. Taking a day off work was the right call. I need Colton and Lucy to know that I'll never punish them for standing up for themselves or each other. I had no idea Colt had been bullied for weeks before it escalated, and I can't help but feel like I failed him.

Perhaps I've been relying on Leia too much. I've definitely been working too much. Trying to keep up with everything Grandpa has me doing has been hard enough as it is. Combine that with my role at Astor College, and I barely have time left to sleep.

I need to do better. Not just for the kids, but for Leia too. I'm asking too much of her. Without me even realizing it, she's taking on the role of their mother, when that was never in her job description. Even now that we're dating, I wouldn't dare ask it of her.

"Can we go on that ride?" Lucy asks, pointing to a long spiral slide, and I nod.

"Go on," I tell her. "Leia and I will wait here. The queue will be long, though. Are you sure you want to go on that one?"

"Definitely!" Lucy says, and Colton nods in agreement.

I smile when he takes his sister's hand and pulls her along, the two of them joining a queue of forty-five minutes to go on a ride that'll last three minutes tops. I never quite understood theme parks, but the kids love them, so here we are.

"You know, Ley? Because of you, Lucy is finally acting like a child again. She's smiling the way she used to, and I owe it to you. Colton too, he coped with the divorce by throwing himself into his games, and you took that and used it to connect with him. You never cease to amaze me, and I'm so incredibly grateful that the kids and I have you in our lives."

She looks at me, visibly emotional, and I smile as I lean in. I tuck a strand of her hair behind her ear, my eyes on hers. I've fallen for her so damn hard. I never thought I'd ever fall in love again, but here I am, staring down at my future.

"I didn't notice he was being bullied. Even worse, it was because of me. I can't help but wonder what it is I did that made him a target. I feel terrible about it, Thor."

I cup her cheek and lean in, pressing a soft kiss to her lips. She sighs and rises to her tiptoes, kissing me fully. I don't think I'll ever get enough of this woman.

"It wasn't anything you did, Leia," I murmur against her lips. "Kids can be mean, and I can only imagine that this boy was jealous of the love you give Colton. It must be hard, you know?

Seeing how much you care, when many parents probably don't care half as much. That's all it is."

She nods, but I see the worry in her eyes. I love that about her. I love how much she cares, how much of herself she gives us. I always thought I'd never find another woman that I'd want to be in a serious relationship with, because I didn't think I'd ever find someone who would love my kids as though they're her own. I think Leia genuinely does, and they love her just as much. Lately I find myself thinking of a future with her every time my thoughts drift. Day dreaming about her has become my favorite hobby.

"Come on, the kids will be back soon," she says, pulling me toward the exit of the ride. "I don't want them to look for us. I'm worried they'll panic if they don't see us straight away."

Yeah, it's official. I'm fucking smitten. "Okay, Princess," I murmur, grabbing her hand. Leia looks surprised, and I smirk. She and I rarely hold hands since we're so secretive about our relationship, but I can't resist today.

I've never felt this way before. I've never felt so possessive. I've never had the urge to touch a woman at all times. This type of need, this connection, it's all new to me.

"Ley! Dad!"

I grin when the kids run up to us. Colton crashes into me while Lucy wraps her arms around Leia, hugging her tightly. "Oh, that was so exciting!" she squeals, and my heart skips a beat. I've missed my little girl. This is exactly what she used to be like, and when Alice and I divorced, I thought I'd lost her. "Oh, Daddy, we should bring Mum here soon!"

Leia tenses beside me, and I force a smile. "You'll have to ask your mum, but if you ask really nicely, she might just bring you here."

Thankfully, Colton pulls Lucy away to go to the next slide, saving me from what I'm certain was about to be a tough conversation. It's one I'll need to have with them, though.

"When will she be arriving?" Leia asks, her tone hesitant.

"Next week."

"Oh." Leia crosses her arms and looks away, her expression torn. I can pretty much guess how she feels. She's happy for the kids, but worried for us.

"I booked her a nice hotel. I haven't spoken to her much, so I'm uncertain how much she'll want to see the kids. I figured we can discuss that in person once she's here. I'd hate to make the kids any promises that she can't keep, but I think she'll want to take care of them, so you'll be able to focus on your dissertation."

Leia nods, but she won't look at me. "Hey," I say, placing my index finger under her chin. I lift her face up and smile at her. "Tell me what you're thinking, Princess. If you won't talk to me, I can't put your worries at ease."

Leia sighs and runs a hand through her long hair. "I'm just worried in general, Thor. I can't help but worry about whether you'll spend much time alone with her, and what it'll be like when the four of you are together again. I know I'm being irrational, but part of me wonders what you'd do if she says she changed her mind, and she wants you back. You never even wanted a divorce, and the kids want nothing more than for you to get back together. I can't help overthinking everything."

"I love you," I tell her. I've never been overly generous with my affection, but I can't resist with Leia. I wish the first time I told her I loved her wasn't while I was fucking her against the door of my office on campus. I imagined roses and champagne, and every other little thing I want Leia to have so she'll never feel like she missed out on anything by being with me, but I've already fucked that up now. All I can do is tell her I love her every single day to make up for the first time I said it not being special. "I love you so fucking much that it hurts, Leia. I have the utmost respect for my ex-wife as my children's mother, but that's all she is to me." I want to admit that I never felt anything like this before, that I never loved my ex-wife the way I love her, but it feels disrespectful to say that, when Alice has given me so many happy years and two beautiful children. It's something I'd rather prove to Leia than say.

She looks at me with wide eyes, and I smile, my heart overflowing. "I love you," I repeat, trying to resist the urge to say it a thousand times over. "All I ask of you, is that you remember my words when doubt inevitably creeps in. *I love you.*"

She smiles, and I see her feelings reflected in her eyes before she says anything at all. "I guess I love you too." She smirks, and I burst out laughing.

"You *guess*? Looks like I'm going to have to up my game, wifey. I'm going to have to go all out to make you fall for me as hard as I fell for you."

Leia grins and rises to her tiptoes to press a quick kiss to my lips. "Can't wait, hubs."

With Leia and me, the time has never been right. Being with her has taught me that the best things in life are worth fighting for, against all the odds and every obstacle.

I'm certain Alice being here won't be easy on us, but I'll do everything in my power to make sure Leia feels secure in our relationship.

Thirty-Eight

ADRIAN

I'm on edge as I drive the kids to the airport to pick up their mother. Alice and I haven't seen each other since the divorce went through, and by the end of it all, things weren't exactly civil between us.

I'm worried about introducing any negativity into the kids' lives. Leia and I have had to work so hard at helping them adjust. They're finally happy again, and I'm not sure what seeing Alice is going to do to them. Even worse is that they'll eventually have to say goodbye to her again, and I wonder if that will set them back too much. I would hate to see my little girl become so quiet again, and I'm worried Colton will withdraw into his games again instead of hanging out with kids his age.

"I can't wait to see Mum!" Lucy says, her smile so wide that it tugs at my heart. I really hope Alice isn't going to let my little girl down. I understand Lucy's love for her, but my daughter seems to have forgotten how strict she's always been, how she suffocated Lucy's interests in favor of living vicariously through her.

Colton has been a bit more subdued, not saying much at all

about his mother visiting. I suspect my son remembers the endless arguments, the way she always favored Lucy over him. I'll have to pay extra attention to him to make sure he's doing okay throughout her visit.

My entire body is tense while the kids and I wait for Alice. If I had any doubts about our divorce at all, I can say with full certainty that they can be dismissed. I'm dreading seeing my ex-wife. Coming to the States has provided me with so much clarity. I didn't even miss her for a moment. If anything, I haven't felt this free in years.

"Mum!" Lucy yells.

She lets go of my hand to run up to her mother, but Colton tightens his grip on my hand. I glance at my son and offer him a reassuring smile. "You've got Leia and me," I tell him, and he looks into my eyes, his insecurity clearly on display.

"Do you think she'll want to play Roblox with me later?"

I nod. "I'm pretty sure she's going to be ecstatic if you ask her to. Why don't you text her later?"

Colton relaxes and nods at me. "I will. I wonder if she misses me. Usually we'd be doing homework around this time."

"I have no doubt that she does." I grin at him, recognizing myself in him. He won't say he misses her too, but it's obvious.

Alice and Lucy walk up to us, and the way Alice's gaze roams over my body makes me uncomfortable. It's strange how you can spend over a decade with someone, yet within a few months, they become a stranger to you. This is the woman I thought I'd grow old with, but now I see how incompatible we've always been.

"Adrian," she says, smiling at me in that seductive way I used to love, yet now it just feels inappropriate.

"Hi Alice. How have you been?"

Her smile falters and her gaze sharpens. "Good," she says, drawing the word out.

I nod and turn to Colton. "Say hi to your mum, sweetheart," I tell him, and he reluctantly lets go of my hand to hug her. At least she truly seems happy to see the kids. For a while she tried to convince me that I could never take care of the kids, that they'd resent me for taking them away from her. Despite that, she never fought to keep them. Everything was always a game to her. I didn't see it when I was in the midst of it all, but I see it now.

Lucy and Alice chat up a storm as we get into the car, and I try my hardest to ignore the annoyance I feel at the way Colton is being left out. The last thing I want to do is get into an argument the moment she's here.

"I've missed you so much, kids," Alice says. "I really wish I could stay with you. It would be so nice if I could make breakfast for you the way I used to."

"You aren't staying with us?" Lucy asks, confused.

I shake my head. "No, sweetheart. Mum and Dad are no longer together, remember? That means that Mum will stay in a hotel really close to our house. She'll be able to pick you up any time she wants."

I look in the mirror to find my daughter's eyes filled with tears. *Fuck.* I should've told the kids she wouldn't be staying with us. I never should've assumed that would be a given. I fucked up.

"Adrian, why don't you just let me stay in a guest room? Lucy told me you have several spare rooms. There's no reason why we can't co-parent while I'm here. I already have limited time with the kids. I'd like to spend every second with them if I can."

"Yes, Dad. *Please,*" Lucy adds, her voice wobbling.

Fuck. Realistically, I don't have a valid reason to say no. I can see how it would benefit the kids, even if it'd make me uncomfortable. My first concern should always be the kids, but I can't help but wonder how Leia would feel if I'm suddenly living with my ex again.

"Please, Daddy," Lucy says. "We haven't seen Mum in forever."

"Okay," I say. "All right, sweetheart."

Alice puts her hand on my leg, and I tense. "Thank you," she says, a sweet smile on her face.

I nod at her curtly, but she keeps her hand on my leg. "I've missed you," she murmurs. "I'd love to catch up with you too. I'm not just here for the kids."

I gently lift her hand off my leg and place it back in her lap. Alice looks surprised, and she narrows her eyes as she looks at me.

"It's good to see you, Alice. It really is."

I need to have a proper talk with her. I have no desire to reminisce with her, and I need her to know that. But not now. Not in front of the kids.

"Good to see me, huh? So you didn't miss me. Or are you still mad at me?"

I smile tightly, unsure how to answer. I didn't miss her. I'm not playing games with her, and I'm sure as hell not mad at her for asking for a divorce. If anything, that was a blessing in disguise.

I can see Alice scheming as she sits next to me, the ride to our house quiet. Whatever it is she's got on her mind needs to be nipped in the bud.

Dread rushes over me as I help her carry her luggage into the house. The very last thing I want to do is welcome her into the home I built after she left us. I don't want to be the bigger person. I guess that's the difference between Alice and me. She always did what she wanted, and I always did the right thing.

I place her luggage in the guest room and smile at Lucy who followed us in. She's trying to drag Alice along so she can show her the house, but it'll have to wait. "Give us a moment, sweetheart. I just need to talk to Mum for a moment."

Lucy's smile melts away, but she nods. "Don't be long," she warns me. "There's so much I have to show Mum."

She closes the door behind her and I turn to Alice. "If you're staying in my house, there'll be some ground rules I expect you to keep to. If you fail to do so, I'll have to ask you to move to a hotel."

Alice looks at me with lifted brows and smiles. "Hmm, I like this new and improved version of you. You never used to be this dominant."

I sigh, already tired of her shit. The reason I was never dominant is because it wasn't worth arguing with her over anything, not when she never truly listened, anyway.

"Any rules that I've made for the kids will remain the same, and they won't be broken. I'll send you a list. If there's a dispute of any kind, I'll have the final say in how it's handled. Then finally, stay out of my room. You're absolutely welcome to make yourself at home, but I ask that you respect my privacy and my home."

She looks at me, her gaze sharp. "Are you sleeping with someone?"

I tense, equal parts surprised and confused by the question. "I literally just asked you to respect my privacy. If you can't do that, I'll have to ask you to leave."

She purses her lips and nods. "Interesting. Very well. I'll abide by your terms, *for now.*"

I nod, knowing that's the best I'll get from her. As I walk through Alice's door, there's only one thing on my mind. How am I supposed to tell Leia that my ex-wife will be living with me for a few weeks?

Thirty-Nine

LEIA

"Leia! Come talk to the tailor in India. You need to tell him what kind of lehenga you want to wear to Priya's wedding!" Mom shouts, and I groan. I guess our weekly family dinner has instead become an outfit design event.

Another wedding. I'm not even sure who Priya is. Third-cousin on my dad's side? Honestly, she might not even be family. She could just as easily be the neighbour's daughter from three generations ago when my family still lived in India, but we'll still have to go. If I so much as try to tell my mom that it's completely unnecessary to go and they won't even notice if we don't attend, since they'll likely have hundreds of guests, she'll lose her mind. Every single time, she insists that we just have to *show our faces*. At least they feed me well at all of these weddings, so there's that.

I walk down the stairs to find my sister holding up a photo of Aishwarya Rai-Bachchan in a Sabyasachi outfit and roll my eyes. Did she print that out so she could show it to him on video chat? Honestly, I can't even. *Yes, Asha. Our cheap tailor is going to make you something similar to Sabyasachi's couture designs worth several thousand dollars.*

"I want the skirt to be quite fluffy, but I don't want the top to be this short or this open," she says in broken Hindi, pointing at the picture.

I have no doubt whatsoever that what she's going to receive is going to be something similar to the items from the cheap Chinese apps that I keep seeing online. The Wish app? Is that what it was called? Either way, it'll look nothing like what she's showing our tailor.

She hands me the phone, and I instantly panic. My Hindi is even worse than hers. "Hi Rajesh," I tell him, thankful I at least remember his name. I glance at my mom when he starts rambling to me in Hindi, and though I understand every word he's saying, I have absolutely no idea how to reply.

"Mom!" I hiss.

She side-eyes me, looking entirely unimpressed with me. "You have a PhD, but you can't even speak Hindi, huh? Why can't you speak Hindi?"

I squint and throw my hand up in an *um, what* gesture. "Because you didn't teach me? You literally always only spoke English to me. How was I supposed to learn?"

She narrows her eyes at me and wags her finger. "Other children learn by watching Bollywood movies. You can memorize whole textbooks, but you can't learn Hindi?"

"Oh my God, Mom," I say, handing her the phone. "Can you tell him I want something simple? Maybe a simple golden nude type of color? How about a sequin top with a plain skirt, or maybe some sequins on the skirt too?"

My mom clicks her tongue and throws me an annoyed look. "Always with these modern modern outfits. No. Wear something normal for once. I will decide for you."

I'd roll my eyes, but no matter how old I get, my mom will still scold me if I do. "Then why did you even ask me to come down?"

She shoos me away, and I shake my head as I walk away. Her

idea of normal is some type of elaborately embroidered thing with lots of stones sown in. I'm pretty sure she's convinced people will think we're dirt poor if I wear what I have in mind. I wouldn't be surprised if she's already planning on parading her supposedly single daughter at this wedding, and the mere thought of it makes me groan. I wish I could take Thor as my date, but my parents would be endlessly scandalized.

I daze off for a moment, my thoughts turning to Thor. If he and I truly get married, would we have a religious ceremony too? I've always wanted a formal western ceremony with a white dress, but I've also always imagined myself in a red traditional dress too. I've always wanted elaborate *mehendi*, and turmeric on my face and body days before the wedding, all of it. I've already got several henna designs saved to my Pinterest board. I want it all, but I might never have it.

Dad chuckles and raises his brows at me. *"Why don't you speak Hindi, Leia,"* he mimics, ridiculing Mom.

I glance at him and shake my head. "I'm going to tell her you did that."

"Kill me, she will," he says, throwing his Yoda charm at me.

My phone buzzes, and I glance at it, expecting it to be Amara. Instead, it's Thor.

Thor: *I'm outside your house. Come see me for a minute?*

I full-on panic. If my parents see him standing outside of our house, I'm dead. They won't care how old I am. I'll be lectured and scolded for the rest of my life.

I don't think Thor understands — sneaking out isn't something I do, not even at my age. I did it last time because it was late at night, but now? It's seven in the evening! "I think Amara wants to talk about something," I tell Dad. "I'll just go see her instead of calling her, since Mom and Asha are being so loud."

Dad looks into my eyes for a moment, and then he nods, a smile on his face. Something is up with him... he didn't see through me, did he?

My heart pounds in my chest as I walk out the door, expecting to see Thor standing right outside, but thankfully, he isn't. I breathe a sigh of relief as I walk around the block, finding him parked in the same spot he's dropped me off at before. He's leaning against his car, and the way his face lights up when he sees me makes my heart skip a beat.

"I missed you," he says, walking up to me to meet me halfway. He throws his arms around me and hugs me tightly. "Finally, you're back in my arms."

I chuckle and rise to my tiptoes to bury my face in his neck, pressing a soft kiss onto his throat. "You saw me yesterday, Thor."

"I know. It's been far too long. Every one of my days starts off messed up because I don't get to wake up with you."

"Is that my cue to swoon?"

"Go ahead," he tells me. "I'll always be there to catch you."

I chuckle and tilt my face up to kiss him. He obliges gladly, groaning in disappointment when I pull away too soon for his liking.

"Not here," I tell him. "My neighbors are honestly all snitches. There's another Asian family a few doors down, and they'll absolutely tell my mom if they see me with you."

He chuckles and takes a step back while keeping his arms around me. "Are you joking? I can't tell when it comes to your family. To be fair, everything you've told me about your family might very well all just be an elaborate ruse created to trip me up when I finally meet them."

The thought of him meeting my family both excites and terrifies me. There's no way they'll easily accept him, but I'm confident that they will, eventually. I smirk and shake my head. "It's all true. Come on, let's go for a drive?"

He nods and walks around the car to open the door for me, sneakily stealing another kiss before I get in.

We're both smiling as we drive away, and by the time Thor parks in a secluded area, I'm giddy with excitement. I've missed him too, but I've also been driving myself crazy with anxiety over his ex-wife arriving today. The fact that he's here with me now puts me at ease.

"Ley," he says, his voice soft. "There's something I need to tell you."

My heart sinks and I clasp my hands as I turn to him. Dozens of worst-case scenarios run through my mind, and before he even speaks, I've already convinced myself that I lost him.

"Alice is staying at my house. I wouldn't have allowed it, but she roped Lucy into it, arguing that she wants to spend every second with them and such. It was near impossible for me to say no without hurting Lucy."

I nod, somewhat understanding the situation, but despising it with every fiber of my being, too. "When Colton and I played Roblox earlier, we spoke to each other on Discord for a bit, but he didn't mention his mom at all. I've been wondering how he is."

Thor smiles, the look in his eyes setting my heart ablaze. "I love you," he says. "I just love you so fucking much, Leia. You have no idea. No idea at all." He runs a hand through his hair and looks away. "As usual, Alice's attention is mostly on Lucy. If you... if you could give Colton some extra attention for a while, I would really appreciate it. It's not me he wants, you know? Today when we picked Alice up, it was you he was thinking about. He was talking about gaming with you later."

I smile, my heart overflowing at the thought of my sweet Colt. "You don't need to ask me that, Thor. I would've done it even if you hadn't asked."

"I know," he says. "If you weren't so stunning, I'd tell you that your heart is the most beautiful part of you, but I think it's an even match."

I smirk and shake my head. "You're a smooth talker tonight, huh? Is it because you're worried about Alice being here?"

He threads his hand through my hair and looks at me. "I'm worried that you're worried."

"I am," I tell him honestly. "I don't like that she's living with you now, but I'm not a child, Thor, and neither are you. I trust you to make the right decisions for your family, I just hope you consider me part of it too."

"You absolutely are my family, Leia. Without a doubt."

He leans in to kiss me, his touch more passionate tonight, more desperate. My heart skips a beat when he drops his forehead to mine. "You know what, baby? Mercury is in retrograde today, and it isn't that dark yet. We could still see it."

I giggle and pull away to look at him. "You're kidding me, right? Your ex-wife rocks up during a mercury retrograde and you still believe there's nothing supernatural about it?"

"No, there isn't. I'm willing to show you some magic, though."

I smirk at him. "Sure, and I'm about to make you see stars, babe. The kind you've never seen before."

He bursts out laughing. "Wow, who is this smooth talker and what did you do to my girlfriend?"

Girlfriend. Such a simple word, yet it does all kinds of things to me. "Lay me down underneath the stars and kiss me really hard, and she'll magically appear."

"Oh, I'm going to do so much more than kiss you, Leia."

I lean in, my lips hovering over his. "I'm counting on it," I whisper, before kissing him. This thing between us... it's strong enough to weather a storm. It has to be.

Forty

LEIA

I squint at my laptop as I try to remember what source I pulled this line of data from. Why would I not have saved the reference straight away? It could take me hours to track that down. I groan and run a hand through my hair. I'm so close to finishing my dissertation, yet it still feels so far away too.

I welcome the distraction when my phone buzzes, hoping it's either Amara or Thor. Instead, it's the kids' school. My heart drops as memories of last time flood my mind. God, I hope the kids are okay. Please, don't let them have gotten into another fight — especially not when their mother is here, without a doubt silently judging Thor's parenting skills.

"Hi, Ms. Sital. Colton has a fever and we advise that you pick him up. He's not been feeling too well."

I check my watch. It's only ten in the morning. How could he have been sent to school at all if he's feeling unwell? "I'll be right there," I tell her, rushing to grab my bag.

I text Thor before stepping into my car, my nerves creeping up on me. I hope he's okay. Colton is so incredibly strong, but everyone is different when they're sick. I always turn into the biggest baby when I'm sick, and I worry Colt might be the same. I'm worried that he needs me, and I'm not there.

By the time I reach the school, I'm shaking with worry. I can't remember which medication we have in the house, and I'm not sure what he needs. I need to call Noah as soon as possible. I need him to come look at Colton.

My heart breaks when I see Colton lying down on a row of seats outside the Dean's office, covered in several blankets. "Colt?" My voice is high-pitched, betraying the worry I feel.

He looks up, his eyes widening when he sees me. He sits up, and I try my hardest to calm my racing heart. He's pale, and he's sweating.

"You came to get me? You're here for me?"

I place my hand on his forehead, only to find him burning up. "Of course, my sweet boy. How could I not be here when you aren't well?"

He throws his arms around my neck, a sob escaping his lips. I tighten my grip on him and hug him back. "What's going on, Colt?" I ask, my voice soft. "Are you hurt somewhere?"

He nods, and I pull away from him to check him over, my hands on his shoulders. "Where, my love? Where does it hurt?"

He places his hand on his heart and looks into my eyes. "Here. It hurts here, Leia, because I missed you so much. I thought you left me because Mum came back."

I swallow hard, trying my hardest to keep from crying. This boy... oh man. "I'm so sorry, Colt. I'm sorry. I should've explained to you that your mother would be taking you to school and picking you up, and that she'd be looking after you. I should've told you that it'd only be for a few weeks. I didn't explain properly, and I'm sorry, Colt. I would never abandon you. Never."

"Do you promise?" he asks, tears streaming down his cheeks.

I wipe them away with my thumbs and nod. "I promise. So long as your dad allows me to be in your life, I will be there."

He nods and throws himself back at me, hugging me tightly.

The two of us walk through the hallway like that, with Colt and I clinging to each other for dear life.

I almost wish the walk to the car was longer, so I wouldn't have to put him down. "Come on, my love," I say, placing him in the passenger seat gently. He looks drowsy and exhausted. It's clear he needs lots of rest. His eyes droop as I buckle him in and I press a quick kiss to his forehead.

As I get behind the wheel, realization dawns. I'm about to meet Thor's ex-wife, and I'm not sure I'm ready. I certainly didn't expect to meet her under these circumstances.

I hesitate for a split second before calling Noah to request that he meet me at Thor's house. I can't get my racing heart to calm. I need a doctor to look Colton over, and who better than my best friend's husband?

I'm nervous as I carry Colton toward the house, unlocking the door clumsily. My darling boy is heavier than he looks.

"Adrian! You're home already?"

I pause in the hallway, and so does the tall blonde dressed in nothing but a silk nightgown that barely covers her. Is that how she's been walking around the house this entire time?

"Who are you?" she asks, and irritation washes over me. Why isn't she rushing over to check up on Colton?

"Leia Sital," I tell her.

"Oh, the nanny," she tells me, her eyes finally settling on Colton.

I ignore her and walk toward the staircase. "Colton has a fever," I tell her. "I picked him up from school."

She follows me and watches as I put him to bed, making no effort to help me lift the covers.

"Make sure you cool him down," she tells me. "Use a small towel and place that on his forehead, refreshing it every few minutes."

I nod, even though her words make the hairs on my back rise. She's the type of mother I've had to deal with many times as a nanny, but somehow I was hoping she'd be different. "Sure," I tell her, struggling to push down my annoyance. What Colton needs is love, not a hands-off approach. He needs his mother, not his nanny. How can she stand there and withhold the love he so desperately needs?

I jump up when the doorbell rings and walk past her. She follows me down the stairs instead of staying to watch Colton, and my opinion of her plummets further.

Noah smiles at me reassuringly as I let him in. "Hey," he says, patting my head because he knows I hate it when he does that.

"Excuse me," Alice says. "I'm going to have to ask you to leave. I don't allow unexpected strangers into my house."

Noah glances at her and frowns. "Good thing this isn't your house, then, isn't it?" He glances at me and tips his head toward her. "Who is she?"

I purse my lips to suppress a smile and slightly shake my head, indicating not to rile her up. Noah is surprisingly good at getting on people's nerves while acting clueless. He's the perfect match for Amara.

"This is Dr. Noah Grant," I tell Alice, smiling apologetically before turning back to Noah. "Can you please take a look at Colton?"

He nods and follows me, but Alice holds her hands up. "Hold on. You're not seeing my son without my say-so. I don't care if you're allegedly a doctor. I don't know you."

I nod, understanding her stance, and grateful that she's finally looking out for Colton. She's right, of course. She just met me, and though she might have heard of me, it's unlikely she'd have heard of Noah.

"Lady, I don't even know who you are, but you aren't keeping me from checking up on my nephew."

He walks past her, and I blink, realization dawning. How did I even forget? "He, uh, he's Amara's husband," I explain. "Amara is Adrian's cousin."

She looks at me sharply. "I know who Amara is," she snaps.

Something about the way she looks at me doesn't sit well with me, but I dismiss it as I walk up the stairs.

"He's going to be okay, Leia. Honestly, when you called me, I thought the kid must've lost a leg or something. You were barely making sense, but it's just a regular good old flu. It's going around right now. Give him plenty of fluids and plenty of hugs. Make sure you keep him cool too, but other than that, he's fine."

I breathe a sigh of relief and sit down beside Colton as Noah packs up his stuff and writes me a prescription. I push Colton's hair out of his face gently, and he smiles at me. "You hear that?" I ask him. "Uncle Noah says you're going to be fine."

He smiles at me and nods. "I knew that, Ley. I've been sick before, you know? I'm not a kid anymore."

I chuckle and nod. "Yes, my little man. I hear you."

Noah's phone rings, and he sighs. "I need to take this, Ley. Amara's grandfather does not like to be kept waiting. I'll see you later, okay?" He picks up his phone and winks at me before walking out.

"You know what?" Alice says as soon as we're alone again. "I'll take it from here. You can go home."

Colton tenses and grabs my hand, his gaze pleading. "Don't leave, Ley," he murmurs, his voice barely above a whisper. "You promised."

"Colton," Alice says, her tone admonishing. "Don't bother the nanny. We don't need her now that I'm here, sweetheart."

Colton bursts into tears, and I pull him into me, letting him bury his face in my hair. "Don't go," he sobs, and I nod, tears filling my own eyes.

"Don't make him false promises," she warns me. "Just go. I'll take it from here."

I shake my head. "No. If he wants me to stay, I'm staying. I won't leave him. Not now."

"Excuse me?" she says, her tone indignant.

"Alice." I breathe a sigh of relief at the sound of Thor's voice. "Didn't you hear her? If she said she's staying, she's staying."

Forty-One

LEIA

Thor walks into the room and kneels by Colton's bed, his expression mirroring my own worries. "Hey buddy," he says, patting his back gently.

Colton tightens his grip on me and hugs me harder. "Don't make her leave, Dad," he pleads. "I... I want m-my Ley."

My heart squeezes so tightly that I have to inhale deeply to keep from bursting into tears. "I won't leave you," I tell him, holding the back of his head, my fingers stroking his hair soothingly. "I'm not going anywhere, Colt, I promise, okay?"

He nods, but he won't loosen his grip on me. Thor looks at me, his gaze questioning, but I shake my head. Nothing really happened. There isn't anything to tell him. "He's just not feeling well, that's all."

He glances at Alice and nods. "I see," he murmurs. I want to tell him it isn't her fault, and that she didn't do anything per se, but I can't be sure that her attempts to make me leave were in Colton's best interest. Something about her doesn't sit well with me, and it isn't just because she's Thor's ex-wife.

"Can you stay over?"

I nod, my entire attention on Colton. He's stopped crying, but he's still so distraught, and I'm not sure how to make him feel better.

"I'll ask Amara to grab some of your stuff from home."

He rises to his feet and walks away, his phone in hand. I can feel Alice's gaze on me, and it puts me on edge. I'm not sure what to make of her, and part of me is worried that my presence is hurting her — not because of Thor, but because Colton seems to need me more than he needs her. I want to explain to her that he's become reliant on me while he's been away from her, and that he's used to me, but I doubt it'd be received well, no matter how I word it.

"Ley, can we watch a movie later?" Colton asks as I put a cold towel on his head. "You told me you always watch movies when you're sick."

I nod and brush his hair out of his face. "Of course we can, Colt. What movie do you want to watch?"

He grins then. "The one about the little girl who goes to camp to find the lady that used to be her dad's best friend. The one with all the dancing."

I frown for a moment, confused. "Oh. *Kuch Kuch Hota Hai*?" I ask, chuckling. I'm surprised he even remembered the old Bollywood movie we watched months ago. One time, when the kids were questioning me about a wedding I'd gone to and the outfit I'd worn, I told them a little about Bollywood movies. One thing led to another, and over the next few weeks, we watched several classics. This one stuck with them. Perhaps it's because one of the main characters is a little girl their age.

"That's the one."

I nod, acutely aware of Alice's gaze on me. "Of course we can, sweetheart. I want you to get some rest, but if you're a little better tomorrow, we can lie on the sofa together and watch it, okay?"

He nods, his eyelids drooping already. He's exhausted, and his body clearly needs the rest.

"You made my kids watch foreign movies during their one hour of TV allowance?"

I glance at her, unsure what to say. I guess it's probably best that I don't tell her that movie is actually three hours long, or that Thor doesn't limit their TV time so long as they finish their homework and do well in school.

"They were curious about it, and Adrian felt it was good to teach them about other cultures."

She nods, but I can't read her. I check that Colton has fallen asleep, and I carefully place him back in bed, tucking him in. Noah said his temperature isn't dangerously high, but I'd still like to see it lower a little more.

"How long have you worked for Adrian?"

I turn around, only half surprised she's still standing where she was earlier, leaning back against the wall.

"Ever since he and the kids moved here, so it's been a few months now."

Her eyes run over me, as though she's appraising me, and I can't help but straighten my shoulders. I have a feeling that she's assessing me as a woman, and not as a nanny.

She smiles, and then she walks away, leaving me standing there in confusion. What just happened? While I expected things to be weird with her here, this is still hard to deal with. Thor told me that she's the one who asked for a divorce, so why does it feel like she wants him back?

Is this simply a matter of not wanting to see your ex with anyone else, or is it more? As far as I'm aware, he hasn't told her about us, so why does she seem to view me as a threat? I'm tense as I walk down the stairs, unable to shut down my endless over-thinking.

"Leia!"

I look up to find Amara standing next to Thor in the living room, a wide smile on her face.

"Hey, babe," I say.

"Hey," Amara and Thor both instantly reply.

209

They look at each other, both of them seemingly annoyed. "She was talking to me," Amara says, and I shake my head. At this moment, it's so obvious that they're family. They're both petty.

They both turn to me with raised brows, and I stare back at them with wide eyes. "Um... I see you brought me clothes," I tell Amara, instead of clarifying who I was talking to.

She smiles and holds up a paper carrier bag for me, and I take it from her gratefully. I peek into it and freeze for a split second before closing it instantly. What did she bring me? That was an awful lot of lace, and was that a sex toy in there? What in the hell is Amara up to now?

She grins at me and throws me a sassy wink. She's insane. I love her, but she's crazy. "Um, *thanks*," I tell her, drawing out the word.

"How's my little nephew?" she asks. "Adrian says he's being super needy?"

I nod. "He's asleep now, but I suspect he'll ask for me if he wakes up and I'm not there." I can tell that there's more she wants to ask, but she falls silent, her eyes moving to the doorway.

I turn to find Alice walking into the room, a serene smile on her face. "Amara," she says. "I haven't seen you in years. I'm sorry I missed your wedding, but I'm sure it was beautiful."

She nods. "It was. I was glad to see the kids and Adrian there. It's so good to have them back."

I blink and glance at Adrian, wondering if he realizes she's slighting Alice, subtly hinting that she doesn't care for Alice, in the way only Amara can. He purses his lips in an effort to hide a smile, and I look down at my feet, biting back my own smile.

"I cleared the upstairs guest room for you, Leia. It's next to Colton's room, so that should be easiest for you," Alice says.

I nod, but I can't help but hate the way she's acting like this is her house. It makes me feel like an intruder, like they're a happy family I'm not a part of. It's completely irrational, but I can't help the way I feel.

"I'll see you later, babe," I tell Amara. "I'm just going to check up on Colt."

She throws Thor a vindictive smirk, as though to say, *see I told you it was me she was calling babe.*

I shake my head and turn away, a smile on my face. I'm blessed to have a best friend like Amara, even if she gave me a sex toy when that's the last thing I need tonight. I have no idea how to even explain that to Thor — even worse, what if the kids find it? I chuckle to myself as I walk up the stairs, imagining the crazy explanations I'd have to come up with.

Colton seems fast asleep, and I lie down next to him for a moment, my fingers trailing over his face gently. My sweet boy. The way he cried today tore my heart up. How has he been feeling with his mother here? It never occurred to me he'd need me as much as he does, and it kills me to know I let him down. I wasn't there when he needed me most.

I lean in close and wrap my arm around him, wishing I'd checked in with him more. Part of me worries that him getting sick is my fault. While I'm not sure it makes any logical sense, my mother always told me that kids' emotional health can result in physical issues, and me not being there seems to have upset him. It's all I can think about as my eyes fall closed.

Forty-Two

ADRIAN

"Goodnight, sweetheart," I tell Lucy, pressing a kiss to her forehead. She grins at me and glances at Alice, who is standing next to me. Her eyes light up when Alice leans in and also presses a kiss to her forehead. The joy in her expression is irreplaceable, and it hurts to know that Lucy's heart will break all over again when Alice leaves.

"Colton is fast asleep," she says as we walk out of Lucy's room. "He's got the nanny with him, so we'd better not disturb them."

"Leia fell asleep in Colton's room?"

She nods, her gaze lingering on me. "The nanny... are you fucking her?"

I stop in my tracks and look at her in surprise. "Pardon?" I ask, even though I heard her perfectly fine.

"You are, aren't you, Adrian?"

I cross my arms and stare her down. "I'm pretty sure I told you to stay out of my private life. Whether I am or not is none of your business. What is it going to be? Are you going to intrude and pack your bags, or are you going to mind your own business?"

She looks shocked for a moment, incomprehension crossing her face. "What happened to you? You never used to speak to me that way."

I sigh and run a hand through my hair. "Alice, I've been perfectly civil with you. Hell, I've even opened up my home to you. All I've asked for in return is that you agree to the very few rules I set. If you can't do that much, then don't expect anything from me in return. You're not my wife anymore. I don't owe you anything."

She glares at me, and I stare at her for a moment. It's odd how I never saw her for who she truly is. I put her on a pedestal and tricked myself into believing she was the person I wished she was.

"Goodnight," I tell her, walking toward my bedroom, even though it's Colton's room I want to go to. The last thing I need right now is for her to follow me into his room, when what I want more than anything is to finally get Leia alone.

I sigh and wait until I'm certain she went downstairs, feeling fucking ridiculous. I can't believe I have to sneak around in my own damn house. This situation couldn't be weirder.

I'm impatient as I walk into Colton's bedroom, pausing when I find Leia cuddled up with Colton. I stand there for a moment, just watching the two of them. It should be Alice lying there with Colt, but it's Leia he asked for. It doesn't exactly surprise me, but it does help me see things clearer.

I lift her into my arms gently, my heart overflowing with love for her. I've fantasized about having her in my bed for months now. There's no way she's sleeping in a guest room tonight.

Leia blinks sleepily as I carry her into my room, her eyes finding mine.

"Thor?" she says, her sleepy voice sexy as hell. I want this. I want to wake up with her and fall asleep with her every single night. I've never been more sure of anything else in life.

I lie her down, and she yawns. "I need to shower," she tells me.

"I've had such a long day."

"Use my bathroom," I tell her. "I'll go grab your bag from the guest room."

She nods, and I watch her disappear through the ensuite door. It just hits me right in the chest. I want her clothes hanging amongst mine, her toothbrush next to mine. They're stupid silly things to want, but I want them desperately.

I sigh impatiently. Just a few more weeks. That's all I can take. No more than that. If we can survive the next couple of weeks, we'll be okay. Leia is supposed to hand her dissertation in next week, and as soon as she's defended it successfully, we'll be in the clear. Then it's just a matter of finding the right time to tell the kids and her family.

I place the bag Amara brought Leia on the bed and frown when I see something purple peeking through her clothes. I reach for it, my eyes widening when I find myself holding a vibrator that looks like an aubergine emoji. What the fuck is this?

Fucking Amara. I have no doubt she designed and built this. What was she thinking, giving that to Leia? And why the fuck is it so big? It's as big as my entire forearm. What does Amara think? Does she think I don't satisfy my girl well enough?

I walk into the bathroom to find Leia standing under the stream, the steamed-up glass hiding most of her body. "Baby," I mutter. "What the fuck is this?"

Leia turns toward me and burst out laughing. "It's... an eggplant. Like the emoji."

"I can see that... what I'm asking is why Amara would think you need this. What in the hell have you been telling her?"

She wipes the glass, exposing her body, and my cock instantly hardens at the sight of her.

"Nothing," she says. "I think the problem is that I haven't been telling her much at all. How am I supposed to tell her I had her cousin's face between my legs just a few days ago?"

"This won't do," I tell her. "I can't compete with that thing. I have to make sure you're so satisfied you'll never reach for it."

I pull my t-shirt over my head, and Leia chuckles. Her smile fades when I undress fully, and the way she looks at me makes my cock throb.

I join her under the shower, her entire body slick and wet. She takes a step back, until her back hits the wall. "Eggplant emoji, huh?"

She laughs and bites down on her lip. "It was all Amara's doing, I swear."

I narrow my eyes at her and shake my head. "It's going in the bin," I warn her, and she chuckles. "Oh baby," I add. "You won't be laughing by the time I'm done with you."

I lean in, my lips hovering over hers for a moment. Leia rises to her tiptoes, throwing herself at me, and I smile against her lips. Her hands roam over my body, until she's got my cock in her hands.

"This is way better than that eggplant," she tells me, and I smirk. It better fucking be.

I lift her up high against the wall, her legs wrapping around my waist. "Can your eggplant do this?" I ask, flicking my tongue over her nipple.

She moans, and I smile to myself as I swirl my tongue around it, teasing her before sucking down it. "Thor," she moans. I love the sound of her. It's one of those things I'll never get enough of. I pull away to look at her, and the expression in her eyes has me ready to burst.

"Are you going to tease me, or are you going to fuck me? I mean... maybe I should grab the eggplant after all."

I lower her slightly to align her with my cock. "Baby, you can barely take my cock, you'd better forget about the eggplant."

Her smile is wiped clean off her face when I push into her. I look into her eyes as I thrust all the way into her, loving the way her lips fall open. This. I want this, for the rest of my life.

I want this intimacy, being able to joke with her, laugh with her, even as I fuck her. I never quite understood the term making love, but I think I do now.

Forty-Three

ADRIAN

My alarm goes off and I silence it instantly, but I wasn't fast enough to keep Leia from waking up. She twists in my arms, and I pull her closer, enjoying the feel of her body against mine, the way her leg is draped over my hip.

Waking up with her is far better than I expected. The fragrance of her shampoo, her softness and warmth... yeah, this is better than my fantasies.

"Morning, Princess," I tell her.

"Mm," she moans, burying her face deeper into my neck. I think a sleepy Leia might be my favorite version of her. I don't think I can go back to a world where I don't wake up with her in my arms.

She kisses my neck, and a low guttural moan escapes my throat, intense need rushing through me. I spent most of last night worshiping every inch of her body, yet I already need more of her. I bury my hand through her hair and tighten my grip. "Don't tease me, baby. I absolutely will fuck you so hard that you'll be feeling me for the rest of the day."

She giggles, and the sound of it just fucks me up. I've never loved a woman the way I love her. *Fuck*. I always thought people were being over the top when they referred to their other half, but she is it for me. She's my missing part. She completes me.

"I have to get to work," I groan, wishing I could spend all day in bed with her. "We need to tell the kids soon, Ley. I can't do this anymore. I don't want to sneak around with you."

She nods, but I feel the way her body tenses. "We need to wait a few weeks," she says. "Just to see how they adjust once Alice leaves."

I nod, my heart once more overflowing with pure love for her. The way she puts their needs above hers, above our relationship. "I love you," I tell her, wishing those words could adequately convey how I truly feel about her. It doesn't seem like enough. The words feel too simple to describe a feeling as all-encompassing as this is.

"I love you more," she says, pushing away from me. "I'd better go. I want to be in the guest room before the kids wake up."

I sit up in bed and watch her as she puts the pajamas I tore off her last night back on. I've never felt this urge to claim a woman. I've never wanted anyone to be mine this badly. My relationship with Alice has always evolved the way she wanted it to. We got engaged when she pushed for it, and we got married when she wanted to. It was similar with the kids. When our marriage started to break down, she insisted on having children. In hindsight, I think it might have been because she knew we wouldn't last without something to tie us together. In the end, we didn't last even with the kids.

I'm absentminded as I get ready for the day, my mind on how to tell the kids about Leia and me. I think Colt is going to be okay, but Lucy might not be. I'm so lost in thought that I don't even notice Alice sitting by the breakfast bar in the kitchen until she speaks.

"So you *are* fucking her, then? What is it, Adrian? A rebound?"

I'm startled, to say the least. "What are you doing here?" I ask, checking my watch. "It's five in the morning."

She stares at me, her expression softer than I'm used to. She looks hurt, and the last thing I wanted to do was hurt her. I don't want my relationship with her to sour. The last thing the kids need is for us to fall apart even further.

"Tell me it's just a rebound, Adrian," she whispers, her voice breaking.

I hesitate, unsure what to do or how to act. Leia and I aren't ready to announce our relationship. When it happens, it has to be on our terms.

"It isn't," I tell her honestly. "It's not a rebound. It never has been with her."

"So what? You're going to marry her? Have her take care of my children? You don't marry the help, Adrian. You need to snap out of whatever phase you're going through."

I tense and force myself to stay calm. "She's a lot more than the help," I warn her. "She's my girlfriend, Alice, and so help me God. If you say one little thing about her that I don't like, you can pack your damn bags and call yourself a taxi."

Her eyes widen, hurt reflected in them. For a moment, I regret being so harsh with her, but I know what she's like. If I don't draw boundaries now, she'll continue to needle me. I don't mind her messing with me, but Leia is off-limits.

"You can't actually... you have feelings for her?"

She sounds so surprised that I almost take offense. "Of course I do," I tell her. "She's incredible, Alice. I never thought I'd ever even date, because I was so worried about the kids. I didn't think I'd find someone who would love them the way I do, someone the kids would love in return. I thought I'd never fall in love again, and I was prepared to sacrifice the rest of my life for Lucy and Colton. Hell, after our marriage fell apart, I didn't think I'd ever want to do it all over again, but I do. I understand that this worries you, but I can promise you that the kids won't be adversely affected by my relationship with Leia."

She looks into my eyes, and her expression absolutely guts me. She looks so devastated that my own heart aches. I have no idea how I'd feel if she moved on with someone else, but after spending so many years with her, thinking we'd grow old together... I can imagine it'd be hard, even if my feelings for her are no longer what they used to be. It must be hard for her too, and nothing I do or say will make it better.

"You need to break up with her."

I frown. "Excuse me?"

She looks down at her feet and sighs. "She's a bad influence on the kids, Adrian. Lucy stopped going to ballet classes, and Colton stopped playing football. She isn't pushing them to fulfil their potential. Of course they like her. She's just doing the bare minimum, letting the kids get away with wasting entire days."

"That was my choice. The kids were unhappy because of all the pressure you put on them. I chose to let them take it easy while they adjusted. When they're ready, they can pick their own interests to pursue."

Her eyes flash and she shakes her head. "Break up with her, Adrian. It isn't just about the kids. This has gone too far as it is. This isn't how it was supposed to go. You and I... we've always been together. We belong together. For a while, I was blinded by the thought that you'd never love me the way I want to be loved, but I was wrong. I let it go too far, and I pushed you away. I never should've asked for a divorce, and there's nothing I regret more. When you and the kids left, I thought you'd miss me so much you'd come begging for another chance. I was certain you couldn't raise them without me, and that you'd need me, that you'd finally appreciate everything I do for our family. You were never supposed to replace me with such ease."

She sniffs, and my heart clenches painfully at the sight of tears in her eyes. "Alice," I murmur. "You did what needed to be done, what I didn't have the courage to do. Throughout the years, we'd grown apart."

She wipes the tears on her cheeks away and shakes her head.

"You don't understand, Adrian. I want another chance. I miss you, and I miss our family. I miss my children. I want everything we lost. I get that you're confused, and you're trying to move on, but this girl... she can't compare to the years of history we have. No matter what you might think, she cannot love our children the way I do. She can't be their mother."

"She isn't trying to be their mother, Alice. She would never try to take your place. That isn't what's happening here. I get that it'll take some time for you to process this, and that's fine, but I just didn't want to lie to you."

She shakes her head. "I don't think you're hearing me, Adrian. I want you back. I want us to be a family again. I still love you, and I know deep down, you love me too."

I straighten my back and sigh. "I don't, Alice. You asked for a divorce, and you got one. The last three years have been hell for us both, and I've finally found some semblance of peace again. The kids have finally adjusted. Whatever is going on in your mind, stop it. You and I aren't getting back together. We ended the moment you asked for a divorce."

She looks at me, her gaze sharp. "What if I'd never asked for one?"

I look away. "Leia asked me the same question, and I'll give you the same answer I gave her. I never would've left you if you hadn't asked me to. I would've stayed for the kids, but make no mistake, that would be the only reason I'd stay. You and I were over long before you asked for a divorce, and you know it."

"I don't think we are, Adrian." She pauses, her gaze calculative. "Lucy told me Leia is also a PhD student. One under your care. How would the university feel about you sleeping with one of your students? Surely that would jeopardize her doctorate?"

I start to see red and pinch the bridge of my nose, praying for patience. "You won't win me back by threatening Leia," I warn her. "If anything, that will just result in the severance of any remaining relationship we have. Is that something you want to put the kids through?"

She looks at me. "I'll give you some time to think about it, Adrian. Consider giving us one more chance. Don't underestimate how far I'll go. If I can't have you, then she won't have you either."

I frown, my gaze roaming over her. The passion I used to love in her just looks like insanity now. How did I never see it before? To Alice, I was always a possession, a box to check. Our relationship has always been volatile, and for the longest time I loved it, because it kept life interesting... but that was before Leia. Before I knew what true happiness and stability felt like. Just being married doesn't equate to stability, and I realize that now.

"I don't know what that even means, Alice, and I'm not interested in finding out. I want you to leave. If you aren't gone by the time I get back from work, I'll physically remove you myself. You choose whether we're doing this the hard way or the easy way. I'm done giving in to you. I won't sacrifice one more moment of happiness for you."

I take a good look at her, a pang of regret hitting me in the chest. Regret for the way this is playing out, and for staying with her far longer than I should have, but most of all, I regret the pain that will continue to haunt the kids because of this.

I walk away, at last at peace with the way Alice and I ended. I didn't see it at the time, but it truly was the start of something new.

Forty-Four

LEIA

"He will never love you the way he loves me." I turn around to find Alice leaning against the kitchen door. I expected her to come find me earlier today, but she's left me alone all day. She didn't even ask me to pick up Lucy and did it herself. I was sure she'd pile every single errand she could think of on me, reminding me that I'm an employee. Other than checking in on Colton and Lucy a few times, she's barely said a word to me. Until now. "This fling might be exciting for now, but he'll never marry you. You're still young, Leia. Don't you want children of your own? Do you really want to spend the rest of your life being a stand-in for me?"

Her words hit me straight in the chest, and it takes all of me not to react. *Stand-in...* I guess that's exactly what I am. I try not to let her words get to me, but they do, and I have a feeling she knows it. "I'm not at liberty to discuss my relationship with Adrian with you," I tell her, keeping my tone as friendly as I can.

She chuckles and runs a hand through her long, blonde hair. "That's cute. So he's keeping you hidden, huh? Let me guess...

he's got you convinced that it's your idea, or that it's for the best. It's probably for the kids, right?"

I look at her, unsure where she's going with this. I'm not stupid. I know she's trying to rile me up, and I'd be an idiot to fall for it, but I can't help but feel hurt.

"Why do you think we got a divorce, Leia?" she asks, a knowing smile on her face. "You're not the first girl Adrian has promised the world to. You're not his first affair. He's charismatic, isn't he? He could charm any girl he sets his sights on, and he does it with such ease. It isn't the first time he used the children, either. Makes him look more broken, you see? As though he's just in need of the right woman's touch. He'll convince you that our marriage was empty, because he's not stupid enough to actually badmouth me. He's too subtle for that. He always is." She laughs, the sound chilling. I should walk away, but I can't. A part of me fears that her words are true. He did, after all, give me the wrong phone number, and he did pick me up in a bar. It's so out of character for him, but maybe it isn't at all?

"He'll tell you he can't date you out in the open, because the kids would never accept that. That part of the story has changed. It used to be that our marriage was over, but we stayed together for the kids. He'd promise the girls that he'd leave me someday, but he never would. You know, if I hadn't asked him for a divorce, he never would have left me at all. I'm the only woman he's ever truly loved, the only one he keeps coming back to."

She smiles apologetically, her eyes filled with pity. "I shouldn't even try to warn you, because you'll end up finding out the hard way. He will never love you, no matter what he says. Don't believe his promises, Leia. He won't marry you. He won't start a family with you. Whatever he promised you, it isn't true. I can't make you believe me, but just think about it. He used to cheat on me each time he went on a trip, picking up girls in bars, spending a night with them. There weren't many that actually lasted beyond one night, but the few who did, didn't last more than a few months. He'd get bored, and he'd move on. It was an endless vicious cycle that I was trapped in as much as these girls were. I got out, and I hope you will too."

She walks away, leaving me standing there reeling. I don't want to believe her, but something in her expression as she spoke to me unnerved me. I mentally go through my first meeting with Thor, the way he wouldn't tell me his real name, and the way he gave me a wrong phone number. Has he done that to other girls, too?

I might not even have been the only girl he slept with on that trip. I was just the one that crossed his path again, unexpectedly. Perhaps I was just the most convenient choice. I'm always accessible to him, and I didn't exactly even make him chase me.

"Leia?"

I look up at Thor and blink slowly, confused as to why I'm seated on the kitchen floor. I don't even remember sitting down. How long have I been here, lost in my thoughts?

"What happened?" he asks, kneeling down beside me. He brushes my hair out of my face and I recoil, my eyes widening.

"Leia?" he repeats, his tone worried.

My eyes find his, and I breathe in deeply. "Did you ever cheat on Alice?" I ask. "Don't lie to me, Thor. Tell me the truth."

He shakes his head. "Never. I swear it."

I nod. "Why didn't you tell me your name that night?"

"Because you wouldn't give me yours. I remember that night vividly, baby. You were wearing a yellow summer dress with shoes that had a sunflower on them, and your lips were bright red. You were sipping a cosmopolitan when I walked in, and you stole my breath. I was supposed to meet Silas there, but when I saw you, every thought just faded. I asked you what your name was, and you told me I could just call you Ley. In return, I told you to call me Thor."

I nod, a sob tearing through my throat. He takes me into his arms, and I burst into tears, my throat burning. "Princess," Thor says. "You need to tell me what happened. What's going on? Is it something Alice did, something she said?"

I nod and tighten my grip on him, my entire body heaving from the force of my sobs. I believed her. For a few moments, I believed her over the man I know so well.

"Leia, look at me," he says, pulling away. He wipes away my tears and smiles. "I love you. I don't know what Alice said to you, but it's clear she made you doubt me. Ask me anything you want. Even if the answers aren't what you might want to hear, I will always be honest with you. I promise."

I nod and drop my forehead to his shoulder, trying my best to get a hold of myself. What was I thinking? How could I possibly have doubted him as much as I did? If Alice could do that to me, then our relationship might not be as strong as I thought it was.

"I asked her to leave this morning," he says. "I'm not surprised she lashed out, but I should've warned you. She threatened me this morning, insinuating that she'd tell the school about us. I told her that doing so would be the end of any relationship I still have with her, and I thought she heeded my warning."

I have a feeling that it's more than Thor is telling me. For her to react the way she did... that wasn't just being unhappy to see your ex move on. She was actively trying to sabotage our relationship. To what end?

"We can no longer keep our relationship hidden, Leia. You need to finish your doctorate as soon as you can. You have to hand in your dissertation. Once you've done that, we can tackle the rest. I'm tired of hiding in the shadows. I'm ready for more, Leia. I'm ready to publicly call you mine, consequences be damned... but I won't let this hurt your doctorate. Please, Princess, please tell me you'll finish your dissertation soon."

I nod. "It's nearly finished. I was going to ask you if we could sit down and review it together next week."

His relief is palpable, and my faith is restored. I was crazy to doubt him. I should've known better. This is Thor, after all. "As soon as you finish your doctorate, we need to come clean about our relationship. The kids might not take it well, but there's no point in delaying the inevitable."

I recognize the worries in his eyes... they reflect mine perfectly. We need to tell the kids before Alice does.

"My family won't take this well either," I admit. "They might not accept it at all."

It would be impossible for him to truly understand, but they won't immediately accept him. It isn't just the fact that he's older, divorced, and has kids. It's his ethnicity and religion too. My parents will be too worried about the way us being together might look, and what it would mean for any kids we might have. They'll worry that I'll lose sight of my roots by being with him, but that's something I will need to worry about when it comes to it.

"I will win them over," Thor says, a smile on his face.

God, I hope so. I doubt it's going to be as easy as he thinks it is.

Forty-Five

LEIA

"You're all better now, Colt. You have to go to school," I tell him, but he shakes his head, desperate for another sick day, when he's perfectly fine now. He was sick for three days, but he's definitely healthy now, despite what he's trying to convince me of.

"Ley, I'm still sick! I can't go to school!"

I glance at Thor who's standing in the doorway of his bedroom, his arms crossed. *"Colton Astor,"* he says. "You'd better be ready for school in ten minutes."

Colton groans and gets out of bed angrily, glaring at his father as he walks to the bathroom. I bite back a smile and shake my head. He's cute when he's angry like that.

"Come with me," Thor says, holding his hand out. I hesitate before taking it, and Thor entwines our fingers, holding onto me tightly as he leads me down the stairs.

"Where are we going?" I ask when he pulls me through the front door, where a black car is waiting for us. "I need to take the kids to school!"

He shakes his head and grins. "No, you don't. Alice is here to take care of them, isn't she? Let her. She'll pick the kids up and take them to school herself, and Lenora just got here to ensure they're ready to go. You and I have somewhere to be."

He holds the car door open for me, and I get in hesitantly. What is he doing? Where are we going so randomly?

Thor walks around the car and gets in next to me, his hand on my knee. "Drive us to the Astor private airstrip," he tells the driver, and my eyes widen.

"Seriously, where are we going?"

He glances at me, taking in the blue summer dress I'm wearing. His hand slips underneath my dress, and he caresses my thigh, drawing circles on it as he smiles at me. "The Bahamas. Looks like you're nicely dressed as it is, but I brought you plenty of clothes too. Amara helped me buy them for you."

"We... we're going *where*?"

He grins at me and leans in, his lips brushing over mine, once, twice, before he kisses me fully. His hand moves to my cheek, and he holds my face as he kisses me, taking his time with me.

By the time he pulls away, my heart is racing. "We're going to the Bahamas, baby. You've been so stressed out ever since Alice got here, and I hate seeing you that way. I promised you that her presence wouldn't affect us, but it did. I wish I could promise you that you'll never cry because of her again, but I can't control what she does or says. Because she's the kids' mother, I can't cut her out of our lives. What I *can* do is promise you that I'll always try my hardest to soothe the pain she brings you. I can promise you that I'll show you how much I love you each time your conviction wavers."

I look at him, my heart thumping loudly in my chest. "You don't need to do that," I whisper. "I'm not with you because of this type of thing."

"I know," he murmurs. He threads his fingers through my hair and looks into my eyes. "I know it's never been about the money for you, Leia. We live a simple life, most of the time. I do it knowingly, because I don't want the kids to grow up spoiled and entitled... but you? I'm going to spoil you rotten. I promised myself that I'd do everything in my power to make sure me having children wouldn't mean that you have to miss out on things. Ever since I found you crying on the kitchen floor, what I've been wanting to do most of all is take you away, someplace where it's just the two of us. If I thought you could bear to leave Colton, I'd have gotten you onto a flight that very day, but there's no way you'd leave him, is there?"

I shake my head. "No," I admit. I'd be uncomfortable leaving him in his mother's care when he begged me to stay with him. "I never would have done that."

He nods. "I know. So I waited till he was better, but no second longer. I'm taking you away for one night. Your family already thinks you're staying over to take care of Colton, so what's one more night?"

I smile and drop my head to his shoulder. It can't be easy for him to cope with my crazy family, but he does his best to understand. "I love you, Adrian."

He presses a kiss to my cheek and grins. "We're here," he says, and I look out the window, my eyes widening in shock.

Thor walks around the car and holds my door open for me, but all I'm focused on is the metallic grey plane in the hangar we're in. "This... what is this?"

He chuckles and pulls me along while the driver grabs our luggage. "This, my love, is the Astor family's private plane. Let's go."

He tightens his grip on my hand, and I can't get my racing heart to calm as he leads me up the stairs. This is insane. What is he thinking? "Thor, this is too much."

He wraps his arm around me and leads me to my seat. "Sit," he orders, and I obey. Thor falls to his knees in front of me and buckles me in. "Nothing is ever too much for you, baby. I should've done this months ago. I'm sorry, baby. I'm sorry it took me so long to realize that I wasn't putting you first the way I should have. I'm sorry that it took you getting hurt for me to realize that I didn't protect you well enough. I'll do better, okay? I promise you, Leia. I'll do better."

I shake my head, shocked. "No, Thor. None of this is your fault. I knew what I was getting into when I started dating you."

He leans into me and kisses me, his touch tender. "Even so," he whispers. "I need you to myself for a night. I need some time away with you."

I nod, and he grins at me as he takes the seat next to me. He grabs my hand as we take off, and I can barely contain my excitement. One night with Thor, just the two of us. It's exactly what we need right now.

Forty-Six

LEIA

This entire morning has been a blur, and I don't think I've ever been happier. "Where are we staying?" I ask when Thor and I walk out of the plane to find yet another car already waiting for us.

He holds the door open for me and grins. "I have a feeling you're going to like it."

I smirk and watch him as he walks around the car and gets in next to me. "Thor," I plead, grabbing his hand. "I can't deal with surprises. I'm so curious that I think I might *die*. You have to tell me where we're staying. Is it a hotel? A resort?"

He laughs as I continue to question him, but he won't give in. "We're nearly there," he says eventually, and I look out the window curiously. We're approaching a gated community with an outrageous amount of security, but the gates swing open automatically as we near them. "Numberplate recognition," Thor says.

I nod and glance around, giddy with excitement. The thought of having him entirely to myself, without having to hide or worry the kids will walk in on us... I didn't realize how much I needed that until we stepped on that plane.

"We're here."

I get out of the car to find myself staring up at a secluded mansion. There are no other homes around for miles, it's just us. "We're staying here?"

Thor nods and pulls me along. "This," he says, smiling at me, "is going to be our summer home. It'll be a good place to go to when we need to get away from the kids without wanting to go too far away, and we can bring them here during their school breaks too."

We walk into the house, and I glance around in shock. "It's beautiful," I murmur. It's done up in warmer colors than his own home, making it feel all summery. This feels much more like a home than his actual home does. "I bought it furnished but without too many decorations, so you can style it however you please."

I follow him into the kitchen, and he reaches for a document on the counter, pushing it toward me. "It's yours, technically."

"*What?*"

He tips his head toward the document and smiles. "The property deed has your name on it, Leia. I bought this place for us, but primarily for you. I know that being with me isn't always going to be easy, so if you ever need to get away, this place will always be here. We can come here together when we need a moment to ourselves. When things get hard, this'll be our sanctuary."

I look at him in shock. "You bought me a *house?*"

He nods. "Sooner or later, everything I own will be yours, so it won't matter. But yeah, technically, it's yours."

"Are you insane?"

"I'm a little crazy about you, yes."

"Thor, you can't... you can't buy me a house!"

He shrugs. "Why not? I'm going to marry you, Leia. I'm going to give you a whole lot more than just this house. This is just a start."

I run a hand through my hair, unsure what to even say.

"Leia," he says, grabbing my hand. "I don't want to argue with you about what is mine and what is yours, okay? I don't want to argue with you at all. What I want to do is take you to our private beach and fuck you until you have sand in places it shouldn't even be able to reach. How about that?"

I grin and nod. He's right. It doesn't matter what I own, or what he owns. Us getting married is inevitable.

Thor grins as he pulls me along, pausing at the sliding doors that lead straight to the beach. I giggle when he pushes them open and bends down, lifting me into his arms. He carries me onto the beach, where a canopied day bed is waiting for us. He lays me down, his eyes on mine as he climbs on top of me, holding himself up on his forearms.

"Leia, I'm so in love with you," he says. "I want to give you the world, and I can't wait to officially make you mine. I know that you're having a hard time, baby. Your silence speaks volumes. There's nothing I don't notice about you. I know Alice being here has been difficult for you, and I promise I'll make it up to you, okay?"

"How?" I ask, smiling. "How are you going to make it up to me, Thor?"

He chuckles and lowers himself on top of me. "What are you thinking?"

I smirk and tilt my head, my lips mere inches from his. "I think I should get an orgasm for each time she upset me."

"That sounds fair. Thirty orgasms coming right up, baby."

I burst out laughing and wrap my arms around him, his lips finding mine. He kisses me slowly, leisurely, and I wrap my leg around his hip. Thor moves between my legs, and I moan when he presses against me. He's already hard, and the way he's moving against me has me feeling impatient.

I tug at his t-shirt, and he pushes off me long enough to take it off, exposing his strong chest and abs. There's something about a man with arms like Thor's holding himself up above you. It's sexy beyond words.

Thor pulls at my clothes, and I chuckle against his lips as both of us turn impatient, tugging at each other's clothes until we're both naked, the sun and a soft breeze caressing our skin.

He moves his lips to my neck and kisses me right below my ear, his touch lingering. "I love you," he whispers into my ear, and I bury my hand into his hair as his lips move lower, leaving a trail of kisses on my skin.

He looks up at me, his gaze intense. "I'm going to love you for the rest of our lives, Leia, and I'm going to make sure you never forget it."

He smiles at me before lowering his lips to my breast, his tongue twirling around my nipple, teasing me.

"Thor," I warn. I push against him until I've got him on his back and straddle him. "I'm not that patient today."

He lies back and moves his hands behind his head. The way he stares up at me makes me feel invincible, and I want more of that feeling.

I grab his cock and align it with me, sinking down just a little. I groan and bite down on my lip. I can't get used to his size, but I desperately want to ride him. I want his eyes on me, and I need all of him.

Thor moves his hands to my waist and looks at me. "Baby," he groans. "Won't you let me make you come first?"

"Can't you feel how wet I already am?" I moan.

He chuckles and tightens his grip on my waist as I take him in a little deeper. "Good girl," he whispers. "Look at you, baby. You're taking my cock so well. Just a little more, baby."

I nod and lower myself on top of him just a little more, shaking my head. "It's too much," I groan. I can't do it in one go, it's just too much.

"You can do this, baby. You can. I know you can take my cock, my love." I bite down on my lip harshly as I sink down on him, taking all of him.

Thor moans loudly and tips his head back, his eyes falling closed. "Fuck, Leia."

He reaches for my pussy, his thumb drawing circles around my clit as I sit on top of him, taking a moment to adjust to him. He watches me as I start to move slowly, hesitantly. "Thor," I moan when his touch becomes too much. He's got me so close already, when what I wanted to do was make *him* desperate.

He smirks as his touch turns rough, my moans uncontrollable. I can't take this much longer, and he knows it. "Come for me," he orders, and I do.

My pussy clenches around his cock, and he watches me as I come, his gaze intense. The way he looks at me... I want more of that. I want more of this feeling.

"Your turn," I tell him, and he smirks.

I'm going to ride him so hard that I'll be wiping that smirk off his face. Today is exactly what we needed, and I already know I'll be hanging onto the memories throughout the rest of Alice's stay.

Forty-Seven

ADRIAN

I'm exhausted as I park in front of the house Alice rented, not in the mood to deal with her. I wish I could've stayed in the Bahamas with Leia. Our night there passed far too quickly, and it made returning to Alice's presence so much harder. I just want more time with my girl. I want more of the passion and happiness we shared.

I sigh as I stare at Alice's house. Every conversation we've had has revolved around her asking me to reconsider our divorce, and I can't figure her out. Why now?

She's the one who asked for a divorce in the first place, so why is she regretting it now? I'm not in the mood for her games. I'm tired of the endless guilt-trip, the continuous reminders of how happy the kids would be to have us back together.

The thought of putting my own needs above the kids' is making me feel sick to my stomach, and Alice knows it. It's my one true weakness, and she's using it against me.

Had I not had Leia in my life, I probably would've caved, and I'd have suffered through a loveless marriage for the rest of my days. It isn't what I want for myself, and it isn't the example I want to set for the kids. I want to show them that it's okay to pursue happiness. Yes, things that are broken can often be fixed, but not always. It's important for them to learn where to draw lines, and how to prioritize themselves.

Part of me worries that that's just the way I try to justify my choice. I'm worried this is just what I'm trying to tell myself to cope with the guilt of choosing Leia over Alice. A bigger part of me knows it's the right thing to do, though.

"Hey, munchkins," I say, opening up my arms for them when they walk out of Alice's front door. Lucy glares at me with red eyes, and Colton shakes his head silently, his expression torn.

"Hey, what happened?" I ask the kids. Colton pauses, hesitating, but then he continues to follow his sister to the car, leaving me at a loss.

I turn back to the front door to ask Alice what's going on, but she's already closed the door. Usually she at least waves the kids off. My heart sinks as a dozen scenarios flash through my mind. Did they fight with Alice? Is this about her going back and leaving them again soon, or is it something else? Something worse?

My thoughts are whirling as I get into the car, noting that neither of them chose to sit in the front. Usually I have to break up fights between them about who gets to ride next to me. Something is definitely wrong, and I have a sinking feeling that I know what it is.

"Are you two going to talk to me, or are you going to sulk first? This isn't how we deal with grievances in this family, and you both know it."

They both remain silent, and I'm at a complete loss. Throughout the entire divorce, we discussed everything. Alice and I made sure to continuously check in with them, to see how they're feeling, and if they needed any support. Dialogue is what kept us together. Never before have they gone completely silent, and it worries me endlessly.

They're out of the car almost as soon as we stop in front of the house, and I frown. I haven't even had a chance to tell them that Leia is here for dinner, and I'm starting to worry having her here tonight isn't a good idea.

The kids freeze in the hallway when they see Leia, and my suspicions are confirmed. "You," Lucy says, her voice wobbly. "Because of you, Mum won't come live with us again. It's all your fault!"

She storms past Leia and stomps up the stairs, soft sobs escaping her lips, the sound of her grief fading away when she slams her bedroom door closed behind her. Colton hesitates in the hallway, his gaze on Leia. Her eyes have filled with tears, and she looks as though Lucy just struck her.

"Ley," Colton says. "I'm sorry."

He looks down at his feet, and Leia kneels in front of him, her hands on his shoulders. "Can you tell me what happened, Colton? Please?"

He looks at her and shakes his head. "Is it true?" he asks. "Are you and Dad in love? Is that why he left Mum?"

What the fuck? She looks at me, but I don't know what to tell her. I know as much as she does. This is coming out of nowhere, and I don't know what the right thing to do or say is. Most of the time I feel like I'm winging it as a parent, and this is one of those moments that makes me feel inadequate.

"It's true that we're in love, Colt," I tell him. "It's not true that Leia is the reason Mum and I got a divorce. You only met Leia after we moved here, remember?"

Colton stares at me, his gaze assessing, as though he's searching for a lie. "Mum says that you knew Leia before we moved here. She told us that maybe auntie Amara introduced you two before, but that you definitely knew each other before."

Fucking Alice. "I didn't meet Leia until after your mum asked for a divorce, sweetheart. By the time I met Ley, our divorce papers were already signed. It had nothing to do with Leia."

Colton just stares at me, looking conflicted. "Mum said that you would say that, but that it isn't true. She said that Leia is the reason you two are no longer together. She told us that Leia is a home wrecker."

I look up at Ley, her expression breaking my entire fucking heart. Fuck. What the fuck is even happening? How the fuck could Alice do this to us?

"It isn't true, sweetheart," I tell him. "I promise you that it isn't true. Your mum and I always would've gotten a divorce. Leia had nothing to do with it. You know her, don't you? Hasn't she always loved you, always taken care of you?"

Colton nods, but he looks unsure. "But you two lied to us. Mum says that you lied and said she's our nanny when she's your girlfriend because you wanted us to get used to her."

I sigh and run a hand through my hair. "Colt... ever since Leia became your nanny, haven't you slowly come to love her? Haven't you started to see her as part of our family? It was like that for me, too. When she started working as your nanny, she truly was just your nanny. But over time, I fell in love with her. Can you understand that?"

He purses his lips and nods. My sweet boy gets it, because he fell for Leia too. Not quite in the same way as I did, but she stole his heart too.

"Mum is still hurt, Colt. You know how you sometimes say things you don't mean when you're angry? Mum is like that too. Mothers and fathers are only human, Colt. Sometimes we say things we don't mean. Mum is a little hurt that Leia has become part of our family. It's hard for her, you understand? That's why she's saying these things, but she doesn't mean it."

He nods and looks down, as though he's processing my words and trying to determine what is true, and what is false. I wish my kids didn't have to go through this at all. Fucking Alice. That fucking bitch. I've done everything I could to ensure we could co-parent, even opening up my home to her at the risk of upsetting Leia. I gave her more than she deserved after she tore our family apart, and she repaid me by stabbing me in the fucking back.

"Go on," I tell Colton. "Go get ready for bed."

He nods and walks up the stairs, his expression pensive. The kids have gone through so much. I can't believe Alice is putting them through even more.

"I'm sorry, baby," I tell Leia. I walk up to her and cup her cheeks before pressing a kiss to her forehead. "I'm so fucking sorry."

She shakes her head. "We knew this was a risk. I... I didn't really expect this, to be honest, but we'll handle it. I'm sure we will."

I look into her eyes, taking in the quiet confidence mingled in with her pain. This is what I love most about her. The pure resilience. I've never once experienced stability like this before, and it's insane how secure it makes me feel in our relationship. Leia isn't going to walk away from me now that things are hard, and I have no doubt that we'll get through whatever awaits us.

"I'd better go check up on Lucy."

She looks away. "I should leave."

I shake my head. "No way. They know now anyway. We move forward now, baby. Together."

She nods, and I press another kiss to her forehead before walking up the stairs, praying I can talk some sense into my daughter when what I want to do is drive back to my ex-wife's house and demand a fucking explanation.

"Lucy?"

I open her bedroom door to find her curled up in a ball, crying. It's the kind of sobs that break my damn heart, the kind that rock her entire tiny body.

"Oh, Luce," I murmur, sitting down beside her. I'm going to tell her everything I just told Colton, but I suspect she won't hear me. Not the way Colton did.

Forty-Eight

LEIA

"Lucy, please talk to me," I whisper. "I miss you so much, Luce. Doesn't a small part of you miss me too?"

She ignores me and continues to eat her dinner. It's been over a week, and she hasn't spoken a word to me. Thor and I weren't sure what the right thing to do was, but we decided that I'd continue to work as their nanny, sticking to our routines as much as we can. Alice picks them up from school, and they spend the afternoon with her. Depending on whether Thor is working late or not, he'll pick them up for dinner. If he's working late, I'm the one who goes to pick them up.

I worry that things will never be the same, no matter how hard I try. I'm worried that the relationship we built is gone. She won't stay in the same room as me unless she's eating — the only time Thor has mandated that she must be at the table. Lucy won't even take the books I keep trying to give to her, and Colton and I haven't played a single game together.

I thought Colton, at least, might not hate me... but I was wrong. He avoids me as much as Lucy does, and it breaks my heart. I don't know what to do or say. I understand that me being with Thor feels like a betrayal to them, but there's no way for me to make them understand that I'm not the reason their mother left them. They're too young to understand that even if I weren't in the picture, their parents wouldn't be getting back together.

I never even realized how much these two kids have come to mean to me. They're right here with me, yet I feel empty. It isn't even about Thor, or them accepting me as his partner. It's not that at all. It's about us, about the relationship I had with Lucy and Colton outside of my relationship with their father.

I swallow hard and glance at Colton, who won't look up from his food. Is my presence harming them? I haven't seen them smile even once in the last week, and the home they fought to build has turned into a battlefield. This isn't what I want for them.

"How was your test, Colt?"

He looks up briefly before glancing back at his plate. "Good."

"Oh yeah? How did you do?"

He shrugs, and I inhale deeply, desperation clawing at me. I miss them so much. I miss the way Colton laughs, and the way he'd teach me Roblox slang. I miss reading with Lucy, and the way she used to confide in me. I miss hanging out, and feeling like we were a united front, even against Thor when we needed to be.

I love them like they are my own, and for a moment, I let myself believe they felt the same way. It was never my desire to steal Alice's place in their lives, but perhaps subconsciously, that is exactly what I was trying to do. I wanted a place in their lives that was never mine to take. I foolishly assumed that there'd be space for both Alice and me, and I'm starting to realize that I was wrong.

I rise from my seat when I hear the front door slam closed. I've never felt unwelcome here, but I do now. I can't be here. Not when my presence is hurting both of the kids.

"Your father is home," I tell them softly. "I'd better leave. I'll pick you up from your mom's tomorrow, so I'll see you then."

I turn to walk away, my mind torturing me with memories of

me putting the kids to bed, helping them with excuses to stay awake a little longer, the three of us scheming against Thor. Those days will never turn from memory to reality again.

"Leia?" Thor murmurs when I meet him in the hallway.

I shake my head. "I need to go," I whisper.

"Don't, baby. Please."

He walks up to me and cups my cheeks before dropping his forehead to mine. "Princess," he whispers. "I'm sorry. I'm so fucking sorry. Seeing your heart break like this... I can't fucking take it. Tell me what to do. Tell me how to make this better?"

I rise to my tiptoes and press my lips against his, recharging myself. "You can't," I murmur against his lips. "There isn't anything you can do, my love."

I take a step away, and he grabs my hand, his gaze pleading. "I need to go, Thor. I can't do this tonight, okay? I just... I can't."

He looks at me with such desperation that I almost cave, but I can't. "We're fine, Thor. We're okay, I swear. I just need a moment, that's all."

He nods, but he doesn't let go of my hand. His hand doesn't slip out of mine until the very last moment, as though he's hanging onto us as much as I am. I wonder if it's enough.

I'm absentminded as I walk to my car, my mind made up as I get behind the wheel. This can't go on like this. I can't see the kids hurting like this.

Before I consciously realize what I've done, I'm parking in front of Alice's house. I second-guess my decision for a split-second, but then I shake my head. Maybe this is the worst idea I've ever had, but I can't not do this. I'll always live with the regret if I don't tell her what I need to.

"Leia." She sounds mildly surprised to see me when she opens the door, her eyes trailing over my body.

"Alice," I say, my voice breaking. "Please stop. I'm *begging* you. Just stop."

She smiles then, pure viciousness flickering in her eyes. "I won't stop until you leave my husband."

I don't even have it in me to remind her that their divorce went through over two years ago, and they've been separated for much longer than that. "Alice, I honestly couldn't care less if you want to pursue Adrian and do whatever you can to win him back. I will never compete with a woman over a man. Never. If you manage to win him over and he decides the give you another chance, good for you. Will I have lost the love of my life? Yes. But it'd be for the best, because if you can seduce him away from me, he was probably never truly mine to begin with. That's something I might never get over, but I'd learn to live with it."

I pause and run a hand through my hair, trying to find the right words. "I'm not asking you to stop trying to get Adrian back, Alice. I'm asking you to stop sabotaging my relationship with Lucy and Colton. I'm not just asking you, I'm begging you."

A tear drops down my cheek, and I swipe it away angrily. I don't want to show her my pain, but it's overflowing.

"I love your kids, Alice. I love them with my entire heart and soul. When Lucy cries, my entire heart breaks, and it feels like I might suffocate. When anyone even remotely mistreats them, I see red. When Colton is sick, I can't sleep because I'm so worried that I can't close my eyes. When Lucy first moved here and would barely speak, hiding away behind her books, I was the one who coaxed her playful-self back out. I did it because I understood. I was once her, too. It wasn't part of my job — I did it because I care. When she's lonely, I'm the one who takes her on a girl's day out on my day off. When Colton has a bad day, I'm the one who plays games I don't even like with him. I'm telling you this not to offend you, or to make you feel like I'm trying to take your place, because that's the last thing I ever expect to do. I'm telling you this to illustrate that I truly, wholeheartedly, love them. I've done all I can to make sure your absence doesn't harm them, that they continue to grow up to be the wonderful people I know they'll be. Even if I walk away now, can you say with full certainty that the woman who comes after me will love them like I do? If there's going to be a woman in their lives who isn't you, wouldn't you rather have someone who loves them as much as she loves their father?"

I take a step back and sniff, my tears falling uncontrollably. "Please think about what you're doing to them, Alice. I'm begging you. Yes, you're killing me, and yes, this is putting considerable strain on my relationship with Adrian. But honestly? He and I are going to be okay. We'll recover from anything you might throw at us. Will the kids? If I end up marrying Adrian, will what you're doing right now be in their best interests?"

I take one last look at her, hoping she heard anything I just said, but knowing that she probably didn't. She's won. My relationship with the kids is destroyed, and it probably won't recover.

Forty-Nine

ADRIAN

I sit up when my office door opens and Leia walks in. I rarely see her at school these days, and each time I do, it just lights up my whole day. "Hey baby," I tell her.

She looks nervous, and I grin when my eyes drop to the document in her hands. "Ah, the elusive dissertation."

She smiles then, and my heart skips a beat. Things have been hard for us lately. The two of us have been under considerable pressure, both of us weighed down by the knowledge that us being together is hurting the kids.

I knew it'd be hard, but I never expected it to be this painful. It isn't just watching the kids hurting that's hard — it's equally hard to watch Leia's heart break over them. It doesn't matter how many times I speak to Alice or the kids, the damage is already done.

Leia places her dissertation on my desk and smiles at me nervously. "I can't believe I finished it. It feels like the end of an era, you know?"

I nod and grab her hand, raising it to my lips. "I've read it a thousand times now, but I'll read it one more time before we arrange your defense. You're going to kill it, baby. Almost done."

She nods and sits down opposite me, looking as tired as I feel. I hate seeing her so weary. Leia has always had this spark, and it's missing today. It has been for a while now.

"I'm going to lock the door and then I need you to come sit in my lap. I really need a hug," I tell her.

The edges of her lips turn up into a small smile, and I breathe a sigh of relief. The door lock clicks and I grin as I walk back to my seat, opening up my arms for her.

Leia smiles at me as she walks up to me and straddles me, placing her head on my shoulder. I wrap my arms around her and hold her tightly.

"It's hard, isn't it?"

She nods.

"You're doing so well, though. I'm so proud of you, baby. You've handled everything that's been thrown at us with such grace."

Ley presses a kiss onto my neck, her lips lingering. "It can't be easy for you either. You worked so hard to get the kids to settle into their new lives here, only for them to be thrown back into turmoil."

I nod and rest my head against hers, my hand stroking her back soothingly. "You did most of the heavy lifting," I admit. "I just keep reminding myself that if we can do it once, we can do it again. The kids are resilient, and they'll be fine. Will you?"

I wrap my hands around her shoulders and pull her away slightly so I can look into her eyes. "Will you be fine, Leia?"

She smiles at me, but there's such sadness in her eyes that I can barely take it. Her hand trembles as she brushes her index finger down the bridge of my nose, over my lips, and then lets it fall away. The way she's looking at me makes me feel like she's committing the image of me to memory, and it kills me. Am I losing her?

"Leia," I whisper as I lift my hand to her hair, threading my fingers through her hair gently, until the tips of my fingers brush over her scalp. I lean in and kiss the edge of her mouth, my touch gentle. She seems so broken at this moment, and all I want to do is keep the pieces of her together. Even if we fall apart, I'll collect every broken piece and keep them safe, so we can rebuild together.

I kiss her again, and she tilts her head, returning my kiss. It's different today. Her touch is laced with heartbreak, and it kills me.

I tighten my grip on her hair and kiss her harder, the way I know she's always liked. Leia moans softly, and I deepen our kiss, giving her all of me. She places her hands on my chest and slides them upward, until she's got one hand in my hair, while she unbuttons my shirt with the other.

I groan when I feel her fingers on my skin. Her touch turns frantic, and she rotates her hips in my lap, grinding against my cock as she pushes my shirt off my shoulders. I tug at the blouse she's wearing, wanting it off, but not wanting to stop kissing her.

Her lips never leave mine as she moves her hand to my trousers, undoing it before reaching for my cock. Leia doesn't say a word as she rises to her knees, tearing her lips off mine for a brief moment as she pushes her underwear aside. I take that moment to pull her blouse off, watching my girlfriend as she lowers herself on top of me slowly, taking the tip of my cock with her eyes on mine. "Oh God," she moans as she takes me in deeper, until she's sitting in my lap. She's so fucking tight, I can barely take it.

I reach behind her and undo her bra, until she's in nothing but the skirt bunched around her waist. Leia rocks her hips, the sensation fucking divine. I'm so deep inside her, and I've got her so close. This is perfection.

She cups my face and leans in, kissing me as she rides me, slowly at first, before she increases the pace, fucking me harder, faster, using me as she pleases.

One of her hands moves between us as she starts to touch herself, and it takes all of me not to come right there and then. I wrap my hands around her waist as I move her up and down my cock, loving the way she takes it all, the way she moans for me.

"Thor," she moans against my lips, "I love you."

I groan and kiss her harder for a moment before tearing my lips off her so I can kiss her neck. "I love you more," I whisper into her ear before kissing her in that spot that always makes her shiver.

"I'm going to come," she warns me, and I nod.

"Then come for me, Princess. Come all over my cock, baby."

And she does, tightening her grip on my hair as her pussy squeezes me tightly, taking right over the edge with her. I come deep inside her, filling her up. Leia sighs happily and rests her head on my shoulder, hugging me tightly, the two of us still intimately connected.

I hold her close and stroke her back soothingly. "Feel better now?"

She nods and kisses my neck, her body entirely relaxed now. "Much better."

I squeeze her tightly and sigh. "I love you, Leia. Throughout all of this, I want you to remember that. I want to be the person you lean on, the one you go to when you're hurting. Will you let me be that for you?"

"You already are, Thor."

I sigh and cup the back of her head, enveloping her in a big hug. I wish there was more I could do. I wish I could take away her pain.

Fifty

LEIA

"How was school?" I ask as we walk through the front door, a brave smile on my face even though my heart is falling to pieces. The kids haven't spoken a word to me since I picked them up, and you'd think that I'd have gotten used to it in the last few weeks, but I haven't. Each day is as hard as the last one.

Thor and I keep hoping for change, both of us hoping that this behavior will only last until Alice leaves next week, but I'm not sure. I think the damage to our relationship is permanent, and I wonder what Thor thinks of it.

It won't be long before he cuts me out of their lives entirely. My presence isn't a good influence on them anymore. The home that was filled with love and laughter has become so quiet and devoid of joy, and it's all my fault.

How can my relationship with Thor even last like this? When the kids make it so clear that they don't want me in their lives, how is he going to summon the willpower to stay with me? What would a future together even look like?

Flashes of a quiet dinner table and reluctant kids on family trips go through my mind, and my heart sinks. We were so happy before they found out about us, until Alice came back. I hoped that speaking to her would help, but it hasn't. If anything, the kids seem angrier each time I pick them up from her house, and I have no idea what she's telling them.

It's hard for me, because the last thing I want to do is be the person who questions them, or who badmouths their mother in any way. I can't even warn them not to believe everything she says without checking in with us first, because it'll just lead to me losing whatever remaining credibility I have.

"Your teacher called me, Colt. Looks like your grades have dropped a little lately. We're going to go through your homework together after dinner."

With Alice taking them after school, I haven't had a chance to check their homework or tutor them whenever I feel they need it. The added turmoil caused by our family situation likely isn't helping either. Thankfully, Lucy seems to be doing okay. I can manage tutoring Colton, since he doesn't seem to hate me as much as Lucy does... but I cannot imagine having to tutor Lucy when it's so clear she can't stand me.

Almost as if on cue, Lucy stomps up the stairs and slams her bedroom door closed. I'm so close to snapping and telling her I'll remove her door if she slams it one more time, but I'm not her mother. I never will be. Disciplining the kids is Thor's job, and I won't be overstepping anymore.

"She doesn't really hate you," Colton says, his voice so soft I nearly miss his words.

"What makes you say that?" I ask carefully.

"It's just because she misses Mum. I don't believe the things that Mum says about you, but Lucy does. She thinks that if you leave, Mum might come back to live with us again."

I nod. I get it, I do... but there's nothing I can do to fix that. I can't make her see reason. Adrian talks to her every single day, and it still isn't enough.

"And what do you believe?"

He shakes his head. "I don't know. I don't want Mum and Dad to fight all the time again, and Dad says he doesn't want to live with Mum again. I think it maybe isn't your fault. I don't really know, Ley, but you're never mean to me. Mum says you're only nice to me because you have to be, but I don't believe that. Our other nannies were never like you. You're different."

I nod, unsure what to say to that. He's far more perceptive than I thought he was. I guess, maybe, the kids do realize what is going on, but I'm just an easy target, someone to blame for their parents' separation so they don't have to deal with the pain.

"I don't know about your mum and dad, Colt. I can't tell you if they'll ever get back together or not, because it isn't my decision to make," I tell him. I sincerely doubt Thor would ever give Alice another chance, but I can't tell Colt that. "But I can promise you I'll always love you. I'm not nice to you because I have to be. It's because you're very special to me, and I love spending time with you. I've missed you, Colt."

He nods and grabs my hands, an apologetic look in his eyes. "I miss you too, Ley... but I'm all that Lucy has. I have to be on her side. Mum and Dad are always fighting, so I have to side with Lucy."

I sink down to my knees and place my hands on his shoulder. "I get it, Colton. But as her brother, it's also your job to guide her when she's wrong. If you think she isn't doing the right thing, you need to guide her back onto the right path. Sometimes, in life, we lose our way. It's because of the people around us that care about us, that we find our way back. Remember that, okay? Not just for now, but for in the future too. You and Lucy should always stick together, but always question if what you're doing is the right thing to do." I tap on his chest gently. "If it doesn't feel right in here, then take some time to think about what's going on, and what you should do, okay?"

He nods and stares into space as I pull out his textbooks. Had I known getting him to do homework with me would've made him talk, I'd have done it so much sooner.

The two of us work together harmoniously until the doorbell rings. I look up in surprise when Amara follows the housekeeper in.

"Hey, babe," she says, a knowing look in her eyes.

Relief rushes over me at the sight of her. I've kept from telling her too much, because Adrian is her cousin. I don't want to put her in a position where she'll feel like she needs to speak to him, because I know what she's like. If she's worried about me, she won't be able to keep her mouth shut.

"Amara? What are you doing here?"

She smiles knowingly at me and places her handbag on the table. "I'm here to hang out with my niece for a bit. Where is she? In her bedroom, I assume?"

I nod, and Amara walks past us, toward the stairs. Did Thor ask her to speak to Lucy? I'm worried this is going to backfire.

"Go on," I tell Colton. "You can go play games now, but we're picking this back up tomorrow. You've done enough for tonight, but there's still a lot left to do."

He nods and takes off running, a smile on his face. It hits me right in the chest. When was the last time I saw him smiling like that?

I'm anxious as I walk up the stairs, terrified of what Amara might say. She's my best friend in the whole wide world, but she's unpredictable and ballsy. Lucy needs to be handled with care right now.

I pause right outside Lucy's bedroom door and lean against the wall beside it, ready to intervene if I need to.

"So, I heard you hate Leia now. Is that true?" Amara asks, and I freeze. What does she think she's doing?

"We should just get rid of her, shouldn't we?" Amara adds when Lucy stays silent. "My mom hired her, so while your daddy can't fire her, my mom can. Shall I ask her to just fire Leia?"

"I thought she was your best friend," Lucy says, her tone accusing.

"Yeah, we used to be, but now she's always here, and she never has time for me anymore. I want her to stop spending so much time with you, so I get her to myself again. She's always taking you to places, hanging out with you, taking you to watch movies and going shopping with you. You even went to the spa without me. If she stops working here, she'll stop spending so much time with you, and I can have her back."

Seriously, what is she doing? My nerves are skyrocketing, and I'm itching to walk into Lucy's room to drag Amara out.

"You can't," Lucy snaps. "You can't have her back."

"Oh, but why? You don't like her anymore, right? We can just find you a new nanny for when your mom leaves next week. You don't need Leia. You don't even speak to her anymore. She's sad here, and I don't like seeing my best friend sad. Every time you ignore her, her heart breaks. I don't want to see Leia cry anymore. If you don't want her, she should go work for a family that loves her. It's not like you'd miss her, would you? I'm sure there's a little girl out there who would love to spend time with Leia, and who would appreciate her and would never ignore her."

"Leia was crying?" Lucy asks, her voice soft and concerned.

"You make her cry every day. Every time you ignore her, her heart breaks. Every time you accuse her because of something your mom told you, something you know isn't true, she cries. I've had enough of it, Lucy. If you don't want her, I'm taking her away. You know just as well as I do that it isn't Leia's fault your parents aren't together anymore, and I'm tired of you hurting her."

My blood starts to boil at the harshness in her voice. Lucy has been through so much already, the last thing she needs is to be chastised like this, but it also doesn't feel right to intervene.

I grit my teeth when I hear the sound of Lucy sniffling, as though she's holding back tears. When Amara walks out minutes later, she glances at me apologetically.

"Someone had to do it, Leia. You won't, and Adrian can't. Someone needs to make sure they stop and think about what they're doing and what's happening."

She walks away, leaving me standing there, surrounded by the sound of Lucy crying. It breaks my heart, and today, more than usual, I wish I was still the person she turns to when she's hurting.

I wish I could take her in my arms and make the pain go away, but I can't. Not when I'm the cause of it.

Fifty-One

ADRIAN

I'm calm as I walk into the dean's office, though I have a feeling I know what's coming. Things haven't been great for Leia and me lately. I didn't think it could get any worse, but I wouldn't be surprised if I'm about to be proven wrong.

"Professor Astor."

I nod at Dean Ferguson and tense when I see Leia sitting in the seat opposite him. Goddamn it. Why the fuck can't my girl and I just catch a fucking break? I sit down next to her, resigned.

"It has come to our attention that the two of you have breached our no-fraternization policy," the dean says, looking regretful. He glances at me, a hint of reluctance in his eyes.

"What happened?" I ask him before reaching for Leia. I grab her hand and entwine our fingers before placing our joined hands in my lap. She tenses, but I shake my head slightly, indicating that it'll be fine.

"Every member of the college's board received a set of photos this morning," Dean Ferguson says. He reaches into his desk drawer and pulls out a manila folder that he slides toward me.

I open it up and clench my jaws when I find myself staring at dozens of photos of Leia and me, most of them taken right outside my front door. Because she's paranoid about her family seeing us together, we make sure we're rarely in public together, yet this folder somehow seems to have evidence of every single time I kissed her goodnight. What the fuck?

Leia gasps, her breathing uneven. She's panicking. I need to fix this as soon as possible. There's no way I can let this affect her. She has too much on her plate already. The look in her eyes tells me she's close to losing it, and I know how much she'd hate to burst into tears right now. I need to get her out of here.

"Leia and I are in a committed relationship. She has already handed in her dissertation, and I wasn't the one who helped her with the majority of it. By the time I joined Astor College and became her advisor, she was already nearly finished with her dissertation. Her previous advisor will be able to confirm that."

Dean Ferguson nods. "We've launched an investigation. If Professor Larson can confirm she wrote most of it without your guidance, then Leia may be allowed to defend her dissertation."

He hesitates and looks away. "I... I can try to save Ms. Sital's academic career, but I can't save yours."

I chuckle and cross my arms. "That's quite alright. My grand-father needs me to take a more active role in the business, anyway. It's about time I give up on my career as a professor. If I really wanted to stay, I'd just have you and the board replaced."

Dean Ferguson's eyes widen, as though realization is finally sinking in. Yeah, I'm not just any Astor. I'm one of Harold Astor's only two grandchildren, one of two direct heirs to his fortune.

"I will, however, be forced to do just that if Leia experiences any issues with her dissertation. She's nearly done, and she worked her ass off. I'll be damned if all that hard work is taken away from her."

He nods in understanding, but I know it isn't just in his hands. Whether or not Leia will walk away unscathed is unknown. It'll depend on the college's board members, and everyone else involved. This won't be easy. Even if they do allow her to defend her dissertation, they'll give her a hand time.

"I'll hand you my formal resignation tomorrow morning," I tell him, before pulling Leia up with me. "Do what you can to save the future Mrs. Astor's academic career, and I'll see to it that an adequate donation is made," I say, tipping my head toward Leia. The shock on his face is priceless, but I think it's the shock in Leia's expression that I love most.

I pull her out of his office, her hand in mine. Since the truth is out, there's no way I'm letting her go.

"Future Mrs. Astor?"

I smirk at her. "You and I both know it's only a matter of time. This is it for me, Leia. You're the one. I don't care if he knows it too — it's not like that knowledge can harm us now that the truth is out."

I doubt she even realizes how much my academic career meant to me. I'd never have given it up for anyone but her, and I didn't even think twice.

My phone buzzes, and I grimace when I see eleven missed calls from my grandfather. I see he's been notified, too.

"Let me drive you home," I tell her. With how anxious she seems, I don't want her driving. "I need to go see my grandfather."

Leia nods and follows me. "Are you sure everything is going to be okay, Thor? I'm so worried. You're losing your job, and I might lose my doctorate. How could you possibly be this calm?"

I lean over and buckle her in, pressing a kiss to her lips before straightening. "I'm calm because I've got you, Leia. All I need is you and the kids. Everything else is replaceable."

I won't ever tell her that my heart is breaking. She doesn't know what my job as a professor meant to me, and I'm going to make sure she never finds out. Leia would never forgive herself, even though she isn't to blame.

My thoughts are still on her by the time I pull up in front of my grandfather's office. Leia seemed distraught when I dropped her off, and I'm not sure what I can do to make things better.

Lately I keep finding myself in completely powerless situations. I can't stop the way my kids are alienating her. I can't stop Alice's behavior without ruining my relationship with the kids. I can't keep my job now that the college found out about us.

It feels like everything in my life is falling apart, and the way I'm clutching at the strands of my life just makes it unravel faster.

"Adrian!" my grandfather snaps when I walk in.

I grit my teeth when I see the photos on his desk.

"I will give you three seconds to explain why you're involved in a major scandal at the college I entrusted you with."

He looks furious, and for a moment, I'm speechless. This isn't how I wanted everyone to find out about Leia and me.

"I'm going to marry her," I say simply.

Grandpa's anger drains away, and he looks at me. "What?"

I nod and gather the photos on his desk into a pile before straightening it. "There's no doubt in my mind. She's the one."

"What are you talking about, Adrian? She's your nanny and a student. I love Leia as much as Amara does, but this is incredibly inappropriate."

I slip the photos into the envelope and hold it against my chest. "Is it? The kids love her, and so do I. I never thought I'd want to be with anyone else again, Gramps. She's different."

"You lost your job over her, Adrian. You were so desperate to be a professor that you've been procrastinating on taking on more responsibility within the company. It was your mother's greatest dream to see you follow her path, and you're giving that up for her?"

I smile at him. "It was my mother's greatest wish to see me happy. Truly happy. She never got to see that while she was alive, but I'm still honoring that wish. I'm happy now, Gramps. I hear you. I know what this is costing me, but you're failing to see all that I'm gaining. Leia is unlike any woman I've ever met before. Alice has been giving us hell, and she's handling it with such grace. Hell, I think she loves the kids more than she loves me, you know? I know what I'm doing. She's worth it."

He looks at me long and hard. "You and Amara... you're both the same. Stubborn to a fault and willing to sacrifice everything for the one you love." He looks away and shakes his head, but I see the reluctant smile he's trying to hide. Leia is worth anything. She's given her all for my family. It's about time I do the same for her.

Fifty-Two

LEIA

Anxiety hits me hard when my head hits my pillow, the events of the last few weeks flashing through my mind. I thought it was bad enough to have Alice back here, but this is infinitely worse.

This could destroy my career. I want to continue my research and become a professor, but that might not be possible. Even if I manage to finish my doctorate, my academic career is likely over. They won't take me on as a researcher if rumors about my lack of professionalism start to circulate.

I bite down on my lip in an attempt to temper my panic. Lucy and Colton hate me, Thor just lost a job I know he loves, and my education and career path are on the line. I wish I could convince myself to regret my relationship with Thor, but I can't. Even as my whole life falls apart around me, I can't imagine leaving him. Despite everything that's happened, I'm certain we'll make it through.

I just wish that they hadn't found out before I finished my PhD. Just a few more weeks, and we'd have been in the clear. I was planning on telling my parents about him after I finished my education and he ceased to be my professor. Similarly, in just a few weeks' time, there's nothing the college could've done, as I'd no longer be a student there.

The timing couldn't be worse, and I can't help but wonder if Alice is behind it. I never should've shown up at her house like I did. I was foolish to think I could change her mind. If anything, I've just made the situation so much worse.

I sit up when my phone buzzes, the edges of my lips tipping up into a small smile when I see Thor's name on my screen.

Thor: *come outside. I'm parked around the block in the usual spot.*

I slip out of bed, my anxiety melting away at the thought of being in his arms. I never used to sneak out of the house before. I used to be far too worried about my parents catching me, yet tonight I've got my robe and slippers on in record time.

My heart races as I walk around the block, my eyes darting around to see if any of the neighbors are out and about, but the streets are empty.

I find Thor leaning against his car, his expression as tired as I feel. "Hey, Princess," he says, smiling.

I smile at him and jump into his arms. He holds me close and buries his face into my hair, inhaling deeply. "God, I missed you."

I sigh and hug him tighter. "You saw me today," I reply, even though I feel the same way.

"I can't do this long-distance thing anymore," he tells me, making me chuckle.

"You live twenty minutes from my house, Thor."

He nods. "That's twenty minutes too long."

My heart skips a beat when I look into his eyes. I've never felt anything like this before. Even when the whole world wants to rip us apart, this still feels right.

"Are we going to be okay?" I ask, a small seed of doubt making its way through.

Thor cups my face with both hands and nods. "We will be. We had a rough start, but we're going to be okay, my love. This sets us back a little until they conclude their investigation, but that's okay. I have full faith that they'll clear you. They'll let you graduate."

"You lost your job, Thor. You once told me that your mother was a professor, and I know how reluctant you are every time you go into your grandfather's office. I know your heart lies with teaching. How can you just give that up? Maybe they'll let it go if we agree to break up. There are just so many signs telling us that we shouldn't be together... how long are we going to ignore all that?"

He tenses and buries a hand into my hair. "We're going to discuss this once, and then I never want to hear you say this again, you hear me?"

I nod, my heart unsettled. It's something that's been on my mind, and though I've tried not to voice it, something feeling right doesn't mean it *is* right.

"Tell me about these signs, Princess."

"It's just everything... the kids suddenly hating me, you losing your job, my dissertation being on the line. We're risking so much, and for what? So you can destroy your family and I can destroy my career?"

"Leia," he says, his voice soft. "The kids love you, and you know it. There's no one better suited for our family than you. You're perfect for me and the kids in every way. I genuinely think you might love them more than you love me, and I wouldn't have it any other way. Lucy and Colton have their mother whispering lies into their ears, and for the time being, we can't do much about that without jeopardizing their relationship with her. Give it some time, and they'll get used to us being together. They'll have to, and we'll do our best to make it as easy on them as we can."

I nod. I know that what he's saying is true, but I can't help but worry. I'm worried I'm hurting the kids, and that's the last thing I want to do.

"When I moved back to the States, I came to an agreement

with my grandfather. He helped me with the kids, the move, and the house, and in return, I would join the family business. He gave me a maximum of three years to learn how the family business works, and to give up on my teaching career. That was always coming, Princess. At some point, I was always going to start working for my grandfather. Your dissertation is something I can't fully control, but they won't want to lose their jobs. When it comes down to it, I'll have everyone who makes a fuss replaced. It's Astor college, baby. They won't want to offend me. Have some faith in me, okay? I'm trying my hardest not to burn any bridges, but for you, I will. Hell, I'll burn down the whole damn world for you if I need to. Being with me won't cost you your career. I'll make sure of it."

I rise to my tiptoes and kiss him, losing myself in him for a moment. Thor tightens his grip on my hair, his touch rough, desperate, as though he's feeling everything I'm feeling. The two of us are holding onto each other as though we're all we've got, and in many ways, that's true.

We're both breathing hard when I pull away, and he brushes his thumb over my lips tenderly. "I love you, Leia."

I look up at him and grin. "I love you more," I whisper.

"It leads me to the next topic I wanted to discuss with you, Princess. I was dead serious when I said you're too far away. I want to meet your parents. I know they're traditional, and I know that there will be several further trials awaiting us, but I want to be with you."

"I... it doesn't really work that way," I tell him cautiously. "We don't really... we don't do that. Having boyfriends isn't really a thing. It's weird, I know, but..."

"I don't think you understand, Leia. I want to meet your parents so I can ask for your hand in marriage."

I stare at him in disbelief. "You... you want to do *what*?"

He bites down on his lip and looks away. "I asked Amara about it, and she said I can't just propose to you. She told me I can't even think about doing that until I have your parents' approval."

I feel the tears gathering in my eyes, and my throat closes up with overflowing emotions. The last few weeks have been so hard that I was certain he'd leave me. I thought it'd all be too much, and that he'd give in to the kids. I didn't think he'd still want to marry me.

"Ley," he murmurs, leaning in to press a kiss to my forehead. "Don't cry, baby. It breaks my heart when you do that."

I wrap my arms around him and burst into tears. "I just love you so much," I sob. "I want nothing more than to be your wife."

He hugs me tightly, one arm wrapped around my waist, and the other buried in my hair. "I'll still propose to you, baby. I want you to have it all. Being with me won't cost you anything, I swear it. I won't let you miss out on all the traditions you love, but I'll also go down on one knee so you'll have that experience too. Being with me won't cost you your career, it won't cost you your dreams. I promise you, Princess."

I nod and tighten my grip on him. This. This is exactly what I needed after a few horrible weeks. Thor and I... maybe we'll be fine, after all.

Fifty-Three

LEIA

The kids were just a little nicer to me today, not ignoring me entirely when I asked them how school was, and it's a little silly how happy it made me that they actually answered. Just a few more days until Alice leaves, and I can't wait. I hope we'll finally be able to repair our relationship once I'm spending every afternoon with them again.

I'm grinning to myself as I walk into my house, but my smile melts away when I find my parents sitting in the living room, both of them looking furious. My mother stares at me with crossed arms, while my father has a letter in his hand, his expression showcasing his rage.

"What is this, Leia?"

He waves the letter in his hands, and I frown. *Please, no*, I silently beg. I can't take much more. After the last couple of weeks, I'm at my breaking point.

"You are under investigation at school? Dating a teacher, huh?" my father says, and my heart drops. This can't be happening. Panic seizes me, and I start to tremble.

"It isn't like that," I try to explain, but my mother shoots me down with a look.

"You aren't dating your teacher? It says in the letter you're dating Professor Astor. Is he Amara's cousin?" she asks, her tone harsh.

I nod, my throat closing. We wanted to wait until the school's investigation wraps up to them tell them about us. This can't be happening like this.

"He's the one you're working for? Divorced and two kids?" Dad asks. His voice is soft, but it's clear to me that he's furious.

"Yes, Dad," I say, my voice trembling. "He's a great man, I promise you. I was going to tell you about us soon."

"What kind of good man would date his student? Open your eyes, Leia. If he cared about you, he would never risk your education. You need to break it off with him. Immediately."

I can feel the tears gathering in my eyes as I shake my head. "Dad, I can't do that. It isn't like that, I promise. We're serious about each other."

My dad holds up his hand and stares me down. "He has two children, he's divorced, and he's your teacher. Not to mention, his religion and culture are different to ours. What will people say?"

I burst into tears and sniff, hating that I can't control my emotions. I never could around my parents. "I get how it sounds, I do, but it isn't that simple."

Dad narrows his eyes and shakes his head. "You're his nanny, no? What does he think? That he can just marry you and get his children a new mother? Who does he think he is? Does he know about your fertility problems?"

I nod hesitantly, and Dad looks away. "So he thinks it's okay for you to marry a divorced man with kids? Because he thinks you can't have any of your own?"

I cross my arms, my heart breaking. "He never said that, Dad. *You* did. He's never once treated me like I'm flawed, like I'm broken. He doesn't care if I can't have children, but he's willing to try."

"He doesn't care because he already has his children, Leia. You deserve better than this. You can't become a stepmother. Is he even willing to marry you, or is he just playing around with you? What about your culture and religion? Will you abandon it all for him? He has already divorced once. What makes you think he won't divorce you too — if he even marries you at all?"

I shake my head. "No. I don't know. Nothing in life is guaranteed, Dad. How am I supposed to tell you we'll never divorce? I don't think we will, and I'm serious about him."

"You're not listening to me, Leia. You have to break up with him. I will never accept him as my son-in-law. You will not marry a divorced man with kids. You're young. You have your whole life ahead of you. What are you even thinking? You work for him. Are you insane? You risked your sister's company by getting involved with him, and you risked your education. What good man would ever let you do that? If he was serious about you, he would have come to see me already. He would have explained, and he would have waited for you. Stop being so delusional and break up with him."

"What would make you accept this, Dad?" I ask, my voice tinged with desperation. "Would you accept it if we had a full-blown Indian wedding?"

Dad hesitates. "You think he would give you that? Think again, Leia. You aren't even the first woman he's marrying. He doesn't understand our traditions. Even if you do have children, are you going to raise them differently to his other children?"

The truth is that I don't know. I don't even know if we can have children, so I haven't thought about how I'd raise them. I'm not overly religious, but my culture means a lot to me.

"What about your sister? You risked her company's reputation, and for what? Does she know about what you've done?"

I shake my head. It's true. Me being with Thor could harm her company's reputation. One of her nannies getting together with her employer could keep some of her prospective clients from hiring her. I bite down on my lip to keep from crying, but hot tears stream down my face nonetheless.

"I will not tell you again, Leia. I will never accept this match. You need to break up with him."

"And if I don't?"

"Then you'd better pack your bags. You can come home when you get to your senses."

I sniff loudly and turn to walk away, my body shaking with the force of my sobs. I can barely see through my tears as I rush up the stairs.

"Leia," Mom says, following me into my bedroom.

"He doesn't mean it. You know what your father is like, don't you? He just wants what's best for you. He's worried, that's all."

I shake my head. "If he wanted what's best for me, he'd at least hear me out. He'd meet Adrian before condemning him."

"He's worried about your reputation, and our reputation as a family. He doesn't want you to be with a man who was your boss and your teacher. That is bad enough as it is, Leia, but he's divorced and has two kids. Can you blame your father for wanting more than that for you?"

I shake my head as I throw clothes into my bag, my heart breaking. "Not you too, Mom. Please."

She sits down on my bed and looks at me, her expression torn. "Leia, you're my baby. You've always been my baby. I want the world for you, and this man... he isn't it. It might seem like he is now, but he can't give you everything you deserve when he has two children that will always have to come first."

I wipe my tears away angrily and shake my head. "You haven't even stopped to ask if I'm happy. I love his kids, Mom. I don't mind the fact that he already has kids — not even in the slightest."

"Leia..."

I shake my head and throw my bag over my shoulder. "I'm going to Asha's house. I'm not coming back until Dad agrees to at least meet Adrian."

Mom sighs as she watches me walk away. Every time I think things can't get worse, they do. I'm not sure how much more I can take.

Fifty-Four

LEIA

Asha opens the door with a knowing look in her eyes, and I burst into tears all over again. She hugs me tightly, and I fall apart in her arms.

"Oh honey," she says, rubbing my back. She just holds me like that until my tears subside, and then she pulls me into the house.

I'm only mildly surprised when I find a cup of masala tea waiting for me. Looks like Mom called her the moment I walked out of the house.

"Adrian Astor, really?" she asks.

I nod and raise my teacup to my lips, unsure what to even tell her. "It really isn't what it seems like," I murmur, my voice barely above a whisper. "I first met him nearly three years ago. Even back then, I knew he'd be special. You know how you always tell me you knew your life would never be the same again when you met Rohan? That's what it was like for me. The time wasn't right then, and I didn't see him again until recently."

"He's your teacher and one of our clients, Ley."

I nod. "I know. It isn't ideal, and neither of us expected this to happen. We tried to fight this thing between us, Asha, I promise you."

Asha nods, a small smile on her face. "But you can't fight fate."

I shake my head. "You can't. When I saw him at Amara's wedding, I walked away, never expecting to see him again. Then he showed up as my PhD advisor, and I thought I could perhaps handle that... but when you assigned me as his nanny, I just... I tried to get out of that, but I couldn't. I should've walked away from that job, but I couldn't walk away from Lucy and Colton. It had nothing to do with Adrian, and everything to do with him."

Asha takes a sip of her tea and nods. "I get it, Ley. When destiny comes calling, there's nowhere to hide. I assume Dad lost his shit because Adrian is white, divorced, and has kids? You know what he's like. In his mind, our entire family and all our neighbors are already gossiping about you, and I'm pretty sure he thinks you just dating him has made you forget about every single one of our traditions."

"Yeah, he wasn't happy, to say the least. He told me to break up with Adrian."

"Will you?"

"No. I can't. I'm well aware that no one will accept us being together, Asha. I know that we're in a precarious position, and that it won't be easy... but despite that, despite everything, my life is better with him in it."

She smiles at me and places her hand on my shoulder. "Then that's all that matters. So long as you're aware that this will be difficult, you'll be okay. You need to speak to Adrian, though. Winning over Mom and Dad won't be easy. If he isn't willing to suffer through a week-long Indian wedding, then I'm not sure they'll ever accept him. Honestly, I don't even know what to tell you. This is going to be difficult, but you have my support."

I drop my head to her shoulder and nod. "I love you, Asha."

"I just want you to be happy, Ley. In the last couple of months, you've looked happier than I've ever seen you before. I don't care who he is or what his story is. If he makes you happy and you're certain he's the one, then you have my blessing. For so long I didn't think you'd ever want to get married, yet here you are, willing to defy Mom and Dad for the man you love. In a weird, twisted way, I couldn't be happier about it. You've never had anything you thought was worth fighting for."

She's right. For years, I just went through the motions, too scared to really put myself out there. Until him.

"You do realize I have to fire you, right?"

I tense, my eyes widening. "*What*?"

"Ley, you're dating a client. You broke our no-fraternization policy."

I sit up and run a hand through my hair. "But who will take care of the kids?"

Asha looks at me and smiles. "I'll send the very best staff members I've got, okay?"

I nod, my heart sinking. Perhaps some distance is exactly what the kids and I need, but it doesn't sit well with me.

Though everything I've ever wanted is now closer in reach, it seems further away. Now that everyone knows about us, there should be no obstacles left, yet at each turn, a new one arises.

Are Thor and I going to make it to the other side unharmed, or will everything we're about to go through leave scars?

Fifty-Five

ADRIAN

The kids look surprised to find me standing in front of their mother's house. I suppose they've gotten used to Leia picking them up every night, but that's all over now.

"Make sure you hug Mum goodbye," I tell them. "She's leaving tomorrow." Good riddance. She and I could've co-parented the kids harmoniously, but she ruined it. As their mother, she's supposed to put her kids first, but she never did.

I watch as the kids run back to hug her one last time. Alice's eyes are on me, and the way she smiles makes a chill run down my spine. "You'll miss me, won't you, Adrian?"

I glance at the kids and force myself not to snap at her. "I'm sure the kids will miss you."

Alice grins at me, a provocative look in her eyes. "How is Leia? Is she still in the picture?"

I grit my teeth and force a smile. "Of course she is."

Alice chuckles, and it takes all of me to keep standing here. "She won't be for long. I hope she's able to graduate, you know? Poor thing."

I take a step forward, tempted to yank the kids away from her, but I resist. I knew it was her. That fucking bitch. Can't she see what she's fucking doing? It's the kids she's hurting most. Now that she's leaving, they'll need Leia, but Ley won't be there. Because of her. Because of her petty foolish behavior, our kids won't have the one person who was able to pull them out of the funk they were in when we first moved here. My Princess and I can weather every storm. No matter what we're put through, we'll be fine. The same can't be said of the kids.

"I've let it go this time, Alice. I won't extend you that same courtesy ever again. You've reached the limits of my patience, and there's nothing I won't do to protect my family. That includes Leia now. It does not, however, include you. Remember that."

She stills, her eyes widening. "You never once cared about me that way," she says. "When I asked for a divorce, you didn't even blink twice."

I smile at the kids and tip my head toward the car. "Get into the car, you two. I just need to talk to Mum for a moment."

The two of them exchange glances I can't decipher before they both nod and walk to the car. I watch them until the door closes behind them before I turn back to Alice.

"You and I are over, Alice. What is the point of reminiscing now? I don't understand what you're doing. You're the one who walked away, so why are you sabotaging my happiness now? The kids love her, Alice. After a couple of extremely tough weeks, she's the one who returned the joy we took from them. Why don't you want that for them?"

"You don't get to replace me so easily, Adrian. This girl came out of nowhere, and you're suddenly smitten? She used our children to get to you, and I won't have it. She's Amara's best friend, so she knows what your net worth is."

I close my eyes and inhale deeply as I pray for patience. She did not just insinuate that my girlfriend is a gold digger, did she? Is this all about the money? My lawyers prevented her from getting her hands on any of my assets, and I know she's still bitter about it.

"She didn't come out of nowhere, Alice. Remember when I came back from my trip to see my grandfather two years ago? I told you about a woman I'd met and slept with, because I wanted to be transparent with you about everything since we were still living together, despite our divorce papers already having been signed."

She nods, the confidence leaving her expression.

"That was Leia. I've thought of her every day from the moment I walked away from her. Hell, even when she walked back into my life, I tried to resist. I get it, Alice. I didn't want to introduce a new woman into the kids' lives either, and perhaps if she hadn't been their nanny and hadn't stolen their hearts, she wouldn't have stolen mine so quickly." I pinch the bridge of my nose, wishing I could make her understand. "She's the best thing that ever happened to me, Alice. I get that you might not want to hear that, considering our history, but she is. You walking away from me is the best thing you ever could've done for me. I'm happier now. I didn't even realize how intensely unhappy I was with you, because it'd just become the status quo. You were right when you told me you never felt loved, like I didn't appreciate you. I wish I could've been the man you wished I were, but it's too late for that now."

It's hard for me to explain that I get it now. I get why she felt so lonely in our marriage. What I thought was love was really just comfort. She and I had gotten so comfortable together that we refused to acknowledge that we'd outgrown each other. We were never right for each other. What I feel for Leia, I never felt for Alice.

"This isn't what was meant to happen, Adrian," she says, her voice breaking. My heart clenches when a tear drops down her cheek. I don't want to hurt her, not after all the pain we barely survived, but I need to make it clear to her that we're over.

"I was so angry when you signed the papers so easily, but I was certain that you'd change your mind, that you'd fight for me. I expected you to realize what you were losing, but you never did. If anything, you seemed relieved."

I look into her eyes and shake my head. It shouldn't surprise me that she asked for a divorce just to see if I'd finally fight for her. That's how emotionally deprived I'd made her. I was never able to meet her needs, and I see that now. I can't explain why it's different with Leia, but it is.

"I'm sorry, Alice. I'm sorry things didn't work out between us. I know it would've been best for the kids if it did."

She nods, and for once, I see defeat in her eyes.

"I love Leia," I tell her. "I won't give up on her, no matter what you do to us. I will, however, start defending my family. Nothing you do will touch her. I'll make sure of it. Remember that all your actions have consequences, though. The kids may be young and impressionable now, but they won't always be. If you want to be a part of their lives, then you need to start thinking about what kind of influence you are, and whether they'll want to keep you in theirs."

I take one last look at my ex-wife and sigh before walking away. What a fucking mess. I hope we make it out of this shit intact, but with each passing day, I'm more worried.

The kids sit up in their seats when I step into the car, their gazes on the back of my head. "What is it?" I ask.

"Why are you picking us up?" Colton asks, his tone annoyed. I smile to myself as I start the car. The kids have mostly been ignoring Leia, and now they're unhappy they didn't get to see her today?

"Leia will no longer be working for us. She's not your nanny anymore."

I wasn't surprised when Asha called me to tell me she was replacing Leia, and since Ley seemed fine with it, I am too. It'll only be for a little while, after all.

"Why?" Lucy asks, sounding shocked, and just a touch scared.

"You guys haven't been talking to her, and it's clear you don't want her around anymore. Shouldn't you be happy?"

The kids look at each other, and though the sorrow I see in their eyes should tug at my heartstrings, it really just reinforces how good of a lesson this is for them. "If you keep pushing people away, they'll eventually leave. You can't expect someone to stay if you don't treat them well. She's left now, so what are you two going to do about it? Do you want her to stay away, or do you want her to come back? I won't talk to her for you. If you miss her, you will have to tell her yourself."

I see the helplessness they exude, but I won't give them the support they need. I won't give them any way to keep blaming Leia for anything.

"Mum said *she* asked for a divorce... is that true?" Lucy asks.

I look at her in my rear-view mirror and nod. "Yes, Lucy. Like I told you before, what happened between your mother and me was just between the two of us. It had nothing to do with Leia."

She swallows hard and look out the window, a distraught expression consuming her lovely little face.

Looks like my kids have a lot to think about, and so do I. Leia's family isn't going to be easy to conquer, but I have to win them over.

Fifty-Six

LEIA

I pin my phone between my ear and my shoulder as I open up my laptop. "Are you really not going home?" Thor asks. "You've been at your sister's house for a week now."

I shake my head, even though he can't see me. "My dad told me not to return until I came to my senses, and I never will. I won't leave you just because he's scared of what people might say about us."

"Why don't you just come stay here? I miss you. The kids hate the new nanny, and they're so sulky I can barely take it. It's obvious they miss you too. Maybe we should just put them out of their misery."

"They miss me, really?"

He chuckles and I hear the sound of rustling sheets. I let my eyes fall closed for a moment, imagining myself in his bed. I miss him, but we've had to be cautious lately. The last thing I want to do is aggravate the college's board, or my father.

"They do. I see Lucy staring at her phone for hours every day, and I don't think it's her mum she's scared to text. Those two still talk on the phone regularly. Colton can't even play the games he's so obsessed with without his expression turning somber. Honestly, it's like I'm watching them go through their first heartbreak, except the one they lost is you. I hope they snap out of it soon and reach out to you. I told them I won't do it for them."

I click on the Discord app that Colton and I often use to chat on, and my heart skips a beat when I see a message from him.

"Adrian," I whisper.

"Wow, full name, huh? What happened?"

"You let Colton go to bed without checking that he doesn't have his laptop."

"I... how do you know that?"

"He messaged me. He's online right now. Don't go intervene, please? I want to talk to him."

"Is it chat or audio?"

"Usually we start off on chat and then we use our microphones."

"Can you put me on speaker, Ley? I want to know what this kiddo is thinking."

I nod and do as he asks, placing my phone next to my laptop. I'm nervous as I click on the chat.

RBLXCOLT

Ley?

I transcribe for Thor as I type my reply.

PRINCESSLEIA

Hi Colt. Everything okay?

RBLXCOLT

Yes. I couldn't sleep, and I just wanted to message you to tell you that I don't hate you at all. I keep thinking about you being sad because you think I don't love you anymore, and it makes me sad too.

Oh, this kid. My voice wavers as I tell Thor what his amazing son just messaged me.

"Told you, baby. The kids miss you like crazy. I knew Colt would be the first to cave. How are you going to respond? You're going to give in immediately, aren't you? Make them sweat a little. We should help them build some character. They should learn that there are consequences to all their actions, and that they can't get away with hurting feelings so easily."

He's probably right, but I can't do that to my Colt.

PRINCESSLEIA

> I know you don't hate me, Colt. It's okay. I do miss you, though. Is your new nanny nice to you?

"Leia," Thor warns me when I read out my message. "You can't let the kids get away with the way they treated you."

I ignore him. They're kids who were heavily influenced by their mother. I won't punish them any further. I just want to restore our relationship as best as we can.

RBLXCOLT

> she's okay but she's not you. I miss you too. I know Lucy does too. Can't you just come home? Please, Ley?

I sniff loudly, my heart clenching tightly. Home, huh? "Thor," I murmur. "What do I say?"

I hear him chuckle over the phone and let my eyes fall closed for a moment, imagining his smile. "It's up to you, Princess... but I'd also like you to come home."

"Should I say that I can come see him? I don't know. What about Lucy?"

"I don't think you should, to be honest. I don't want them to think that you'll always forgive them. I doubt Alice is done messing with us, and I want to be sure they won't respond this way the next time. They need to learn that they can really lose you. I don't want this to become a vicious cycle."

"I get it," I tell him. "I do, but how can I possibly deny him? I miss him too. I want to see him, Thor."

He sighs loudly, the way he does when he's trying to be patient. I get what he's saying, but my heart hurts at the thought of Colt sitting in his room with his laptop, mustering up the courage to message me. I just want to hug him and tell him everything is okay.

"I'll just tell him that I would love to see him, but that I'm still a little hurt and worried that Lucy won't want to see me. How about that?"

"Yes, that's fine," he agrees. "They're blessed to have you, you know? We all are."

I smile as I type my message to Colton, hoping it'll set him at ease while still teaching him what Thor wants him to learn.

Colton turns his mic on, and I warn Thor to remain quiet while I speak to him. I'm more than willing to let him in on this conversation with his son, but I don't want Colton to feel betrayed.

"Ley," Colton says. "I miss you. I'm sorry that I went along with Lucy and ignored you like that. It was mean, and you always tell us to be kind."

"I miss you too, Colt," I tell him honestly.

"If I talk to Lucy and she wants to see you too, will you come? Lucy was really shocked when she heard Mum say that *she's* the one who asked for a divorce. I never believed that anything was your fault, but Lucy did. I think she feels guilty. When she gets like that she just gets quiet because she doesn't know what to say, but I'm so sure that she really misses you."

"You really know your sister well, huh?"

"We're *twins*, Ley."

"All right, Colt. Talk to your sister, and if she wants to see me too, I'll come over. How does that sound?"

"Yes!" he says, his relief and excitement evident in his voice.

I chuckle, I can't help it. "Shouldn't you be asleep right now, sweetheart?"

He groans. "I'm going to bed now, Ley. I promise. I just wanted to speak to you."

I love this kid. I really do. "Okay, go to bed now then. I'll speak to you soon, okay?"

"Can I message you tomorrow? Will you play Roblox with me tomorrow after school, like we used to?"

Thor would probably want me to hold back a little, but I can't. "Yes," I tell him. "I'll be online. I promise."

My heart is overflowing with happiness when I close my laptop after making sure Colton went offline. "You couldn't help yourself, could you?" Thor asks the moment I unmute him.

"Nope," I admit. "I can't wait till I see them again!"

He bursts out laughing, and I snuggle into my pillow, imagining myself in his arms. "I love you, Leia. You're already the best mother to my kids, but I still can't wait to have a daughter with your eyes and smile. I bet she's going to be beautiful."

I bite down on my lip, speechless for a moment. "It won't be easy," I whisper. "We might never have a child."

Thor sighs, the sound of sheets rustling coming through the phone. "Princess, I didn't even believe in fate before I met you, but how could this be anything but? I met you two years ago and never forgot you. Within days of me returning to the country, you showed up in front of me. Each time I fought our connection, you showed up in another part of my life. This was inevitable. You and I are meant to be, and you know it. I'm certain we'll have a child together. I can already see her when I close my eyes."

I swallow hard, my emotions getting the best of me. "I love you so much, Thor. I'm so worried about everything. The kids, my parents, my education... everything."

"Don't be, baby. I called your sister today. My family and I are going to see yours tomorrow."

"What?"

"Asha recommended that we sort of ambush them, which I'm

not sure I agree with, but I'm going to follow your sister's lead on this. I get that it won't be easy, baby, and yeah, right now it does feel like all the happiness we fought so hard for is turning against us. But here's the thing... all relationships have ups and down, just like life does. We're going to face obstacles together, and the ones we've faced so far would've broken up most couples, but not us. If anything, it just made us stronger. I've never felt more certain about anything in life. You're it for me. I might not be the man your parents might want for you, but I'll spend the rest of my life proving that no one could ever love you like I do. I swear to you, Leia. You'll never regret choosing to be with me. I might not fully understand your culture, but I'm willing to learn. You won't miss out on anything by being with me. I'll make sure of it."

Hot tears stream down my face as I clutch my phone tightly. He's right. Through all these trials and tribulations, my heart has stayed calm. He's the one for me — now we just need to make the world accept it.

Fifty-Seven

ADRIAN

Amara comes crashing into the living room, looking just as flustered as I feel.

"Are you ready?" she asks.

I shake my head. "No. I'm terrified."

My grandfather and Aunt Charlotte walk in with a mountain of gifts in their hands, and my palms start to get clammy. I wipe them on the suit trousers I'm wearing and straighten my tie. We can't fuck this up. I don't think I've ever been more nervous.

"What's going on?" Lucy asks.

I turn to the kids, unsure what to say. I know Colton and Leia are talking again, but I'm not sure about Lucy. While I absolutely can't delay this any longer, with Leia and her father at odds with each other, I also don't want to tell the kids anything if it's going to worsen their relationship with Leia.

I pause for a moment, but in the end, I decide on the truth. "I'm going to Leia's house to ask her parents if she can officially join our family," I say, my voice soft. "Her family is very traditional, so I have to ask them for permission. In Leia's family, it would be customary for me to go to her family with my family. We'll be bringing them gifts and sweets, in the hopes they'll say yes."

Lucy's eyes widen. "If they say yes, Ley will come home?"

I straighten my tie, worried about how Lucy might react if I clarify the situation further. It doesn't escape my notice that she used the word *home*, just like Colton did. They already consider this Leia's home too, even if things aren't what they used to be between them. "If they say yes, I'd like to marry Leia. She'd come to live with us, forever."

"*Forever?*" Lucy and Colton repeat in unison.

I nod. "If your family is supposed to go, then why aren't we coming with you?" Colton asks, his tone high-pitched and upset.

"Since you don't seem to like Leia much these days, I didn't think you'd want to come."

Lucy crosses her arms, a stubborn expression on her face. "Who said we don't like her? We never said that."

I run a hand through my hair as I stare down my two kids. "I don't think you understand how important this is. If her parents say no today, we would lose her forever. Maybe that's what you want, I'm honestly not sure anymore, but I can't let that happen."

Lucy sniffs, tears gathering in her eyes. "We don't want that, Dad. We love her. We *do*. I was wrong... I was mean to her, but I didn't... I-I love her."

Colton wraps his arm around his sister and nods. "Yes, Dad. We love her, and we want Leia to join our family, too. You have to let us come with you."

"You want to come with me?" I ask, confused.

They nod. "I... I don't know. If you come with me, you have to be on your absolute best behavior. This is extremely important, you understand?"

"We know," Colton says.

"Great!" Amara says. "I've brought you clothes to wear."

I look at my cousin, who's holding up a suit for Colton and a pretty dress for Lucy. What the fuck? I thought we agreed the kids wouldn't be coming with us, so why the hell does she have clothes for them?

She winks at me as though she knew this would happen, and I shake my head. Amara scares me sometimes.

"Go on, get changed then," I tell them.

Amara nods and hands them their clothes. "You'd better be on your absolute best behavior," she tells them. "If you aren't, Leia's heart will never recover. She's already hurt, but if today goes wrong, her heart will always stay broken. You understand that, right? This is your chance to make up for how you ignored and hurt her," she warns.

The kids nod, both of them looking determined. They rush up the stairs with their outfits in hand, and I pray it goes well.

"It's going to be okay, Adrian," Grandpa tells me. "We aren't strangers to Leia's family. They'll hear us out at the very least, even if it's just because they love Amara so much."

I nod, but I can't seem to calm my raging heart. I'm so scared something will go wrong today. The worst part is that I totally understand why they think Leia can do better. I just hope they'll give me a chance. It hurts to know that the kids I love so much are part of the reason I'm not deemed a suitable partner for Leia, when I'm so proud of them.

The kids walk down the stairs with Star Wars items in their hands, and I frown. Colton is holding a limited-edition Millennium Falcon LEGO set he got from my grandfather, and that likely cost a bomb, while Lucy is holding a Baby Yoda replica.

"You said we were bringing gifts," Lucy says. "Leia's dad likes Star Wars. That's why he named her Princess Leia."

"Um, right," I mutter.

"Aren't you the sweetest?" Amara says. She ushers them out the door and to her car, and I follow along.

"I'll take your aunt," Grandpa says, heading to his own car. I nod as I join Amara. They both went all-out, taking what appears to be the most expensive cars the Astor family owns. We're definitely aiming to impress today, and I hope that won't backfire.

I don't think I've ever known genuine fear before today. The thought of them saying no scares me. Where would that leave Leia and me? I'm not sure she can take yet another blow. She might act stubborn right now, but I know how much her family means to her.

I barely even realize when we pull up in front of Leia's house — I'm totally consumed by my fears. Grandpa has had me negotiate multi-million dollar deals in the last couple of weeks, and that didn't faze me. This? This has me feeling completely terrified.

The kids are clutching their gifts as we approach their front door, and my heart nearly stops beating when Amara presses the doorbell.

Asha opens up almost instantly, as though she was expecting us. She tries to look surprised, but fails miserably. "Amara!" she yells. "Come in!"

She opens the door wide and lets us in, mouthing 'quickly', as though she's scared her parents will throw us out the moment they realize what's going on.

We follow Amara's lead and take off our shoes before following her into the living room. Leia's parents sit up in shock when they see us, and for a moment they just stare at us. For some reason, I expected really traditionally dressed people, but they're anything but. Amara's dad is wearing jeans and a t-shirt, while her mother is wearing a summer dress. They look just like my family does.

"Auntie, Uncle," Amara says. "Let me introduce you to my cousin, Adrian."

Fifty-Eight

ADRIAN

Leia's father rises to his feet, anger crossing his face. "Amara," he says, his tone reprimanding. He looks at Asha next, who looks down at her feet.

Amara smiles at him, and much to my relief, Grandpa steps forward. "It's good to see you again, Akshay."

The two men shake hands while my aunt greets Leia's mother, and I wait for Grandpa to turn to me before I take a step closer to Leia's dad. From what I understand, my parents are meant to lead this meeting, but since mine are no longer with us, the task falls to Grandpa. It seems somewhat unusual to me, but I'll do what I can to play by the book if it makes them more inclined to give me a chance with Leia.

Akshay's eyes drop to the kids, who seem just as nervous as I am, and much to my surprise, he smiles at them reassuringly.

"We brought you some gifts," Grandpa says, and Amara jumps into action, presenting them with one gold-colored metal plate filled with Indian desserts and fruits, and another on which she's placed several presents that look like folded fabric to me.

Asha perks up at the sight of them, her eyes wide. "Are those seriously genuine Sabyasachi saris?"

Amara smirks and nods. "Of course they are. Would the Astor family give you any less than this?"

She reaches for them, but her father pushes her hand away. "Don't take them," he warns. I can't quite tell whether he's angry or not, but he certainly doesn't seem happy to see us.

"Why are you here, Harold?" he asks, ignoring me altogether.

Grandpa wraps his arm around my shoulder and tips his head toward me. "I'm sure that you've been made aware that my grandson lost his heart to your daughter. We are here today to formally ask you for her hand in marriage. We want Leia to join our family."

Leia's mother gasps, her hand rising to her chest in shock. "Sit," she tells us, earning herself a warning glance from her husband, who she ignores.

We sit down in their living room, and I wipe my clammy palms on my trousers. Leia's dad hasn't so much as looked in my direction, and that doesn't bode well. Asha warned me not to speak unless spoken to, and to leave this conversation to my grandfather, but I'm itching to fall to my knees and beg the man for his daughter's hand.

"I brought you this gift, Grandpa," Colton says, walking toward him with his LEGO set. Everyone falls silent as we watch Colt, and I hold my breath, praying he doesn't snap at Colt for calling him Grandpa. Since when are my kids so courageous?

I breathe a sigh of relief when he actually takes the LEGOs from him. "I'm Colton. I can't wait to become your grandson. Our Princess told us so much about you. She says you love Star Wars."

"Your princess?"

Colton nods. "She's our Princess Leia."

Lucy jumps in and pushes her gift toward him too. "Ley told me you always let all the kids read as much as they want, even after bedtime. Is that true?"

He nods at her and stares at the Baby Yoda toy she gave him, trying his best to keep from smiling and failing. "Wow," Lucy says. "I can't wait to become your granddaughter. Maybe I can read past my bedtime then, too."

He chuckles then, and I tense, strangely even more scared. I watch as he puts the toys down and glances at me, his gaze trailing over my face slowly. He hesitates, but then he shakes his head. "I won't let you marry my daughter."

My heart fucking drops and a rush of panic floods me. "I understand that I'm not the man you would've chosen for her, but I swear to you I'll spend the rest of my life proving to you that I am the right man for her."

He stares me down, and I straighten my shoulders. Until today, I'd never met a man more intimidating than my grandfather.

"Is that what you were doing when you ruined her education? When you damaged Asha's company's reputation? A good man would have waited for Leia to finish her PhD. A good man wouldn't have kept her working as a nanny. What is my daughter to you? Are you trying to turn her into a free housekeeper? Why would I let her be with a man who would risk her future?"

"Akshay," Grandpa says, holding his hands up. "You know that I love Leia as much as I love my own granddaughter. If I thought Adrian had any wrong intentions, I wouldn't be sitting here today. He loves her and wants to marry her. I support their union and would gladly welcome Leia into my family."

I scoot forward in my seat and look at him, trying my best to portray sincerity. "I completely understand where you're coming from," I admit. "I can promise you that no harm will come to Leia's future. I've given up my career as a professor to ensure that." I hesitate then, unsure whether I'm supposed to address his other comments or not. "Leia is absolutely free to pursue any career she wishes. I do not in the slightest expect her to be a stay-at-home parent. I wholeheartedly support her ambitions."

He crosses his arms then and stares me down. "So, what

happens when you find another young nanny? Will you fall in love with her, too?"

I struggle to stay calm and grit my teeth. "That would never happen. Truthfully, I have known your daughter for years. I don't believe in fate, sir. Or, well, I didn't use to. Not until Leia. Fate has pushed us together in every way possible, and I'm certain she's my destiny. Nothing and no one will ever replace her."

"Tell us about yourself," Leia's mother says, offering me an encouraging smile. "Our impression of you prior to today hasn't been good, but I can acknowledge that you're here today in an attempt to do the right thing. You've embraced our traditions and brought your grandfather, aunt, and cousin, as well as your two kids. You did your research, and you've impressed me enough to warrant some curiosity. Tell me why I should allow you to marry my daughter."

"The truth is that I want to marry Leia for selfish reasons. I'm well aware that she would be able to find someone much better with ease, but I cannot imagine a life without her anymore. I know that she could find someone younger, someone who is at the start of their careers, their lives... but I love your daughter beyond compare, and I think I can make her happier than anyone else can. Of course Leia would never have to work if she marries me, but there's no stopping her, and she's got her sights set on an academic career. As an Astor, I can pave the way for her. She won't let me, but I can. I can offer her opportunities she'd other-wise have to fight for, and I can make sure she'll never lack anything. Above that, I can offer her a life filled with love and joy. I will make sure that every single day, she feels appreciated and cared for, and each day, I'll remind her she's perfect just the way she is, that her flaws aren't flaws at all, that she's enough as she is."

I fall silent and look away, wishing I was better with words, so I can make them understand how much I love their daughter. "Truthfully, I want to give your daughter the entire world. If she asks me for it, I'd try to take the moon out of the sky to give it to her. There's nothing I won't do for Leia."

She nods, seemingly satisfied with my answer, and turns to the kids. "Lucy and Colton, right?"

They nod, and I place my hands on their shoulders.

"Do you like Leia? Is she nice to you?"

Lucy straightens and nods. "Leia is my best friend. I think I might love her more than I love my dad. She's always nice to me, and I never have to tell her how I feel, because she always knows. Daddy is right. I can't imagine a life without Leia anymore, and if you don't let her join our family, I think it would really break my heart."

Oh, my beautiful little girl. I should probably feel bad about the way she's guilt-tripping Leia's mother, but I really don't.

"Lucy is right," Colton says. "Leia is my best friend, too. She's always there for us, and she always stands up for us. We really love her, more than she even knows."

These kids, man... I'm so glad I brought them. I don't think this meeting was going well until they spoke up.

"How do you feel about Leia becoming your stepmother? You already have a mother, after all."

The kids both tense and look at each other before nodding. "We would like that," Colton says. "Lucy and I have thought about this a lot. She's already our kind of like our mother, even if she never marries Dad. It would be nice to have two mothers."

Both of Leia's parents look surprised, and truthfully, I'm pretty shocked too. So far, I've only mentioned Leia joining our family, but I never explicitly mentioned her becoming their stepmother. I was worried it'd affect them aversely, but it looks like I was worried for nothing. I suppose having Alice needle them the way she did ensured that they started to think about Leia as their stepmother.

"I'll give you a chance," Leia's mother says, and the relief is fucking unreal.

"Pooja," Leia's father warns, but she holds her hand up and silences him.

"I've seen my daughter move forward in life seemingly

completely numb. She's been lonely and guarded for years now, until you. I saw the change in her and suspected it was a man, but I didn't say a word because I wanted her to be happy for once. Leia has suffered enough. I never thought she'd find someone who would make her see her worth, but you do. I see the way she smiles, the way she's stopped hiding behind her work. She's present now, in every interaction. She's no longer lost in thought, or escaping when faced with a difficult situation. Somehow, you've made my baby feel whole again, and for that, you deserve a chance."

She places her hand on her husband's knee and looks at him pointedly before turning back to me. "We will not agree to you marrying her until we see you resolve the mess you made. I want my daughter to graduate without a single speck of dust on her reputation, and the same goes for Asha's company. If you can do that, we can talk again."

The relief we all feel is palpable, and Amara sinks back in the sofa. This isn't quite what we were hoping for, but it's more than I expected. So long as they're giving me a chance, I'll win them over.

"You won't regret this," I promise them. What they're asking for is already in the works. Just a few weeks, and I'll be sitting right here again, asking for her hand once more.

Next time, they'll say yes. I'll make sure of it.

Fifty-Nine

LEIA

I'm a little nervous as I walk through Thor's front door. I haven't seen the kids in a few weeks, and though Colt and I have started gaming together again, and Lucy and I have been texting a little, I'm still worried it'll be awkward to see them.

"Leia!"

They both jump up from the sofa when they see me and run up to me, hugging me with such force that I stumble backward.

"I can't believe you're really here," Lucy says, and Colt nods as he tightens his grip on me.

"I missed you," I tell them.

"We missed you too!" Colton says.

Lucy pulls away and hesitates, looking guilty. "I'm sorry," she says, and Colton nods in agreement.

I hug them again and shake my head. "It's okay. It's all okay."

The relief I feel is unreal. I was so worried things wouldn't be the same between us anymore, but we seem fine. It's almost as though the divide Alice tried to create has vanished entirely, and I hope that's true.

"Are you back for good now?" Colt asks excitedly.

I shake my head and grin as I pull them over to the sofa. "No. I heard you tried real hard to convince my dad yesterday, though? I'm really proud of you for speaking up and trying to win him over. You did really well."

"He still said no."

"It wasn't really a no," I explain. "More of a maybe? It's like when I tell you that you can play games, but only after you finish your homework. So long as Daddy sorts some stuff out, we'll be okay."

They nod, but I can tell they're having a hard time truly understanding the situation. I don't blame them. Thor and I did create a bit of a mess.

I smile when Emily, their new nanny, walks in. I've worked with her before, and she's always been really lovely.

"Good evening, Leia," she tells me, nodding politely. Emily has over thirty years of experience working with VIP clients as a nanny, and she's probably the best Asha's firm has got.

"Hi, Emily! It's so good to see you."

She grins at me before tipping her head toward the stairs. "It's about time you guys get ready for bed."

They both groan, and I run a hand through Colt's hair soothingly. "I'll come tuck you in, okay? You have school tomorrow, so you'll need to get an early night, but I'll come back to see you tomorrow too."

Now that my parents have essentially given Thor permission to court me, they should be okay with me going to see him every once in a while. I would hate to upset my parents, but I also won't give up on Thor and the kids. I suspect my mother knows that.

I sit back on the sofa and let my eyes fall closed as I listen to sounds of the kids messing around in the bathroom. I missed this. It might sound crazy to some, but I genuinely missed this. I've always loved how lively this house is, and soon, I might actually become part of this all too.

I sit up when I hear the front door close, followed by footsteps. Thor pauses in the doorway when he sees me, his eyes widening.

"Leia," he murmurs, my name a prayer on his lips. "You're here."

He walks over to me and pulls me to my feet. I crash into him and smile at his excitement as I rise to my tiptoes, his lips finding mine instantly. He kisses me with such desperation that my restless heart stills.

"How are you here?" he whispers against my lips.

"I told Asha I'd be staying with you tonight. I'm going back home to my parents tomorrow, but before I do that, I wanted to spend a night with you. I have a feeling they won't make it easy on us, and I need this. I need you."

He drops his forehead to mine and inhales shakily. "You have no idea how much I've missed you. Honestly, last week has been hell. Only being able to speak to you on the phone, I hated it. I was so damn close to rocking up on your sister's doorstep, demanding to see you."

I shake my head and press a soft kiss to the edge of his lips. "You did the right thing. I needed time with my sister, and I definitely needed some time to think about the situation with my parents. I cannot believe you went to ask for my hand. What were you thinking?"

He chuckles and cups my cheeks. "Should I have proposed to you first? Amara told me that that's not how it went for your sister, so I thought... was I wrong?"

I smile and shake my head. "You did the right thing. I'm just shocked that you went out of your way to do that for me. One of the things my family is worried about is that I might lose sight of my culture, and you're proving to them that I won't, without me even having to ask it of you."

"Leia, I've always said that you won't lose out on anything by being with me. I mean it. I know how important your family is to you, and I would never ask you to change anything that helped shape the woman I love. There are going to be things I don't understand, and there are going to be times I might behave insensitively, but I'm willing to learn."

I nod and wrap my arms around him, hugging him tightly. Throughout all of this, my heart hasn't wavered, but I'm worried. I'm worried my parents won't change their minds, or that the investigation about my dissertation wraps up unfavorably. It feels like I'm trying my very best, and it's never enough.

"Come with me," Thor says, grabbing my hand. He leads me to his bedroom and sets up his telescope, lowering it to my height. "It's a clear night tonight, so we should be able to see a lot."

I nod and follow along as he positions me in front of it. "Remember how to look for Orion's belt?"

He wraps his arms around me and presses a kiss to my neck as he talks me through the constellations I should be able to see.

"You know, Leia?" he says, his lips brushing over my ear. "Years ago, you asked me how I could love astronomy without believing in astrology. I still think the two are separate, but I also think you may have had a point. The way we found each other twice, the way life kept pushing us back together when we tried to resist... I know everything feels hard right now, and I know you think the obstacles we face might be signs that we shouldn't be together. But, my love, there are just as many signs telling us we're meant to be. Ultimately, I believe we create our own destiny, and you are mine. I'll always choose you, Leia. No matter what."

I nod and turn in his arms, the way I did back then, my arms wrapping around his neck as I rise to my tiptoes.

"And I will always choose you, Adrian."

He smiles and leans in to kiss me, my worries melting away at his touch, even if it's just for a few moments. It feels like faith is all I've got left, all that's keeping me going.

Please, I silently beg. There's nothing else I've ever wanted out of life. Just this. Him. Please, for once... let the path to happiness be unobstructed.

Sixty

Leia

My heart aches as I stare at my front door, part of me unwilling to walk in. It's been over a week, but my argument with my parents is still fresh in my mind.

If my mother hadn't called me, asking me to come home, I never would have. I wonder what my dad would have done. Would he truly have let his pride and stubbornness ruin our relationship? Would he truly want to lose me over this?

I inhale deeply as I unlock the door and walk in, the house quiet. I drop my key in the little bowl we've got in the hallway, feeling conflicted. I'm still hurt and angry, and I know my parents will only make it worse.

"Leia."

I look up to find my mother standing in the doorway, her expression regretful.

"You're home."

I nod and walk past her toward the stairs, unsure what to even say to her. I know what my parents are like. It doesn't matter what I say, they won't listen, anyway. They're more concerned with what people will say. Their pride and ego will take precedence over my happiness.

"Leia," Mom repeats. "Come have some tea."

I want to say no. I don't want to play this game where we act like everything is okay, even though they're breaking my heart. I don't want to put up pretenses. I don't have it in me.

"Mom," I say, my tone weary. "I'm tired."

"It's just a cup of tea, Leia. Just a few minutes, okay? I haven't seen you all week."

Her tone sounds concerned, and my heart squeezes painfully. This is so incredibly hard on me. I know she means well, and I know she's worried about me, but those same worries are going to cost me everything.

"All right," I say in the end, unable to deny her when she's looking at me that way, looking as hurt as I am.

I follow her into the kitchen and sit down at the breakfast bar as she pours me a cup of steaming milky masala tea. I watch as she adds a huge helping of sugar for me, my heart aching.

Mom rests her elbows against the kitchen counter and looks at me, her expression guarded. "So, Adrian Astor came to our house yesterday."

"I know. You called me to tell me about it, remember? And so did Asha."

She nods and purses her lips. "What do you like about that man?"

I take a sip of my tea, both of us ignoring the way my hands tremble. "I like the way he makes me feel, Mom," I tell her honestly. "He makes me feel like there's nothing I can't do, nothing I don't deserve. He makes me feel whole and worthy of everything my heart desires. When I'm with him, I'm truly happy, in a way I've never been before."

"What about his kids? Are you ready to handle teenagers?"

I smile and shake my head. "Is anyone ever ready for that? What I do know is that I genuinely love those kids. They aren't mine, but they feel like they are. Things won't be easy, and there are going to be times that they'll hate me. When they first found out about Adrian and me, they were so upset they wouldn't speak to me for weeks. They're children, Mom. Of course it won't be easy, but I'm getting into this knowing that. I have no illusions of a perfect life and a perfect family that never falls apart. I know there are going to be times that things will get messy, and there will be times that I might envy them for not being able to have as much of Adrian's time as I want to have. I know that. I'm only human, Mom. I know there are going to be times that I'll mess up, or they will and I'll get hurt. But it'd be the same if they were mine."

Mom nods, her gaze thoughtful. "What about his ex-wife?"

I shake my head. "She's... problematic. She's not happy to see Adrian move on, and she's making that very clear. What I can tell you is that Adrian and I have handled everything she's thrown at us as best as we could, and we'll continue to do so."

"So you've thought this through, huh? You're sure about him?"

I nod. "Yes. I have no doubts."

Mom sighs and looks away. "You know what he said about you when he came to ask for your hand?"

I shake my head, curious.

"That he's going to make sure that you always feel appreciated and cared for, and that he'll always remind you that what you think are your flaws aren't flaws at all," she says, pausing. "He also said he's willing to learn about our traditions."

I smile to myself, my heart warming.

"That wasn't what convinced me to give him a chance, though. It was his children. You know what they said about you?"

I shake my head.

"They said they already see you as their mother, that they're okay with having two mothers. You might love those kids, Leia... but they love you just as much in return."

Considering everything the kids and I just went through, that surprises me. "They said that?"

Mom nods. "They even brought your dad Star Wars toys. He'd never admit it, but those two stole his heart instantly."

My eyes fill with tears, and I sniff. Though things have been better between the kids and I, I didn't think we'd fully recover. Maybe I was wrong. Maybe we're doing much better than I thought we were.

"I still don't like this, Leia," Mom says. "I don't want you to have to deal with kids that aren't your own, or an ex-wife that might try to mess with you through the kids. I don't want any of that for you, but I can see that you love Adrian. I can see that he loves you too."

She hesitates and taps her finger on the kitchen counter, the way she does when she's thinking.

"I don't like it," she repeats. "But you have my blessing."

I stare at her in shock. "What?"

Mom smiles at me and nods. "He's a good man. He's not the kind of person I'd have picked for you, but so long as you're happy, then that's all that matters. I nearly lost you once when you were diagnosed with cancer. Just having you sitting opposite me right now is a miracle, Leia. If this is what you want, if you're sure about him, then you have my support. I cannot promise you that I can convince your father, but I will try."

She places her hand over mine and squeezes. "Just be happy, okay? That's all I want for you."

I nod, a tear running down my cheek. "Thank you, Mom. This... thank you."

She smiles and tips her head to the tea on the counter. "Finish your tea, then come help me make parathas for tonight. Your sister fired you anyway, might as well put you to work."

I suppress a smile and nod, my heart warming. I didn't expect this at all. I was so certain she'd put appearances above my happiness, but she didn't.

Sixty-One

LEIA

Thor stares at Dean Ferguson with a chilling smile on his face. I know he has already picked the woman who will replace the dean if he doesn't ensure that I walk away unscathed.

What neither of us counted on was the amount of people who would attempt to go against us just because of Adrian's surname. It's almost as though they tried to turn him into an example, to prove that they're independent from the name the school bears.

In the last few weeks, Thor has shown me what being an Astor at Astor college truly means. He's had several board members who were likely to vote against me replaced outright, and we're now left with what I expect to be a unilateral decision to dismiss my case.

I worked myself to the bone for my PhD, and by the time he became my advisor, I'd already done most of my research. My prototype was already built, and the design didn't change much. All I did was integrate some more hardware. I'd actually already written most of my dissertation, too. I definitely earned my PhD — or I will, as soon as they let me defend my dissertation.

"Professor Astor."

"Mr. Astor," he corrects them. It's still surreal to me that he gave up his job for me. It makes me feel bitter and resentful. It's such a high price to pay when no one was harmed because of the choices we made. I received no unjust benefits from my relationship with him. All he's ever done is protect me, but he's never overstepped his role as my advisor, not when it came to my dissertation. I never received help I didn't ask for, and I never asked him for more than I'd ask my previous advisor.

I fully understand that we're to blame for being in this situation, but to know that Thor lost his job because of me fills me with irrational anger and a feeling of overwhelming helplessness.

The dean turns toward me and smiles. "Our investigation was thorough, involving conversations with every party connected to your dissertation. They all confirmed what we already suspected: that you finalized the major elements of your dissertation before Professor Astor joined as faculty staff. As such, we will allow you to defend your dissertation and finish your PhD. You may also resume teaching your classes. Your suspension is lifted as of now."

The relief I feel at his words has me feeling faint, and I inhale shakily. This is about more than just my dissertation. Had they said no, that would've also meant that we'd lose our chance to convince my father that Thor and I can handle the consequences of our actions. He'd never give us his blessing if the result today had been unfavorable.

"Thank you," I tell him, smiling politely. I have no doubt they're going to give me a hard time when it comes to defending my dissertation, but that's okay. All I need is a chance.

The dean looks at Thor and smiles tightly, as though he wants to apologize but knows he shouldn't. Thor ignores him and rises to his feet, but I see the bittersweet look in his eyes. He's happy for me, but it can't be easy for him to be here today, knowing he'll never teach another class.

We're both quiet as we walk out of the building, and Thor grabs my hand. I look at him, startled, and he smiles. "You know how fast gossip travels. There's no way no one knows about us. Besides, there's no need to hide it anymore."

He entwines his fingers with mine, and I smile as we walk through the square in front of our campus. "You know," he says. "My mother was a teacher. She was a university lecturer, and she was my hero."

I look up at him, surprised. "You never told me that."

He shakes his head. "I don't speak of her often, because each time I do, it still hurts. We lost her five years ago, and I'm convinced my dad followed her a year later due to heartbreak. Most days I'm fine, but then I think of her, and the pain just comes rushing back."

I pause and turn toward him, raising our joined hands to my chest. "So you followed in her footsteps career-wise?"

I nod. "Yeah. I tried to, at least. My mother was the perfect teacher in all aspects of life. She always had advice for me, no matter what was going on in my life, and she always had an endless amount of patience. I didn't just want to follow in her footsteps as a teacher, I also want to follow her lead as a parent." He pauses and raises his free hand to my face to push my hair behind my ear. "She would have loved you."

I look into his eyes, my heart breaking for him. It's clear he's missing her more than usual today, and I wonder if he's worried that he let her down by losing his job. "I'm sorry," I tell him, my voice soft. "It's because of me that you lost your job."

He shakes his head and cups my face, his thumb tracing over my bottom lip. "Don't be sorry, baby. What I'm trying to say, albeit badly, is that I know she'd be proud today. She loved being a teacher, and even if I can't follow in her footsteps, knowing that you are... I think she'd have loved that. Besides, what my mother wanted for me, above all else, is true happiness. If she could see me today, she'd understand."

I rise to my tiptoes and wrap my arms around him, hugging him tightly. "I love you, Thor."

He lifts me off my feet and hugs me back just as tightly. "I love you too, baby," he says, putting me down, his eyes on mine. "Now we just need to convince your family. Your father's requirement was that there'd be no consequences of our actions, and today, at last, we've fulfilled that."

I nod, instantly nervous. Dad and I have barely spoken since we fell out. It's clear to me that he doesn't accept us being together, no matter what he may have told Thor. If anything, he may have said it because he didn't think we'd be able to walk away unscathed from the mess we made.

"Hey," he says, tilting my face up to look at him. "Don't worry, baby. Leave this to me. I won't let you down."

I'm not worried he'll let me down. I'm worried my father will.

Sixty-Two

ADRIAN

I'm nervous as I sit in my car parked opposite Leia's house. She's at Asha's house today, which means her parents are home alone.

I breathe in deeply, worried about what they might say if I show up uninvited again, like I did last time. "Mum, Dad," I whisper. "I never believed in the supernatural and all of that stuff, but Leia does, so I'm giving this a shot. If you're truly out there, I ask for your blessing tonight. I need them to say yes."

I run a hand through my hair and shake my head as I get out of the car. I really must have lost my mind.

I hesitate when I reach their front door, second-guessing everything. Maybe I should've brought my grandfather with me, the way I did last time. I don't know what the right thing to do is. All I can do is my very best and hope it's enough.

I inhale deeply as I press the doorbell, my heart racing as I wait for the door to open. Leia's mother appears, her surprise evident as she stares at me.

"Adrian."

"Hi, Mrs. Sital. May I come in?"

She nods and stands aside to let me in, her eyes on me as I take off my shoes in the hallway.

"Did you eat?"

I look up, surprised. "No, ma'am."

She nods and tips her head toward the dining room. "You can eat with us."

I nod and follow her, unsure what to do or say. I've gone over this visit a dozen times now, trying to find the right words and failing.

Leia's father stands when I follow his wife in, his expression unreadable. "Mr. Sital," I say, nodding.

He purses his lips and sits back down, ignoring me.

"Do you like lamb?" she asks, and I nod as she grabs a plate and loads it up before sitting down opposite me.

She watches me as I pick up my spoon. Her gaze is so intense that I'm almost scared to take a bite, but I do it anyway.

My mouth starts to burn almost instantly, but I chew and swallow down the food anyway. I reach for the glass of water she poured me and drain half of it. The food is insanely spicy, but there's no way I'm saying a word. "It's really good," I tell her, grinning.

I hesitate as I lift my spoon back to my lips to take another bite but force my way through it.

"*Bechara*," Mr. Sital mutters, shaking his head, and I frown. I've heard Leia say that word before. Doesn't it mean something like *that poor thing?*

"Here," he says, pushing a bowl of yoghurt my way. "This makes it better."

I smile gratefully. He's right. The yoghurt makes the food so much less spicy, and I manage to actually enjoy the remainder of my meal.

It's clear that Leia's mother invited me to sit down for dinner to give me a chance to convince Leia's dad, but I don't know how to. Neither of us are speaking, and the silence turns more awkward by the second.

"Why are you here?" he asks eventually.

"For the same reason I was here last time," I admit.

"No," he says, shaking his head.

I rise to my feet and start to stack the empty plates, clearing the table. Leia's mother sighs as she takes the plates from me, disappearing into the kitchen. I wish she'd stayed. Being left alone with Leia's father makes me oddly nervous.

"You asked me to resolve the issues Leia and I caused by being together when we shouldn't have been, and I did. Her dissertation defense went smoothly today, and her education is now officially behind her. I resigned as a professor and now work for my grandfather, and not a single rumor has touched Asha's business. I told you I'd ensure no harm would come to Leia because of our relationship, and I've kept my word. Tell me what objections you have, and I'll do my best to ease your worries."

He stares at me and inhales deeply. "How will you ensure my daughter doesn't lose sight of her values and religion?"

"I'm not particularly religious, but just a few weeks ago, the kids and Leia made their own diyas from clay for Diwali. We lit them before she came home for a religious ceremony, but honestly? I'd have been fine with it if she'd wanted to do it at my house. I don't think there's anything wrong with believing in more than one God. Ultimately, I think they're all the same."

He nods, but his expression tells me that he doesn't like my answer, and I can't quite tell why.

"You already have children, but my daughter wants her own. Will you grant her wish?"

I nod. I'd better not tell him that Leia and I are already trying, because I have a feeling that'll get me thrown out of the house quicker than anything else I might say. "Yes. I'd love to have a child with Leia, provided we're blessed with one."

He nods again, his expression worsening.

"If you marry my daughter, I don't want her to miss out on anything she'd have if she married someone we approved of. It means a big Indian wedding, with several religious ceremonies

Sixty-Three

LEIA

"Leia," Dad says. "Come to the store with me."

I nod and jump up from the sofa. I've been meaning to find the right time to talk to Dad. Maybe now would be good. Now that I've officially finished my education and we've obliged all of his requests, I want to ask him about Thor again.

Just the thought of bringing up the subject has chills running down my spine. I don't mind confrontation, but it's different when it comes to my parents. I'm anxious as I follow Dad to the car, trying to think of what to say and how to bring this up.

"Leia," he says, a few minutes into our drive. "Does that man make you happy?"

I look up in surprise and nod. I didn't expect Dad to bring Thor up himself. "He does, Dad. I've been happier than I've ever been before. I didn't think this kind of happiness was meant for me. After I went into remission, I thought... I just thought I was so lucky to even be alive that I shouldn't dare hope for more, until I met him. He's a really good man, and he treats me well."

Dad nods, his eyes on the road. "He'd better. I'll make him regret ever asking for your hand if he breaks your heart."

My eyes widen at his words. "Does that mean… are you saying you'll let me marry him?"

He smiles at me and parks the car, and it isn't until that moment that I realize we're nowhere near the stores. We're parked in the same spot Thor takes me to see the stars. I can see bright lights in the distance, and my eyes widen.

"Dad? What's going on?"

He grins then and tips his head toward the fields in front of us. "Let's go find out."

I'm shaking as I step out of the car, and Dad walks around to meet me. He offers me his arm, a sweet smile on his face. "Come on, sweetheart."

I nod as I follow him, a gasp escaping my lips when my eyes adjust to the darkness. Tears start to gather in my eyes when I see a gazebo that wasn't there before, Thor standing underneath it, surrounded by countless fairy lights.

"Go," Dad says, his smile bittersweet. I look up at him, and he nods. "I just want you to be happy, Leia. He isn't who I would have chosen for you, but he makes you happier than I've ever seen you before. That's enough for me."

He wipes away a tear I didn't even realize had fallen and sighs. "Go, before I change my mind."

I rise to my tiptoes and press a kiss to his cheek, startling him. I've never seen my father looking as emotional as he does today. This must be hard for him, and I want him to know I appreciate what he's doing.

My heart races as I walk toward Thor. He's wearing a suit that looks impossibly sexy on him, and the look in his eyes mirrors how I feel. Hopeful, excited, scared.

He grabs my hand the moment I'm within reach and lifts it to his lips, kissing the back of my hand. "Leia," he says, his voice soft. "My Princess Leia."

"Thor," I murmur, trying my hardest not to burst into tears. Is this really happening? Is this what I think it is?

"I think I knew you were the one from the moment I walked into that bar and saw you sitting there. Something about you called to me, and my heart and soul both responded. Taking a seat next to you is one of the best things I ever did, but asking you to come watch Mercury with me was an even better decision. Every aspect of you has been seared into my mind from that moment onward, so much so, that I couldn't forget you even as I walked away in an attempt to do the right thing for my family. For two years, you were the one I saw when I closed my eyes."

He grins at me and takes a step closer, cupping my cheek as his thumb brushes over my lower lip. "You're the one that featured in every single fantasy I had, the one I never got over, the one I compared everyone else to. When I saw you at Amara's wedding, I couldn't believe it. There you were, the one who got away, standing right in front of me, looking even more beautiful than you did in my dreams. I didn't see it then, but I believe it now. You and I were inevitable. No matter how we fight this, no matter what life throws at us, we will always find our way back to each other, and we'll always make it out on top, always."

He drops to one knee and takes a ring box out of his suit pocket, and I burst into tears. "Leia Sital, you're the woman of my dreams. I love how you occupy my every dream, but I want to start every day with you too. I want you to gang up against me with the kids, and I want to be the one that makes you smile. I want to buy you ridiculous looking heels for the rest of our lives, and I want to watch the stars with you on days that feel hard. For the rest of our lives, I want to be the one who gets to love you, gets to grow old with you. I want it all with you." He pauses and looks at me, a hint of nervousness in his expression. "Leia, will you marry me?"

I nod and swallow down my tears. "Yes, Thor. *Yes.*"

He slides an engagement ring onto my fingers, and I stare at it in shock. "It's beautiful," I whisper. It's beautiful, and it's *huge*. I have no doubt this ring cost him a fortune.

"It's perfect for the future Mrs. Astor."

He rises to his feet and wraps his arms around me, turning us around so I'm hidden behind him. "Your father terrifies me, but there's absolutely no way I'm not kissing you right now."

I giggle and rise to my tiptoes, my lips finding his. He kisses me underneath the stars, in the same spot our story started.

I can't wait to find out what else life has in store for us. This is only just the beginning.

Epilogue

ADRIAN

"You're here, son," Leia's father says as he opens the front door, his eyes on our little one. "Riya, my darling," he adds, holding his arms open.

My daughter jumps out of my arms and into his, giggling. She's about to turn three, and it's crazy how time has flown by. Leia and I struggled to conceive, and it took us several rounds of IVF before we were able to welcome Riya. It wasn't easy, but it was worth it. The way Leia burst into tears when she finally took a pregnancy test that was positive will forever be seared in my mind.

Her pregnancy wasn't easy, but she never complained, not even when her morning sickness lasted a full nine months, or when she ended up being in labor for thirteen hours. The moment she had Riya lying on her chest, every second of agony just faded away. I could just see it in her smile.

"Well, hello to you too, Dad," Leia says, side-eying her father.

"Yeah, *Nana*," Lucy adds, using the Hindi word for maternal grandfather. The kids have quickly become part of Leia's family, as much as I have. It's amazing to me how they don't differentiate between the kids. Riya is their sweetheart because she's the youngest, but my in-laws always make sure to spend just as much time with Lucy and Colton.

It helps that Colton and Lucy both took an interest in Star Wars once they realized Leia was named after one of the characters. They spend every Sunday watching movies or building LEGO sets with my father-in-law, while Leia and I sneak off on a date.

"Adrian," my mother-in-law says, grinning as she waves me over. "Come see what I made you."

"What is it, Mom?" I ask as I walk into the kitchen.

Amara is sitting on the kitchen counter and narrows her eyes at me. "Why are you here again?" she asks, and I bite back a smile.

"I'm actually part of this family? Why are *you* here every week?"

My mother-in-law places her hand on my shoulder and shakes her head. "Will you two stop arguing, please?"

Amara crosses her arms and glares at me. "Before you, I'd always get all of my favorite foods here. Now it's all about what *you* want to eat. It's unfair."

My wife walks into the kitchen, her eyes bouncing between Amara and me, and she sighs. "You're arguing again, huh? How do you two think I feel? I got married, and suddenly both my parents forgot about me!"

"Come look, Adrian," her mother says, illustrating Leia's point as she holds up a jar of mango chutney she made for me. It's the only type I can actually stomach. My tolerance for spice has increased, but it certainly isn't at the level Leia can handle.

"Mom," she complains as she walks up to me. "You're spoiling him too much."

My mother-in-law huffs at her and turns back to me, smiling. "Come try it."

I oblige and grab a spoon, tasting the chutney she made. "It's perfect," I tell her. She made it sweet, and it's exactly how I like it. She's made spicy versions of this before that I struggled with.

Leia yanks my spoon away and throws it in the sink, her eyes flashing with jealousy. "Babe," I murmur. "Don't be like that."

She glares at me. "Before I married you, my mom would make me nice food. How are you going to make this up to me? You stole my parents!"

I bite back a smile and nod. "Okay, I guess I'd better repent, huh?"

She nods, pouting. Fucking hell... my wife is far too fucking cute. I can't deal. One look, and I'm a goner, and she knows it.

"Adrian," my mother-in-law warns. "You're spoiling her too much!"

I grin and shake my head. "I can't help it. She's just too adorable."

Amara groans. "You both sicken me," she says, grabbing my jar of mango chutney. I watch as she sticks it into her handbag. She's crazy if she thinks she'll get away with that, but I'll deal with her later. First, I need to appease my darling wife.

"How about I take you on a date?"

Leia nods, the frost in her eyes melting away.

"Come on then," I say, grabbing her hand. "Mom, can you take care of the kids for a few hours? I've just been informed that I've wronged my wife by stealing your love."

My mother-in-law rolls her eyes and waves us off. She's used to this from us now, and they love babysitting the kids. We have a full-time nanny, but my in-laws prefer to babysit when they can. They love having all three kids over.

I entwine our fingers as we walk out of the house. "You know what, baby?" I murmur. "Mercury is in retrograde tonight, and we still have a few hours of sunlight."

Her eyes widen. "No way. Every time we try to catch mercury in retrograde in our spot, something happens, and we miss it."

I look up at the blue skies above us and shake my head. "Looks like a perfect day to me. How about we give it a try?"

Leia nods, and I lead her to the car. I glance at her, my heart still racing at the sight of her. I don't know what I did to deserve her, but I thank my lucky stars she was in that bar tonight.

If she hadn't been, I'm sure I would've fallen for her nonetheless.

Leia and I have always been inevitable.

Want to see a scene of Leia and Adrian's big fat Indian wedding? The bonus scene can be found at catharinamaura.com/bonuses or by scanning the following QR code:

More from Catharina Maura

Lexington and Raya: The Secret Fiancée
Raya never expected that ruining Lex Windsor's shirt would lead to an evening filled with games and laughter. She walks away the next day never expecting to see him again — until he shows up as her professor, offering her class an internship. He knows something she doesn't: None of their meetings were coincidental, and the two are arranged to be married.

Silas and Alanna: Bittersweet Memories

When her boyfriend breaks her heart, Alanna goes after his older brother in a quest for revenge. It would have been simple — if he wasn't also her new boss. As they spend time together, she realizes he knows her better than he should. He knows about the memories she's lost.

Author's Note

Hi! You made it to the end of Leia and Adrian's story, and what a wild ride it was! Those of you who know me, probably realised that this book was an #OwnVoices book, meaning that Leia and I share the same ethnicity and culture. That means that the way Leia's culture was portrayed was based on my personal experience and my own upbringing — it's not meant to reflect a universal experience.

I've always wanted to see people like me in the romance books I read, and writing an Indian heroine has been a dream come true for me. I will admit that it was incredibly scary, though. I felt vulnerable every step of the way, with every word I wrote.

I was scared it wouldn't resonate, that people wouldn't love a heroine like Leia, and that I couldn't do her justice. Just within Indian culture, we have so many differences, that it's impossible to write a character that every single Indian person can identify with.

We have different traditions and speak different dialects, despite sharing so many similarities. It's also what makes writing an Indian heroine pretty hard, because there's no universal experi-